SAIGON

SAIGON

RALPH PEZZULLO

atmosphere press

Published by Atmosphere Press

Cover design by Ronaldo Alves

Atmospherepress.com

"When men lack a sense of awe
there will be disaster."
Lao Tse (6th century A.D.)

"When men lack a sense of awe
there will be disaster."
Lao Tse (6th century A.D.)

CHAPTER ONE

The air feels like water. And we're sinking down. Between the rattle, the roar and the pitch of the wings, it seems like the plane is struggling. Like this new place we're reaching doesn't want to accept us. But we have the speed and power of a Boeing 707 behind us. We're on Pan Am Flight 753 bound for Vietnam.

I sit hugged tight by the darkness, hands clasped in my lap, wondering, What will I find in this new place? Why have I arrived with these people?

In many respects they're like strangers to me. Not the passengers, who huddle around the windows. I'm talking about my family. My father, our leader – tall, broad-shouldered, with a mean crew-cut and a nose that juts out like a mountain. My mother, soft and vain, always out of reach — as though she's living in her own dime-store novel that she writes in silence and shares with no one.

I have a younger sister and a brother, too. You have to watch out for my sister. She's the sneaky one with mischief in her eyes. Not only will she steal your candy, she'll pull your confidence right from under you, if you give her a chance. My brother, Corey, at six, is still half-formed. I think our parents hold the last, precious piece that he needs to function in the world. For some reason they haven't given it to him. Maybe they don't want to. Maybe they don't know how.

I've just turned thirteen years old. It's August 1962. John Fitzgerald Kennedy is our president. My father says that we're traveling to Vietnam to fight communism like it's some kind of disease. But I don't understand how it infects peoples' brains and causes them to act like zombies.

We've traveled from Washington DC via Los Angeles, and then Tokyo. All first class with tangerine sherbet served in its skin, rack of lamb with mint jelly and all the Swiss chocolate we can eat. This is the last leg of the trip. Dozens of questions bounce around in my head. My parents have been meager with details about our future. They don't like to be bothered. We children go where we're told, we do what we're supposed to do. They provide the roof over our heads, the food to sustain us, they put us in school.

Even though the flight has been long, my sister, brother and I have enjoyed the little luxuries: free slippers, steaming hot towels, eye shades. Usually there aren't a lot of extras in our lives. Officially, my father is a Foreign Service Officer with the State Department. He makes us feel that we're all on some kind of mission that requires rigorous intelligence and discipline, except he hasn't explained what we're supposed to do.

We've been told to trust him.

The pilot is addressing us in French. I'm pretty sure he's telling us to fasten our seat belts. My mother snores lightly with my brother in her lap. My father stands behind us in Tourist smoking a cigarette with a man wearing black-rimmed glasses. I go back to tell him that we're landing. He tells me gruffly to hurry back to my seat.

My father's a man of few words, to his family. But he

seems to have a lot to say to other people, especially men who wear white shirts and thin dark ties like him. They speak under their breath like they're telling secrets. Like they're playing a special game.

It's one that feels cruel to me. Why? I can't explain. I've always had a way of sensing things since I can remember. The only one who ever really understood me was my grandmother.

She died a year ago while I was staying with my other grandfather in Long Island. One night I had a dream. My grandmother whispered into my ear, "Goodbye, Michael," she said, "I have to go now. I'll miss you. I'll always miss you, but I'll be here, too. Be a good boy. You are a good boy. Grandma's got to go now. I love you. Goodbye."

I felt her lips on my cheek. And when I reached out to touch her, I awoke. I walked to the kitchen where my other grandmother and grandfather were drinking coffee. My grandfather sat in a white terry cloth robe. I told him my father's mother had died. He put down the newspaper he was reading and asked, "What are you talking about?"

I asked him for the section of the *New York Times* that contained the obituaries. Turning the pages, I found my grandmother's death notice and showed it to him. He looked up at his wife who barely spoke English, and she said, "He's right."

I knew.

Don't ask me how. It's the same way I know we're getting into something now that we don't understand. I sense we'll be forced to learn many lessons as we descend through the midnight sky. My father is back in his seat now. The plane sinks lower and lower like we're descending through water.

I see blue runway lights rush by. The dark outline of jungle. Scattered yellow lights. I feel the thud of the tires under my seat. We've arrived.

CHAPTER
TWO

I've only seen a man wearing a white suit in the movies. Now I'm seeing one in real life. He appears to be waiting for someone on our plane — tall, American, with dark-rimmed glasses, a cigarette dangling from his full lips. He leans limply on a black Mercedes with white seat covers. Standing at attention beside an identical Mercedes are two Asian men in white shirts and black pants. Low buildings hidden by tropical leaves loom in the background.

The man in the white suit seems dapper, confident and self-satisfied. His hair is wavy and parted in the middle. He has a worldly air about him; and is more sophisticated than my father.

"Who's that?" I ask my father.

He doesn't answer me, but turns to my mother, who's still half-asleep. "There's Brad," he says to her.

My mother looks up annoyed that she was roused from her dream. Annoyed that she's being forced to look up and face reality. But seeing Brad waving at us from the tarmac, she smiles and is quickly transformed. Instantaneously she's as beautiful as a movie star in her sleek yellow suit.

The air outside is rich with oxygen and perfume. Everything's wet, which gives off a feeling of growth and decay.

On the tarmac, my dad and Brad vigorously shake hands. Then they go off, talking in private, while the Asian men are taking care of things for us, handing our passports to customs officials, fetching our luggage, ushering us into cars.

I steal another look at Brad and remember an afternoon visit to his house in Washington DC. A big, old place with lots of rooms. Our parents were downstairs drinking cocktails. We kids were sent upstairs to play. That's where I met Brad's son, Brad Jr. — two years younger than me, burly and bursting with wild energy. His older sister, Samantha, who is my age, was quiet and shy with freckles on her nose, long amber hair and blue eyes the color of a summer sky.

That afternoon Brad Jr. was trying to impress me with his huge collection of toy soldiers and tanks, and the BB gun given to him by his grandmother. To show off his physical courage he climbed out the third-story window onto the limb of a tree. But when it was time to shimmy back in, he got scared. He didn't want to climb down either.

Maggie and I tried to throw him a rope, but that didn't work. His sister Samantha found a broom and tried to stretch out the window so he could grab hold of the handle, but it wasn't long enough to reach him. So, I went downstairs to ask for help.

I caught my mother saying, "I love these daiquiris and adore the color." Then, she giggled, and Mrs. Relaford giggled, too. The daiquiris were pink and sweet-smelling, the room brown and musty.

Brad – Mr. Relaford to me – spotted me standing near the stairway and whispered something to my father who laughed hard.

My father asked harshly, "What do you want?"

Remembering to stand up straight, I told Mr. Relaford that his son was stuck on a branch of the tree and needed help getting down. Mr. Relaford seemed annoyed by the interruption. He stood and shoveled ice into a blender, then said, "He got up there, didn't he? Then he can get down by himself."

I glanced around the room expecting one of the mothers to disagree. But neither one of them seemed to show any concern.

When I returned upstairs and told Samantha, she shrugged and said, "I thought so," implying that I was foolish for going to the adults, but brave.

Brad Jr. wept. My sister scolded him for going out on a limb in the first place. With my heart in my throat, I jumped from the windowsill to the branch and hung on. Trying not to look down, I shimmied past Brad, Jr. and helped him down the branch, to the trunk of the tree. Foot by foot, we climbed down to the ground.

Mr. Relaford patted me on the back as we left. "Sorted it out, did you?" he asked with a wink.

Now, six months later, Brad Relaford and my parents ride in the lead car. We three kids sit in the second Mercedes with a man named Minh at the wheel. Everything we pass is a stagnant shade of yellow in the murky light: men on bicycles, women carrying double baskets hanging from poles across their shoulders, oxen pulling carts. People sleep on the side of the road — women with peaked straw hats over their faces, men in little shorts. We pass two huge water buffalos and I close my eyes.

I open them as we're being ushered into a hotel. All the eyes we pass are half-closed. The clock on the wall says 3:15.

It's a grand, old place with thick, white walls and high ceilings. We enter a lacy bronze cage and step into an elevator run by a boy in white gloves. He looks down at his shoes, then presses an ivory button marked three.

Minh carries my brother, Corey, into the room and lays

him on a vast four-poster bed surrounded by mosquito netting. Another Vietnamese man in white sets my sister Maggie on the other bed. They bow gracefully and leave. I sit on the bed where my brother is sleeping and look around. Two big fans on the ceiling stir the thick air. The one over my sister's bed wobbles as it turns. I've never seen windows this big or this tall. They're covered with large louvered shutters.

I consider opening them and looking outside, but my body pulls me down onto starched sheets. I see a little lizard dart up the white wall. Others wait on the ceiling, in the cornices.

Outside through the hallway, I hear my parents arguing. A door slams. My dad sticks his head in. I can tell from his face that something is wrong. He says, "Go to sleep," but I can tell that he needs help.

For years now, when he can't deal with my mother, he turns to me. Now I go on bare feet to where he stands in the white-walled hallway and ask, "Dad, is something wrong?"

His forehead furrows as though he is wrestling with something big. "Wait here," he says.

His long black shoes echo off the tiled floor. I try to read the pattern — white, white, black, white, green. I love patterns. But this one doesn't make sense.

I hear my father trying out his new French and someone explaining in a long fluid line of words, like a bird floating on air. I could sleep on my feet, drift back to Arlington, Virginia and my friends in Mrs. Miller's class and the time Willie and I dug spent bullets out of a tree with our pocketknives during a field trip to Manassas. My eyes close, my mind trails off, into the buzz of the jet engines, which still echo in my ears.

I feel a big hand squeezing my shoulder and look up into my Dad's gray eyes. He says, "Your mother doesn't like this place. She wants to leave."

"Now?" I ask. "Corey and Maggie are asleep."

"Yes, now. Do you like it?" he asks, as though my opinion matters.

"Yes. A lot," I immediately reevaluate my assessment, which I confirm with a nod. "It's ...kind of ...interesting."

"Interesting" is one of my father's favorite words. He scratches his head. "She says it smells of mildew."

It smells like the rest of the city – a mixture of sweetness and rot.

"She refuses to stay here," says my father, looking anxiously at his watch.

"You want me to talk to her?" I ask, catching my strange reflection in a mirror.

"Yes." With a big hand on my shoulder, he guides me to the door to their room and stops. I knock gently. The wood is so hard and thick that it barely makes a sound.

"Mom?" I ask, whispering into the darkness. No reply. I step in and wait for my eyes to adjust. I sense her round body, the warmth of her womb, I smell her French perfume. "Mom?" I whisper again.

I see her curled on the bed her knees tucked against her chest. She's removed the yellow jacket, but she still wears the matching yellow skirt. I push aside the mosquito netting and carefully remove her brown shoes, then take a sheet from the other bed and drape it over her, gently.

When I find my father, I say: "She's asleep."

He exhales long and hard so that the tension flows out of him. "Good. Go to bed," he says, pulling at his narrow tie and shirt. "In the morning after breakfast, we'll change hotels."

Why? I want to ask.

* * * * * *

In the morning I'm too busy gathering myself, getting my bearings, pushing my body, which is thick and slow. We cross the street like visitors from another planet to another hotel, which has a restaurant on the second floor, overlooking the street.

There's so much to take in – a Cathedral with two tall spires, lots of delicately boned people in white. Women wear flowing silk pajamas and peaked straw hats. The men appear to be sly and intelligent. Everyone moves slowly, elegantly, like they're pushing through the air.

"Pancakes," my father says to the Vietnamese waiter, who wears a black waistcoat, white shirt and black tie.

He doesn't understand. "Pain-an-cak? *Quelle et pain-an-cak?*"

"*Come les crepes,*" says my sister smartly.

The man nods and scribbles something onto his pad. Sweat beads appear on his flat forehead. A white fan overhead stirs the air.

"No, I don't want crepes," says my mother slowly in English, as though by speaking slowly the waiter will understand. "I want pancakes with real maple syrup."

Now the waiter seems completely confused. He pivots and hurries to the kitchen. A young woman in perfect white pajamas with an orchid behind her ear sets down small glasses of juice. She leaves with a sweet smile and a deep bow. Outside the window, a man on a bicycle pedals up to the curb pushing an upholstered seat on wheels.

"They call that a cyclo-pousse," announces my father.

I'm admiring the strength of the skinny driver, while his passengers argue in French. The woman's mouth is pinched; her face powdered; her hair an unreal shade of red. The man sees me staring and tips his white hat.

That's when I hear my brother scream: "Yuck!" He's tasted the orange liquid in the glass in front of him and is spitting it out and grabbing his throat for effect.

My mother comforts him. "Corey. Corey, are you alright? Oh, my God!"

I don't know why she's so alarmed. Corey is always getting sick and complaining in a dramatic way. Last year when we were living in Arlington and my father was away with the

Secretary of State on a trip to Greece, Corey complained so strongly to my mother of pains emanating from his hips that she took him to a hospital where he was examined, x-rayed and put in a cast that covered his stomach, hips and both legs all the way to his feet. The doctors said he was suffering from something called 'Legg-Perthes disease.'

A swarm of waiters, waitresses and other attendants buzz around him now and remove the offending liquid, but not before my father tastes his and pronounces: "It's canned pineapple juice."

My mother screams back, "Get it out of here!"

I want to drink mine, but it's gone. The frightened-looking waiter appears to tell us there is no such thing as pancakes with maple syrup. My mother threatens to leave. The waiter pleads with her in French.

My sister asks in English, "What's wrong with you people?"

I want to slink underneath the table and disappear. My father says something about eggs, which he repeats in French and the waiter throws open his arms in great relief.

"*Oeufs, Monsieur. Bien sûr!*" he exclaims.

"Can you make SCRAMBLED eggs?" my father asks.

My mother picks up a fork and mimes scrambling eggs on her plate. "Scrambled. You know ... like this."

The waiter caught between his ignorance and his desire to please, nods and bows at everything my parents say.

"Scrambled eggs for everyone," proclaims my father. "And lots of toast with butter and strawberry jam."

"Tell the chef we don't like them runny," warns my mother. "If they're runny we'll send them back."

The waiter bows so deeply his forehead almost touches the floor. Thankfully, we are alone in the dining room, except for two couples who are further inside, obscured by curtains and shadows.

When the eggs arrive, they're not scrambled, but in the

form of omelets, which is fine with me. But my mother, sister and brother send theirs back, with more instructions from my mother in sign language about how to make scrambled eggs.

"This is pathetic," she groans, glaring at my father, who is looking to me for help. I gulp down my omelet, wash it down with a glass of powdered milk and ask to be excused.

"Where do you think you're going?" my father asks harshly.

"I want to look around," I answer. "I'll go to the cathedral."

"Go ahead," he grunts. "Meet us back at the hotel."

* * * * * *

I'm so relieved, I practically fly down the narrow, crowded sidewalk, past cafés with men reading French newspapers, bars with names like Pink Pussycat and Love Lounge, fabric stores lined with bolts of silk and rich brocade, shops hawking newspapers and postcards, beggars with withered legs, French women with white umbrellas, wearing the determined expression I've mastered from years of being out on my own. It dates back to my first day of first grade when my father drew a map through suburban Virginia for my mile and a half trek to school alone.

I pass Vietnamese soldiers standing at attention, their helmets pulled down so far they practically cover their eyes. Some hold their fingers on the triggers of submachine guns. One of them watches me warily. At thirteen years old, I stand five foot three. The soldiers in boots barely reach my ears.

I scurry along Tu Duc Street catching a glimpse of my dark hair and big brown eyes reflected in a window. It's a quarter past nine and the air is thick with moisture.

The red brick Cathedral sits on an island in the middle of the street across from a building that hangs a limp yellow flag with three red stripes.

Looking both ways, towards bicycles, motorcycles and

strange-looking French cars, I cross. I don't see the jeep coming from a side street, which honks. Two American soldiers salute from the front seat. One of them shouts: "Hey, kid, which way to the beach?"

I don't know anything about a beach. All I know is that I'm in South Vietnam, in a city called Saigon. It was once a French colony, but now it's an independent country that is trying to resist the communists from the north led by Ho Chi Minh.

I climb the stone steps of the Cathedral and step into cool air, thick with incense and the smell of burning candles. I genuflect, kneel in a dark wood pew and pray for me and my family and my friends.

Above me stained windows depict scenes from the gospels peopled with dark figures in Vietnamese clothes. I notice a dozen men in dark pants, white shirts, and sunglasses leaning against the columns. I get up from my knees and move closer to the altar, where a priest in green and gold robes holds an infant in his arms.

I sit thinking about my grandmother and wondering about heaven, which has always been described to me as paradise with harp-playing angels and doesn't seem real in a way I can imagine. I decide to light a candle to her in a little chapel along the right apse. It flickers and burns higher than the others. My chest swells. She feels close.

As I exit the chapel, I run into an impeccably groomed Vietnamese man in a blue suit. He looks at me and asks in perfect English, "Why are you so sad?"

I explain that I've just arrived in the city from the United States and came to say a prayer to my grandmother who died last year.

"I wish I could feel sadness sometimes," the well-dressed Vietnamese man says. "But my position prevents me."

His face is long and weathered with deep creases in his brow. I imagine that his dignity won't mix well with the swagger of men like my father who like to give instructions.

"Are you here by yourself?" he asks, looking over his shoulder towards the waiting guards.

I start to tell him that my father, who is working for the US Embassy, is waiting with the rest of my family in a hotel down the street. As I speak, a priest appears in a black robe. He looks American with a round, pink face and short black hair. He lays a friendly hand on my shoulder and asks in English, "What did you say your name was, my son?"

"Michael," I answer. "Michael Sforza."

The priest takes my hand in his. "Father Kevin McDaniel," he says. "And this is Mr. Tu."

Mr. Tu bows gallantly. "Welcome to my country."

"You're new here, Michael? Your father is here on business?" asks the priest.

"No," I answer. "My father works for the United States Embassy."

"Sforza, you said?" asks the Vietnamese man, mispronouncing my name.

"Yes."

He turns and whispers to the priest. I consider excusing myself and leaving, but that would be rude.

Father McDaniel separates from Mr. Tu and approaches me. "Didn't your father tell you that it's dangerous for a boy your age to walk around the city alone?" Father McDaniel asks with the smell of red wine on his breath.

"No, Father. He didn't," I answer, waiting for him to scold me. But his eyes are kind.

"Mr. Tu is a very important man in this country," explains Father McDaniel. "He has lots of problems to deal with because his country is struggling. It's a special place; filled with grace. I compare it to a sensitive young man or woman who isn't ready to face the world. Does that make sense?"

"Sort of," I say, swallowing hard.

"The world can be harsh, Michael," he says.

His last words penetrate. I'm thinking that there are many

things I need to learn as Father McDaniel escorts me down the aisle to the front door of the Cathedral. Outside, a black Cadillac limousine waits surrounded by jeeps filled with men wearing sunglasses.

"You'll come visit us this Sunday?" Father McDaniel asks.

"Yes, Father."

"God bless you, Michael," he says. Then, pointing to the black limousine, he adds, "Mr. Tu has offered to drive you back to your hotel."

One of the men wearing sunglasses holds the back door open with a smile as sharp as a razor. I look back at Father McDaniel, who nods at me from the front steps as if to say it's okay.

As soon as I settle into the cream leather seat, the limousine speeds off smoothly. A soldier in camouflage with a submachine gun in his lap sits facing Mr. Tu and me on a jump seat. The gun looks menacing. Mr. Tu wears sunglasses that hide his eyes and directs the driver in Vietnamese.

We turn right from Tu Duc Street onto a wide tree-lined avenue called Norodom, when a phone rings. Mr. Tu reaches into the armrest and picks up the receiver.

I look out the window at passing buildings as Mr. Tu talks excitedly in Vietnamese. Two jeeploads of men ride in front of us, two in back. Mr. Tu barks something to the driver, who honks three times. The jeeps in front swerve to the side of the road, then we pull over, too, and stop.

Mr. Tu barks something out the window to the drivers of the jeeps, then he turns to me and says, politely, "I'm sorry, Michael. There's been a change of plans. I must return to Gia Long immediately."

"Okay," I say, wondering what Gia Long is and what he does there.

"My driver will drop me off, then take you on a short tour of the city, before returning you to your hotel."

"That's very nice," I say, regretting that he won't be

accompanying me.

He smiles as the window closes automatically and we continue. Up ahead is a massive iron gate. Mr. Tu says, "That used to be the palace, until it was bombed by air force officers who turned against us."

The driver bears left, past the bombed-out palace which is now a pile of rubble behind a very high fence. Mr. Tu asks, "Are you superstitious?"

"I try not to be," I answer, honestly.

"A wise woman told me that my country will experience big political changes every nine years, when the sum of the last two digits is nine," he explains. "In 1945 the Nguyen dynasty fell. In 1954 the French army was defeated by the Viet Minh at Bien Vien Phu. Three months from now it will be 1963." As he finishes, he looks out the window and studies something in the distance.

We enter an older neighborhood with large stucco houses and high trees with delicate fan-like leaves that cast the street in intricate shadow. Policemen in white uniforms open a barricade to let us pass. The limousine stops. Mr. Tu turns to me and offers his hand, "Until next time, Michael," he says. "We will meet again."

"Thank you for the ride," I say.

He's already out of the car and surrounded by the men wearing sunglasses, who escort him into a very large white building. It's old and larger than the White House with rows of columns, large windows and balconies. It flies the same red and yellow flag I saw before.

The only ones remaining with me in the limousine are the driver and the man in camouflage, who has moved to the front seat. We glide down wide streets clogged with motorbikes, motorcycles, pousse-pousses and more bicycles than I've ever seen in my life. People we pass try to peer through the darkened glass.

The camouflaged man speaks in broken English, pointing

out the window and saying, "That's the French Embassy. The Cercle Sportif. The Opera. The National Assembly. The zoo. The Buddhist Temple. Cholun, the central market. The American Embassy."

The city alternates between elegant beauty and desperate poverty. You can almost smell disease breeding in pools of tepid water alongside the road.

The limousine turns left and follows the river. Naked children jump into the green and brown water crowded with little boats, floating garbage and water buffalo.

I'm trying to imagine how I'm going to negotiate the poverty and suffering, the gap between rich and poor, East and West, American and Vietnamese, when we enter a prosperous business section and turn left again. The limousine stops in front of our hotel on Tu Duc Street and the man in camouflage steps out. "Wait here. Wait," he says to me as he hurries inside.

Minutes later he returns with a portly Vietnamese man in a light blue suit who is gesturing wildly. The camouflage man says, "They moved to the Majestic."

"What?" I ask.

"Your family is not at this hotel," he answers.

Then, I remember that we were supposed to change hotels.

CHAPTER
THREE

Two weeks later my father sits in a red-checked shirt reading the local English-language newspaper, *Times of Vietnam*. We're seated on the porch of our temporary residence. It's one of six identical houses on a piece of property called the Norodom Compound, which is off the main avenue — the one that intersects the Tu Duc. The ruins of the palace stand a mile down the street.

My father rests his feet on a bamboo ottoman covered with coarse green cotton. Over his shoulder I see a photograph of Mr. Tu on the front page of the newspaper; he's standing on a platform beside another man. They're both wearing white suits.

"That's him!" I say, gesturing to the newspaper.

"Who?" asks my father.

I point at the picture and say, "That's Mr. Tu, the man I told you about."

"You mean the man you met in the Cathedral?" he asks. We're living temporarily in a ranch-style house that looks like it could have come from a development in Arizona. Beyond the screen porch is an enormous tamarind tree.

"Yes."

Two days ago, a huge green snake fell out of the tree and almost hit my father's head. The snake slithered quickly through a hole in the screening, onto our porch, up onto the same chair where my father is sitting now.

"That's not Mr. Tu," he says with disgust. "That's Mr. Nhu, the president's brother. The man he's standing beside is President Diem."

My father killed the snake with one of his golf clubs. Beat its head to a bloody pulp.

"Maybe I heard wrong," I say, "but it's the same man."

"It's not the same man," my father groans.

When I told my parents two weeks ago about meeting Mr. Tu and Father McDaniel in the Cathedral, they didn't seem interested. When I told them the part about the bodyguards with sunglasses, my mother shook her head and said, "We know how you exaggerate, Michael," in a condescending way that made me want to scream.

I know that if I press the point with my father, the result will not be good. I can't prove that the Mr. Tu I met is really Mr. Nhu, or that's he's the man in the photograph, or that I rode in his limousine which was surrounded with four jeeps full of bodyguards. I have to wait for the opportunity to prove it to him and hope that it arrives.

* * * * * *

The calendar says December 14th and my mother wants a Christmas tree, which seems almost impossible in a tropical country. Nevertheless, after breakfast my father escorts me to our new Mercedes 190. It's a handsome dark green with white seat covers just like the ones Brad Relaford has. My father has even hired a chauffeur named Mr. Fu, because my mother doesn't know how to drive.

I sit next to Mr. Fu on the front seat. He perspires and nods at my father, who keeps up a constant stream of instructions from the back seat that I'm almost certain Mr. Fu can't understand.

"You told me you could drive, goddammit," my father yells. "You're going to ruin the clutch. That's not the way you let it out... Shit! Watch out for that car! Use your signal – the goddamn turn signal. THE SIGNAL!!!"

My father is an anxious man. I sense that he's under a lot of pressure at work.

For a moment I'm afraid he's going to punch Mr. Fu in the face. Mr. Fu is, too. He recoils when my father reaches out to grab his shoulder, then ducks under the dashboard.

"Watch the road!" my father shouts.

Tires squeal. More curses follow. We narrowly miss a bus, which in fairness isn't all Mr. Fu's fault.

He's out of the car now shouting at the bus driver, who curses back at him through an open window. My father climbs in the driver's seat. From behind the wheel he tells Fu to wait for us. "We'll be back in an hour."

We drive away leaving a defeated-looking Mr. Fu behind. I feel bad for him, but my father doesn't want to hear about it. "If you say you can do something, you'd better be able to do it," he explains, adding, "How hard is it to drive a fucking car?"

I can't answer that, because I don't know how to drive one.

There's a checkpoint ahead with armed American soldiers, barbed wire and sandbags. The sign reads, US Air Force Base at Tan Son Nhut Airport. My father shows his ID to a Marine guard and we're waved in. "We'll try the PX," my father explains.

I've been here before several times with my mother who complains that all they stock is cigarettes, booze and candy. They have other things, too, like toilet paper, toothpaste, comic books, deodorant and tennis rackets. But I doubt they sell Christmas trees.

My father asks the manager, a very thin American man with a bald head. His name tag reads: Rick Sharp.

Recognizing me, he drawls, "How ya doin', sonny?"

"Fine, sir," I answer, cringing. Three days ago when I came here with my mother looking for tissue paper, which she couldn't find. I saw some big blue and white boxes on a high shelf with "Kleenex" printed on the side. I pointed them out to my Mom.

"No," she said.

"Kleenex, mom!" I said growing exasperated. "Right there!"

Instead of explaining, she walked away. I grabbed the package and chased her down the aisle.

Mr. Sharp saw the package I was carrying, my mother running, assessed the situation and stopped me. "What's the problem, sonny?"

As I explained, he raised an eyebrow.

"What we got here is a communications problem," he said. "Your mother wants Kleenex tissues and you're carrying Kleenex sanitary napkins. Kleenex is a brand. They make a whole line-up of products. Tissues is just one of them. You want me to put these back?"

I still didn't understand. Mr. Sharp leaned into me and whispered, "Nobody's told you what sanitary napkins are for, have they?"

"No, sir."

"They're for women. For their monthly period." He took the package from me. "I'll put these back."

My mother didn't mention the incident during the ride home. Now Mr. Sharp is listening to my father ask if he has any Christmas trees in stock.

"Christmas trees?" Mr. Sharp asks, letting a hiss of air escape through the space between his front teeth. "We had a couple of those little plastic babies, if that's what you mean."

"No," my father says sternly. "I want a real one."

"A real one?" Sharp asks. "An honest-to-goodness blue fir Christmas tree? Here, in Vietnam?" He looks at my father like he's asking for a piece of the moon.

My father isn't amused. He won't be deterred either.

Mr. Sharp sees that and excuses himself. "Sorry, I can't help you, sir. Good luck."

Now my father is perplexed. As we sit on the front seat of the Mercedes, he fixes me with piercing gray-blue eyes. "A Christmas tree... Where the hell are we going to find one?"

I shrug, but that's not good enough. He only stares at me harder.

"Think, Michael! We need a goddamn Christmas tree. Help me out."

"How about a nursery?" I suggest.

He nods. "It's worth a try." He starts to put the car in gear. "Have you seen a nursery around here?"

"No." But this doesn't seem to bother my father. He drives north, through streets tangled with bicycles, pousse-pousses, cyclo-pousses, troop carriers, ox-drawn carts, buses and taxis, into a residential neighborhood with big houses behind high walls topped with barbed wire and sharp glass. He pulls in front of a modern house with a high yellow gate. Three young Vietnamese soldiers with submachine guns stand guard.

"Wait here," he says.

I'm used to this routine. Since the age of five I've had to sit alone in cars waiting for my father for up to an hour. "How long are you going to be?" I ask.

"Ten minutes," he answers.

I roll down the side window and let the warm, fragrant air waft in. The morning smells vaguely of cinnamon. Brilliant curls of orange, red and vermilion bougainvillea cascade over masonry walls. Black birds with startling yellow markings chase each other over the red tiled roof of the house.

The gate opens. A dark blue Mercedes that's even bigger than ours rolls out and idles right in front of me. From his features I guess the driver is either Indian, or Malaysian, or Pakistani. He gets out and opens the back door for two women who saunter out the open gate. One is a tall, blond-haired woman with her hair pulled back. She looks unhappy. Seeing me sitting in the car, she smiles.

"Michael, what the devil are you doing out here?" she asks.

It's Mrs. Relaford. My parents call her Barb.

Stepping out of the car, I take her hand. "Hello, Mrs. Relaford." She wears a tight white dress that's cut to reveal the top of her breasts.

Hiding behind her, standing with the same straight posture, is her daughter Samantha, who is in my seventh-grade class. Her long hair has been woven into a thick braid. She wears orange pants that reach her ankles.

"Samantha and I are going to buy some birds," Mrs. Relaford says. "Brad bought himself a pair of monkeys, now I want a bird. A beautiful one with red and yellow feathers. Maybe we'll get a big one. Who knows…"

She throws her blond head back and laughs.

"Too-da-loo!" she says gaily, like she's singing. She takes Samantha by the hand and leads her to the long Mercedes.

Samantha waves to me demurely from the back seat. I wave back as they drive off.

I can't get her image out of my head. She's one of the prettiest girls in my new class, doesn't talk much and looks at you calmly with sparkling blue eyes. Her lips are often drawn into a secret smile.

School is a peculiar place. There's the larger world, the world of my family, and the world of school.

The thing that makes it unlike any other school is the tight security. At 7:35 every weekday morning, my sister, brother and I wait inside the gate of Norodom Compound with the five or six other American kids who live there. The blue school bus stops outside the gate. It looks like most school buses except the windows are covered with heavy wire so that no one can throw a grenade inside.

A US soldier carrying a submachine gun gets out and

escorts us to the bus. Inside the bus waits another fully armed US soldier.

The school itself is on the road (Cong Ly) which leads to Tan Son Nhut Airforce Base. It's a series of six two-story concrete structures that stand parallel to one another. Soldiers patrol the roofs with automatic rifles. More soldiers with guns and German shepherds guard the entrance. The walls are topped with circles of barbed wire. There are no trashcans in the halls, and no one is allowed to leave a lunchbox or any other package unattended except in our classrooms.

Despite the exotic surroundings it tries to be a normal American elementary, junior high and high school in one. Our principal, Mr. Orr, is a tall, sandy-haired man from Ohio. Almost all the teachers are American. Kids dress in gingham shirts, khaki pants and white bucks. Girls tease their hair. We have a yearbook called the *Gecko*, which is named after the big, knobby-headed lizard that lives in the local banyan trees.

A majority of the kids at our school have fathers who work for the US Armed Forces. Officially there are 12,000 US military advisors to the government of South Vietnam. That number doesn't include thousands of support personnel — like accountants, clerks, purchasing agents, etc.

Samantha and I are in Mrs. Fisher's seventh grade class. Two weeks ago it was Mrs. Beckel's class. But Mrs. Beckel left the country quickly with her children after the Viet Cong attacked US MacV headquarters with grenades. Twenty-three people were killed including six Americans. The following night four GIs were killed when a bomb went off in a bar on Tu Duc Street.

My father explained that Viet Cong, who are communists, are trying to get the US military advisors to leave. "We aren't leaving," my father declared. Some of the advisors have decided that it's safer for their families to live in the States.

When school started in September there were twenty-two kids in my class. Now we're down to seventeen.

My father works with Samantha's dad, Mr. Relaford. They're both employed by the US Embassy. Judging from the size of his house and the way my father says his name, Mr. Relaford must hold an important position.

When I asked my father if he reports to Mr. Relaford, he said, "In some instances, yes." When I asked him who his boss is, he said, "That's a difficult question. I guess you could say it's the Ambassador."

My father's official title is Liaison Officer. It's his job to coordinate maintenance facilities, carpools, travel and security and the different agencies – State, AID, USIA, MACV, MAAG, TVA, VAA, etc.

* * * * * *

I've been waiting twenty minutes. I try to make eye contact with the three Vietnamese soldiers guarding the house, to get a sense of what they think of me, and by extension, all Americans. But every time I catch their eyes, they look away.

They're small men with delicate hands.

I'm trying to imagine what their lives are like, when my father walks out. "Let's go," he says, briskly.

He's grinning and seems pleased.

"Did Mr. Relaford know a place?" I ask.

"What kind of place?" my father says reaching into his breast pocket for a Marlboro.

"A nursery," I answer.

My father turns to me and frowns from the driver's seat. "A nursery?" Facing forward to negotiate the traffic at the intersection, he says, "Oh, that...."

A traffic cop dressed all in white blows a whistle and waves us through. He stands on a little circular platform, like the ones the elephants use in the circus.

"What does Mr. Relaford do?" I ask my father as he steers the Mercedes north with a lit cigarette clenched in his teeth.

"He works at the Embassy," he answers after cursing a cyclo-pousse driver who has cut in front of him.

"I know he works at the Embassy," I say. "But what is his job?"

My father glances at me quickly with eyes of disapproval. When he doesn't want me to know something, he doesn't answer.

We pass the Embassy, then over a bridge to the other side of the Bén Nghé canal. He turns right past a series of warehouses that look like airplane hangars. He parks in front of one and climbs out.

"Are you coming?" he asks over his shoulder.

I'm always ready to look through any window into my father's world. He steps into an office to the left of the entrance. I follow. A big, round American with a wide, pale face sets a doughnut down on his desk and stands.

"Michael, I want you to meet Mr. Bowers," my father announces.

"Nice to meet you, Mr. Bowers."

"It's a pleasure." He smiles, I suspect for my father's benefit, because there's something smug and disapproving about the way he sizes me up over the top of his glasses.

Everything about him is standard — the plain black-rimmed glasses, the short-sleeved white shirt, the black pants and narrow blue tie.

Mr. Bowers and my father start talking business — schedules, budgets, personnel. I know what my father expects me to do. So I quietly leave, stand in the wide entryway and wait. From inside the warehouse I hear the rasp of saws cutting wood.

Two minutes later, the two men emerge. I can tell from my father's expression that Mr. Bowers doesn't interest him. He takes my shoulder and says, "Mr. Bowers runs the entire Embassy shop and maintenance operation. He's doing a first-class job."

Mr. Bowers nods in appreciation.

Slapping me lightly on the chest, my father announces, "I'm going to show this young guy around."

We enter the shop where we're greeted by the smell of sawdust. It brings back memories of my grandfather — my father's father — who used to own butcher shops in Harlem and the Bronx.

My father stops in front of two men at a long, rough workbench who are trying to fit together two smoothed arched pieces of wood that will form the back of a chair.

They have darker skin and thicker bodies than the Vietnamese and speak in hushed tones completely unaware that they're being watched. The taller, older-looking, black mustached man takes the two pieces of wood and crosses to a big machine that looks like a lathe.

My father steps in front of him. The man bows so that his long, curly black hair falls forward covering his face. He stands quickly and pulls his hair back revealing strong features and a very old expression.

His partner — a shorter, heavier man —smiles with friendly amber eyes.

I can't figure out where these men are from. I imagine the Holy Land, but they very well might hail from a place like Indonesia, India, Malaysia or the Philippines. I don't understand enough about these countries and their ethnic and religious differences to know.

They give the impression of hard-working men who take pride in what they do. I know that my father admires those qualities, because he tells me so at least once a week.

The taller man watches intently as my father sketches a chair on a sheet of yellow paper. When he's finished, the mustached carpenter takes the pencil from my father and makes some suggestions, which my father appraises carefully.

"Yes," my father says. "Mr. Relaford would like four of them by the end of the month."

The stouter man studies the drawing and holds up four fingers. "Four?"

"Yes, four." My father steps back, while the men talk hurriedly in a language that isn't Vietnamese.

"What kind of wood?" the tall man asks.

"He would prefer teak," my father replies, matter-of-factly.

"Mahogany is better," the stout one says.

His partner concurs, "Mahogany. Very strong."

"Fine," says my father. "Then make them out of mahogany."

The two carpenters exchange some quick shorthand about the cost of the lumber, which my father doesn't seem to be interested in. I'm thinking: *Did we stop at the Relaford's house so that he and my father could talk about chairs? Why does my father seem so happy to be doing this favor for him?*

This only adds to the many mysteries surrounding my father and what he does. I always have to be careful about what I ask him. If I'm too direct or act too interested, he'll say I'm "prying," which is something he detests.

My curiosity is sometimes a problem. I see it as a function of wanting to know the truth. In my current circumstances, I also see it as a matter of survival. I'm learning not to trust men who are so sure that they're right.

My father's face softens as he watches the two men work on the chair. "They're artisans," he whispers.

"Yes."

He's a complicated man, harsh and judgmental one minute, accepting and sentimental the next. As we walk to the car, he explains that the shop is the headquarters for a complex operation whose purpose is to maintain and modernize over forty houses and assorted other buildings owned by the US Embassy. "We employ almost eighty men — plumbers, electricians, masons, carpenters..."

My father reaches to start the ignition when a funny-looking man in a wrinkled golf shirt slaps the hood.

Normally my father would yell at anyone who touched his car, but this time he speaks warmly through the open window. "Hey, Sy. What's doing?"

"The usual nonsense," the man answers. "Same ol' crap."

His irreverence grabs my attention. I lean forward to get a better look and see a man of medium height and build with unruly brown hair that is thin on the top, and small skeptical eyes obscured by black-framed glasses. His dress and manner are looser and less careful than other men my father associates with. Seeing me studying him, he says, "Hi. Who are you? I'm Sy."

"My name's Michael," I answer. Sy doesn't seem to care that he's interrupted my father.

"Nice to meet you," he says, reaching across my father and offering his hand. I note that unlike other men my father knows, Sy seems genuinely interested in me.

The two of them continue their conversation outside the car while I watch a tiny Vietnamese woman ladle soup from a cart for a line of men. Those who already have their bowls of soup squat on their haunches and eat with chopsticks, shoveling the broth and noodles into their mouths. Others sit on a low wall that separates the road from the canal. Less than twenty feet away an old, stooped man with long whiskers urinates against a car.

Practically every street and sidewalk of this city is a hive of activity. In the space of two blocks, you're likely to see mothers nursing their babies; people defecating; barbers cutting hair; women selling chickens, ducks, peppers or fruits; boys throwing coins; cyclo-pousse drivers taking naps; men patching bicycle tires; girls selling orchids; boys hawking newspapers; children rolling paper to make drinking straws; men playing cards; kids eating strands of funnel cake.

It must be ninety-five degrees, and yet the men slurp down hot soup in the sun. A dull ache arises from the pit of my stomach. I'm reminded that it's past one and we still haven't had lunch. If I were alone I'd buy a bowl of the noodle soup called *pho*, but I know that my father wouldn't approve. So I won't even ask.

Sy's shadow falls across the window. My father has ducked inside the warehouse again.

"You seen the shop?" he asks.

"Yes," I answer. "It's really interesting," I say wishing I didn't sound so formal.

"Next time you come around, I'll show you some stuff," he offers wiping the sweet off his brow with the back of his hand. "You in school?"

I explain that school is okay except for all the security and the fact that our teachers keep leaving. I tell him that starting next month they're shrinking our hours to 8:30 AM to 12:30 PM.

As my father's wide torso approaches, the woman with the soup cart raises her voice to a very high screech for a reason that isn't apparent to me. Sampans filled with baskets of chickens pass silently on the canal below.

My father and Sy say goodbye. "Nice to meet you, Michael. See you again," Sy says, squinting through his glasses.

"Nice to meet you, Sy," I reply, conscious of the fact that I'm addressing a man who is practically a stranger by his first name.

We glide over the little bridge and push through the traffic that's slower than usual on a Saturday afternoon. People seem to be moving in a dream, oblivious to the clouds building overhead.

"What did you think of Sy?" my father asks unexpectedly. He does this sometimes. He'll ask my impression of people and listen carefully to what I say. A year ago, he confessed that he's not a very good judge of other people and depends on my mother's intuition. I can't help thinking that's a dangerous way to live.

"He seems like a nice man," I answer.

My father measures me carefully, then says, "I like him, too." But I can see from the way he pulls in his lips that he has doubts. He tells me that Sy works for Mr. Bowers and the two of them don't see eye to eye.

"I'm not surprised."

As the first heavy drops smack the windshield, I remember the chauffeur waiting for us by the side of the road. "Dad, we forgot about Mr. Fu."

"Screw him," he growls back. "He can walk." He switches on the wipers which can't keep up with the pace and intensity of the rain. In seconds visibility reduces to a very few feet.

My father refuses to stop. We push through streets slathered with thick sheets of water. Everyone else has taken shelter under entrances, awnings and trees pulled perilously low to the ground.

I'm about to ask where we're going, when my father says, "Sy said there's a nursery on the road to Ben Hua."

My hunger has reached my face, expressed as supreme discomfort. My father asks, "Are you afraid of the storm?"

He's always taken a perverse pleasure in scaring me. For example, he can't resist the urge to sneak up behind me and push my head under water every time I'm in a pool. This time it's not fear he's seeing, it's hunger.

"No, Dad," I answer. "But when are we going to eat lunch?"

Taking his eyes off the road for a moment, he consults his watch. Then he checks the rearview mirror and makes a sharp right. Passing the Kinh Do movie theater, which shows films in English, he turns and parks in front of a new two-story building that I recognize as the bowling alley.

I imagine the taste of burgers and fries. Instead my father hands me a hundred piasters and says, "Run inside and get us a couple of cokes and those little bags of peanuts."

I dash through the warm rain past two MPs who guard the

door. Inside I'm greeted by the sharp smell of cleaning fluid and the crack of pins.

Three minutes later I return to the front seat where I rip open the plastic bag with my teeth. My father warns: "You spill on my seats, and I'll break your neck." Under normal circumstances my brother, sister and I aren't allowed to eat or drink in the car.

When we finish the nuts and sodas, he hands me his empty can and bag and points to a trash receptacle at the front of the building. I know what I'm supposed to do.

CHAPTER
FOUR

The tree we've come back with is pathetic — a spindly trunk five feet tall with six branches that stick out irregularly at odd angles.

It's the only fir tree we could find.

I thought my mother would appreciate our efforts. Instead, she sits on the tile floor surrounded by boxes of glass decorations with her face in hands sobbing. Our puppy, Chico, waits at her feet and wags his tail.

"Chico likes it," my sister says as we watch from outside through the screen door.

A minute ago my father stomped to his room shouting, "Ungrateful bitch!" and slammed the door.

The electric charge created by his anger still cleaves the air. It settles slowly onto banana fronds that wave behind my shoulder. A long green snake slithers up a tree to our right. My brother, Corey, trembles beside me.

"It will be okay, Corey," I say.

"When's Mom going to stop crying?" he asks.

I don't have an answer. There's no consoling her when she gets like this. My sister, Maggie, starts sobbing, too. Then the dog begins to howl. Corey looks up at me with big brown eyes that beg for relief. It feels like the world could end.

I push open the screen door and step inside with Corey clutching my hand.

"Mom," I say quietly. "Mom, we tried to find a better one, we really did. It's the best we could find."

She hugs my brother to her chest and wipes a tear from her dark brown eyes. "It's just not like Christmas," she says with a sob.

"I know that, Mom. It's ninety-five degrees outside. There aren't any lights or decorations in town. But we're together, right?"

"Yes."

"We're together. That's what's important."

She nods.

"We'll have a nice Christmas. I promise."

The way she's purses her lips and narrows her eyes, lets me know that I've said enough. She puts an arm around me and Corey and whispers to me, "You'd better go see if your father is alright."

I walk through the living room with its tiled floor and bamboo furniture, past the bamboo bar, into the hallway, past the bathroom and arrive at his room. The door is locked. I knock twice.

"Dad, it's me. Michael." In the background I hear Bing Crosby singing *White Christmas* over Armed Forces Radio.

"What do you want?" he asks gruffly.

"Can I come in?"

Thirty seconds creep past. I consider retreating to the yard, away from the emotional cobweb of my family. But what would I find there? Danger? Emptiness? More spiders?

"The door's open," he finally says.

I step inside. As mad as he is, I'm grateful to be with him. At least he makes sense. When he's mad, I know he's mad. When he's happy or sad, I can usually understand why. He's more dependable in a sense. As incredibly warm and wonderful as my mother can be, she can be just as disappointing and, even, maddening sometimes.

They're both filled with mysteries.

My mother's are deep and drenched in sadness. They're so deep that she doesn't even talk about them. For example, I didn't know she had a brother until I was six.

I was visiting my grandfather (my mother's father) at his house in Long Island. One night I went into his study that reeked of old cigars. My grandfather, who owned a men's clothing shop in New York City, sat in a big, high-backed burgundy leather chair reading the *New York Times*. Behind him on a bookcase stood a photograph in a carved wooden frame. The face in it looked familiar, because the man in the picture looked like me.

"Who is that?" I asked my grandfather.

He removed his glasses, folded the newspaper in his lap. "That's your uncle Gianni," he said with affection.

"My Uncle Gianni?" I responded. "Who's Uncle Gianni?"

My grandfather seemed surprised that I didn't know him. "Your mother never told you about him?" he asked with the same precise tone he used with his customers.

"No," I said, trying to imagine why my uncle's existence had been hidden from me. In the picture he had such an open, handsome, friendly face. "Where does he live?"

"He died before you were born," My grandfather answered in a voice that told me he missed him very much.

"How?" I asked.

My grandfather held the photo in one hand and rubbed his cheek with the other. "When Gianni came back from the war, he was sick. Very sick. Much sicker than we realized at first..." His voice trailed off. "We lost him some months later..."

His loss seemed incomprehensible. The size of it, the way it had shaped my big white-haired grandfather frightened me. I started to turn away.

My grandfather handed me the framed picture and said, "Here. Take this."

"No, grandpa. I can't."

"I want you to," he said with tears in his eyes. Then, "Michael, you remind me of him... a lot."

The picture felt like a treasure. A totem of a special life. A key to a spirit, a time and place. I hugged it to my chest past the brocade sofa covered in plastic, past the carved antique floors, over the lime green carpets, down the hall to the room where I slept.

The moment I closed the door, I realized that this had once been my Uncle Gianni's room. The objects that seemed dull before vibrated now with meaning — the metal model car, the books and drawings of Italy, the framed print of Saint Sebastian with arrows in his chest.

I studied his photograph. He was handsome with a smile so bright that it threatened to break out of the frame. *What had happened to him?*

"He was sick. Very sick," my grandfather had said. "Much sicker than we realized."

I wanted to know the name of the disease.

Heavy with wonder and sadness my head sunk into the pillow. My eyes closed. I dreamt that I was walking through a crowd of people bigger than me. Their faces distorted as I looked up to the sky. Panic shook me because I didn't know where I was. Then I realized someone was holding my hand.

"Michael," the rich voice said.

It was my uncle, his smile and eyes bursting with life. I felt a life current pass between us when he squeezed my hand.

His face showed so much compassion that I couldn't understand why people didn't stop and embrace him. Maybe he didn't belong.

Then I thought of Christ. I saw his naked body on the cross, blood dripping from his head, hands and feet. He looked down at me with eyes full of pain, sympathy and intelligence.

Then it struck me that each one of us is like Him in a little way. Each one of us has a soul — a piece of God — that we forsake, that others deny and denigrate as they sin against themselves.

Gianni turned to me and said, "Michael, learn to live with the treasure you have been given and find your way in this imperfect world."

What chance do I have? I wanted to ask. I'm a boy who knows so little.

The crowd turned noisy, and people jostled and pushed.

My uncle guided me through.

When I returned to the apartment in Arlington, Virginia, where my family was living at the time, I placed the photograph of Uncle Gianni on the little table next to my bed. The next morning my mother saw it when she was cleaning my room, and screamed, "Oh, my God!" like she'd been shot.

When my father learned the cause of her reaction, he pulled me aside and asked sternly, "Where the hell did you get that picture?"

"Grandpa gave it to me," I answered.

"Put it away someplace where your mother can't see it," he said urgently. "Keep it out of sight. You understand?"

I nodded, then asked, "Did you know him?"

"Yes."

"What was he like?"

"A great guy. Good-looking, well-liked..." He scrunched up his forehead like he was trying to make sense of his memories. "He came back from the war and died. He was sick..."

"What was wrong with him?" I asked.

"I don't know," my father said. "He didn't eat. He wasted away. It was terrible for your mother. She loved him very much."

That's all he said. My mother added nothing. She just looked at me with suspicion and has ever since.

Is it wrong to want to know the stories of your relatives?

Is it difficult for her because I look so much like her brother?

All I could do was adjust to her attitude and learn to live around her.

* * * * * *

At school we're lined up and inoculated with a vaccine against cholera. As the days grow hotter and drier into January, I watch a red bump rise on Samantha's smooth arm and then turn brown and fade.

Is cholera the disease that killed my uncle?

"What happens to someone who gets cholera?" I ask my father.

He hates being interrupted when he's reading the newspaper. I'm just trying to connect the dots, trace the lines between one little island of knowledge and another.

My father doesn't answer. Our dog, Chico, lies curled at his feet. He looks up with mean eyes that aren't aligned properly so he seems to be looking a few feet behind me.

My father pats Chico's head, then takes off his glasses and rubs his eyes. When he feels like it, he's willing to discuss things with me. Sometimes he even talks about the Embassy.

He says, "Sy asked if you'd like to help out around the shop. After school."

"Sure," I answer.

My father fixes me with little greyish blue eyes that seem weary from the weight of many concerns. I assume that they relate to his job.

"Is something the matter, Dad?"

He looks past me into the distance as though he's trying to locate something. "Are you still studying colonialism in school?" he asks.

A week ago I showed him a book report I wrote about the British Empire. The author concluded that British colonialism was the result of the industrial revolution and exaggerated confidence in their system of government, values and religion.

I also know that Vietnam is called the rice bowl of Indochina and is rich in spices and minerals.

"Do you think we'll ever make South Vietnam our colony?" I ask him now, trying to put two and two together.

My father grins. "I don't think there's much fear of that," he answers.

I'm glad to hear it. He turns off his reading light and we sit together in the dark. He says, "We're here at the invitation of the South Vietnamese government to help them fight the Communist insurgents."

I've learned that the country was partitioned between north and south at the 17th parallel in 1954 at the Geneva Convention. I've learned that an election was held the next year to reunite the two parts of Vietnam under a common government, but the south refused to participate because of aggression from the north. I've learned that President Nhu Dinh Diem established the Republic of South Vietnam in October 1955 and the United States has supported him ever since. I've learned that Ho Chi Minh leads North Vietnam and he's a communist and a nationalist. He's determined to unite the two countries that once was Vietnam.

"Do think we'll win?" I ask in the dark.

"Eventually," answers my father. "Yes."

"How come?"

"Because people prefer to live under a democratic form of government where they're free to do what they want, live the way they want and believe what they want."

I have more questions, but my father is finished and gets up from the chair. "Take Chico out and put him on the porch," he says. "I'll talk to Sy."

Even though Chico's only six months old, he's already thick and muscular. The only person he responds to is my father. But I'm grateful to him because he introduced me to softball.

We got him from a US colonel with a square face named Higgins who's from Tennessee. Higgins told us he bred all his dogs to be "strong and mean," which pleased my father who wanted "a good watchdog."

Colonel Higgins told my father about the softball league, which my Dad joined as a member of the US Embassy team. Up until last week, when he tore a muscle sliding into second base, he was the team's third baseman. When he joined, I volunteered to be the batboy, but the manager — a short, grouchy man named Lucas — said I'd only get in the way.

I offered my services to the Special Forces softball team instead and they accepted. We're currently tied for first place with USIA.

Games are played at Pershing Field, which is across the street from our school and near Tan Son Nhut Air Force Base. You reach it by a little dirt road that leads off the main road. Surrounding it is a wooden fence. The wooden stands are painted green. The field has lights, so teams can play after dark, and a concession stand in the back that serves American beer, sodas and grilled hamburgers.

Our team is undefeated because our pitcher is impossible to hit. His name is Rolands and rumor has it that he was flown in from Camp Pendleton, California just to pitch for the team. He's got a big beer belly, which makes him unlike most of the other players who are tall and lean. Before he throws a pitch, he leans forward and glares at the hitter, then leans back and goes into a windmill motion. His arm and the ball move like a blur, then the ball pops into the catcher's mitt. Pow! After each pitch he kicks the dirt and grumbles to himself.

Rolands rarely speaks and never meets your eyes. Our first baseman Leroy who is my favorite player, says, "He's a hell of a pitcher, but a real strange duck." The only two things Rolands seems to enjoy are playing softball and drinking beer. Sometimes he even carries a Budweiser can out to the mound with him.

Leroy is tall with a black crewcut and comes from Alabama. He bats left-handed and smashes line drives that whistle over the heads of first basemen and right fielders. One day I want to be tall, strong and confident like him.

Besides Leroy and Rolands there's Coop, Wag, Sarg, Bonner, White, Scott, Smithy, Richie and Adams.

It's the bottom of the fifth inning. The score's zero-zero. The heavy night air clings to us. Thousands of gnats, moths and mosquitoes gather in the haloes of the lights.

Even though this is an important game between the league's top teams, the talk tonight is about the Air Force captain who nearly lost his eye on the handball court, located on the other side of the stands.

"Ball hit him right under the left eye," Scott reported. "Darn thing nearly popped clear out of the socket. It was hanging there by tendons."

The image burrows into my head. "What's going to happen to it?" I ask.

"Once they get him to the hospital they'll probably pop it right back in," Scott reports.

"And it will still work?"

"Oh, yeah. Teach him to wear protective goggles next time."

I made a mental note: Wear protective goggles when playing handball – even though it's a sport I've never played.

Leroy has walked to first. Coop is up. He's big and stocky with thighs like fire hydrants.

"Come on, Coop. Hit one out!" I shout.

I'm crouched in front of our dugout, about halfway between home and first. The team's eight wooden bats are propped on the screen behind me which protects the people in the stands. Coop wears our only batting helmet, because three weeks ago a pitch almost hit him in the head.

"A little bingo, baby. Just a little bingo," says Sarg coaching third. The Embassy pitcher winds up and slings a curveball that grazes the outside of the plate.

"Stree-rike!" shouts the ump.

A collective groan rises from the players behind me. Coop winces and stomps the ground.

"Come on, ump," yells Scott. "That was way outside."

"A little bingo, baby. Just a little bingo."

"You can do it, Coop!"

The pitcher winds up and throws the same pitch again. This time Coop leans across the plate and tomahawks the ball towards right. The second baseman jumps up, but the ball whizzes three feet over his glove into the gap, then hits the ground and bounces all the way to the wooden fence.

Leroy runs hard around second into third. Sarg waves him home, yelling, "Dig! Dig! Dig!"

We're all on our feet shouting. The right fielder scoops up the ball and in one smooth motion fires it to the second baseman, but Coop has already slid safely onto the base.

The second baseman quickly wheels and throws a strike towards home. Leroy grits his teeth and goes into a slide. I see the catcher field the ball and turn towards Leroy. They're both engulfed in a big cloud of red dust.

The ump shouts, "You're OUT!"

There's a great roar of cheers and protests. "No!" yells Sarg.

"Come on, ump!"

The Embassy pitcher alertly retrieves the ball and fires it to second base. Coop dives back.

At home plate, I watch Leroy rise and dust himself off – his face red, his jaw clenched. There's a hush from the crowd as he faces the umpire. Everyone expects an argument, even a fight.

The ump sticks his padded chest out. "You're out!" he shouts again.

Towering over him, eyes blazing, Leroy bites hard on his disappointment and says, "Yes, sir." Then turns and walks away.

The tension in the crowd fades. Blindly, I hand a bat to Bonner.

"Close call," Bonner says to Leroy, patting him on the back.

"Yeah, good hustle," Adams adds.

Amazed at Leroy's mental discipline, I follow Bonner to the plate and retrieve Coop's bat.

Bonner rests a hand on my shoulder as he knocks the dirt out of his cleats. "We're Green Berets, Michael," he whispers by way of explanation. "We're trained to never lose our heads."

We go on to win 1-0 after Wag hits a homer over the left field fence in the bottom of the eighth.

After the game, after I've put away the equipment, I help Sarg hand out Shasta sodas — orange, lemon-lime, grape and cola. Even though there's one more playoff game against Embassy in two weeks, the guys are in a mood to celebrate. We pile into two jeeps for the ride into town.

"We're going to Brodard's," Coop announces. "You want to come?"

"Yeah," I answer. "Thanks."

As we speed down Cong Ly, Richie passes cans of Schlitz beer from a cooler. The guys razz Coop and Leroy for being "goodie two-shoes" because they don't drink alcohol. Then the guys compare notes about their Vietnamese girlfriends.

I learn that all Vietnamese girls know how to please their boyfriends, which is good. They all want to get married, which is bad. They all like dancing and American movies, which is good or bad depending on what you're in the mood for.

Leroy dates an American nurse named Penny. Sarg and Bonner have wives who live on a base in North Carolina.

"The Brodard" on Tu Duc Street is modeled after a US malt shop with a soda fountain, jukebox, tables and booths. We crowd into the largest booth near the window wearing our blue and white "Special Forces Softball" t-shirts. Ritchie and

White drag up extra chairs, while Coop inspects the jukebox. He selects "Venus" by Frankie Avalon.

"Good song, Coop," I say.

"You like it, Mikey?"

"Yeah," I reply. "He sings it like he really means it."

Three Vietnamese men at a table to our left turn and smile in our direction. They wear white short-sleeve shirts and slicked-back hair. Another two Vietnamese men sit at the counter.

"Where're the girls?" Ritchie asks the waiter. Ritchie has a face that's covered with freckles and the widest smile I've ever seen.

The Vietnamese waiter ignores the question and takes our order. Hamburgers, French fries and milkshakes for everyone. "But no mayonnaise or mustard on the burgers," instructs Coop. "Just bring ketchup. Lots of ketchup. That's the way we like them in the States."

It's a celebration. Everyone smiles and laughs except for our pitcher Rolands who sits by himself sipping Budweiser and looking out the window at nothing. He refuses to drink the local beer — 33 Export (which he calls "fish oil") or Tiger (which he calls "tiger piss.")

"You struck out eighteen tonight," says Sarg, slapping Roland's big shoulder.

"Yeah," grunts Rolands, continuing to stare outside.

Bonner explains to Leroy and me that Rolands has seen some "real nasty stuff." "He still hasn't gotten over his first tour of duty in the Delta before they shipped him back." Bonner points to his forehead. "The wires got crossed."

A fly has landed in Ritchie's vanilla shake. "What you going to do?" White asks.

Ritchie doesn't order a replacement, or spoon it out. Instead he sucks it down with a straw and caps it off with a satisfied burp.

"A true short-timer!" Wag shouts. The men laugh, except

45

for Rolands who reaches under the table and pops open another beer.

"You know what they say?" Leroy offers.

"No," I answer as I bite into my burger, which has a strange taste. Bonner has already told us that they're probably made of dogmeat.

"They say that if you get a fly in your drink during your first year in 'Nam, you order another," says Leroy. "After you've been here two years, you remove the fly and enjoy your drink. But if you've been in-country three years, you drink it down fly and all."

When we finish our food the guys talk about returning to the quarters, showering and meeting at the Pussycat Lounge where they know a certain hostess named Miss Wong. Bonner suggests that they bring me along.

"Would you like that Michael?"

What am I supposed to say? I'm curious, of course. But I'm scared, too. I blush.

"Leave him alone," says Smithy. They raise their glasses to toast their favorite ballboy. I blush some more.

As Leroy drives me home, he tells me that he might miss the championship game in two weeks because he's got to go up north.

"We need you, Leroy," I say. "What's it like up there?"

"I'm part of this team that's working with some Montagnard tribesmen near Pleiku," Leroy explains.

"I've heard of them." In fact, I overheard my father tell someone that the Montagnards are tough and fiercely independent.

"This isn't the kind of war that people usually think of," Leroy says as the wind pulls at his short black hair. "It's not a war we can win."

I look at him to make sure I heard him correctly, because it's not what I expected to hear from a Green Beret. He wears the resigned expression of a man who realizes that all his efforts and all his friends' efforts will be in vain.

"Most of these folks just want to be left alone," he says. "They want to grow their rice and raise their families. They don't care whether they're aligned with the South Vietnamese government or the Vietcong."

"Really?" I ask. Somewhere, somehow, I suspected this might be true.

"In terms of propaganda the Vietcong have the advantage," Leroy continues. "They're basically nationalists. They say they're fighting to liberate their country from foreigners."

I remember reading that the Vietnamese have been fighting foreign domination for most of their history — the Chinese, the Japanese and the French.

Like we always do when we enter the city, we pass a large modern monument to the Trung Sisters who led a successful rebellion against the Chinese in the first century. This time it means something to me.

"But aren't the Vietcong communists?" I ask Leroy.

He looks at me like he's considered the question many times before. "What does communism or democracy mean to a Vietnamese peasant?" he asks back as he turns into the Norodom compound. "They just want to live in peace."

CHAPTER
FIVE

It's Sunday morning and I'm getting ready to walk my sister to church. My father, who is still in his bathrobe, hands me fifty piasters for the collection basket.

I ask, "Dad, do you think we're doing enough to fight communist propaganda?" He looks at me like I asked him to swallow a fly. "What?"

"Isn't propaganda important?" I ask. "Isn't that what we use to convince people that our form of government is best?"

"Yes."

I ask, "Don't the communists have good propaganda?"

"They do."

All the way to the Cathedral, all the way through Father McDaniel's English-language sermon when he talks about the power of forgiveness and tolerance, even as I'm taking communion, I'm thinking about propaganda. I'm looking at the Vietnamese people we pass on the street, the vendors we step around as we enter the Cathedral, the sinewy cyclopousse drivers who wait and puff cigarettes, and I'm thinking of how I would convince them that our form of government is best.

I could tell them about the Boston Tea Party and Patrick Henry's speech in front of the Virginia House of Burgesses. I could tell them about the Declaration of Independence and our Constitution. I could tell them all the lessons I've learned in history and the people and events that make me proud. But what would these stories mean to them?

Nothing, probably. Their experience is different. Freedom of speech, freedom to choose your own religion, free press. What do these concepts mean to a Vietnamese peasant who is struggling to feed his family?

I feel deflated. My mother is the first one to notice when we arrive home. She fixes me with her big, brown eyes and asks, "What's a matter, Michael? You don't seem yourself."

I know that she wants me to cry on her shoulder, and tell her why I feel bad. Then she will wrap me in her soft warmth. She'll tell me that she loves me and that we're alike, and my father doesn't understand us.

I don't want that, because her sympathy will make me feel weak and stupid, and I'll end up feeling that I've betrayed my father.

Mom is all about feelings, the opposite of my father who values intelligence, discipline and reason. Neither one of them seems to accept that emotion and reason are both important. I hope to find a way to balance the two.

My mother doesn't seem to care why we're here. She's more concerned about the quality of the food we eat and how we look. She's an intelligent woman, who, for some reason, doesn't like to think about the outside world. The bigger issues matter to me because they interest my father and affect other people's lives.

* * * * * *

I try discussing my dilemma with friend and classmate,

Gregory Hecht. He's a smart, funny guy with a sly almost Asian smile, who likes to ridicule teachers, parents and anyone in authority. Greg lives in a big, modern house behind a white iron fence on Rue Pasteur. His Dad works for AID and his parents are never home.

"You want a soda?" he asks.

"Sure. Thanks."

I follow him into the kitchen. Like all the houses I've visited, Greg's has high ceilings with fans and tiled floors. A maid in black silk pajamas chops greens in the kitchen. She blurts something to Greg in strange, slurred French that I don't understand.

"You want a grilled cheese sandwich?" he asks.

"Okay. Thanks."

Greg and I spend a lot of time together because we're both mobile. Given the perilous security situation, a lot of families won't let their kids leave their homes. You might see them at school or at the Cercle Sportif on weekends, but that's all. The Cercle Sportif is an old French swimming and tennis club that's located directly behind the grounds of the bombed-out presidential palace.

I'm one of a very few kids my age who are allowed to travel around alone. If I'm going somewhere nearby, like the Cathedral or Tu Duc Street, I walk. Otherwise, I take a cyclo-pousse or taxi. Taxis are my preferred mode of transportation, because they're fast and cheap and have meters, so you don't have to haggle with the drivers.

Most taxis are little blue and white Renaults in terrible states of disrepair. I've ridden in taxis where the windows were missing and the doors were held on with wire. Sometimes they even have holes in the floor, so what when it rains the back fills up with water and you have to ride with your feet in your lap. The drivers are usually skinny, coiled-up men who chain-smoke unfiltered cigarettes.

Greg and I bite into our sandwiches and drink Shasta

sodas, which are sold in the PX. I start to tell Greg what Leroy told me, when he cuts me off.

"I don't care about that stuff," he says with his Asian smile. "We're stuck in this hell-hole for a couple of years. Let's make the best of it."

I agree. Soon we're laughing about the disgusting habits of various teachers and the superintendent of our school, Mr. Orr, "Don't you hate the way Mr. Orr always picks his nose?" Greg asks.

"Yeah, gross."

"You know why they call him 'the superintendent' instead of 'the principal'?" he asks.

"Because he's running a loony bin?"

"Good answer," Greg says. "You see the way he signs his name? He makes big block letters like he's in third grade. The guy's a complete moron. All he can talk about is 'productive citizens.'" Greg imitates Mr. Orr, "We're going to make you into productive citizens."

"A productive citizen always picks his nose."

Greg likes that. He bounces when he laughs. Now he's onto his favorite subject: the girls in our class. More specifically, the growth of their breasts. "Have you seen Debby Bradford? She's going to be stacked!"

Although I've noticed, I'm not nearly as fascinated as Greg is.

"And what about Niki Clifford? Her's are starting to pop!"

"Yeah, Greg, I say. "You like her?"

"I'd like to feel her up!" He bounces up and down and giggles, then leads me upstairs to show me his father's *Playboy* collection. The maid calls up the stairs, probably warning us not to go in his parents' bedroom. Greg pulls me by the arm. "Don't listen to her."

Soon we're on the tile floor comparing centerfolds, but acting like we're more interested in their 'likes and dislikes' than their bodies. "This one says she's attracted to men with tans and motorcycles."

"Miss December says she dislikes buzzards."

"Who likes buzzards?" I ask.

We both laugh.

"Hey, Mom, can I have a buzzard for Christmas?"

We leaf through issue after issue of girls with big boobs and lacquered hair.

"You got a boner?" Greg asks.

"Yeah."

"Me, too."

The whole area of sexual relations is a huge mystery to me. I'm interested in girls and sex, but the idea of actually going all the way is inconceivable to me.

"You still going steady with Patty Hunt?" Greg asks.

"I guess so." Patty Hunt is a cute girl with a ponytail and bangs who rides my bus. We sit together in the back and talk and sometimes hold hands.

"You give her a ring yet?" Greg asks.

"No." The ritual of going steady at our school involves the guy going to one of the shopping arcades off Tu Duc Street and buying his girlfriend either a ring or a silver ID bracelet for about 200 piasters (approximately $3.00) and getting his name engraved on it. I'm not likely to do that. It's not that I'm cheap or don't like Patty, it's that I'll catch hell if my parents find out.

"I thought you had the hots for Samantha?" Greg smirks.

I feel myself blushing. "She's just a friend."

"Did you hear what happened to Charles Shumate? When he broke up with Niki she flushed his bracelet down the toilet."

We both laugh. Charles is what we call 'a pain.' Not only is he constantly reminding everyone that his father is the number two man in the US Embassy, but he thinks he's smarter and better looking than everyone else.

Now that we're finished with the *Playboys*, Greg and I decide to head to the Cercle Sportif for a swim. It's powerfully hot like all the afternoons in Saigon, except in the rainy season when it pours for an hour or so and, then, clears up. We walk in the shade.

The city turns lazy after lunch and most of the shops close until four. In the shade cyclo drivers, vendors and whole families curl up and take naps. We pass a woman with teeth stained black from chewing betelnut. She's picking bugs out of a naked child's hair.

The streets are practically empty and the few people out move like the ooze of heavy oil. We're in a neighborhood of wide boulevards with gated houses on both sides and large old trees. Butterflies fly over flowered fences hunting for nectar. Above us I hear the screech of a monkey.

"What does your father do?" I ask Greg. The world feels immeasurable this afternoon.

Greg wipes sweat from his red face. "He works for the Agency for International Development — AID."

"Doing what?"

"He's helping the South Vietnamese government build strategic hamlets."

"What's a strategic hamlet?" I ask.

We're about halfway there, when Greg stops. "You sure you want to do this?" he asks, his cheeks bright red, his hair hanging limp.

"Yeah. Why not?"

The heat soaks up energy and ambition. We trudge with our towels and bathing suits rolled up under our arms.

"What's the difference between a preacher and a woman in a bathtub?" Greg asks.

"Beats me."

"One has hope in his soul and the other has soap in her hole."

The Cercle Sportif is an old French club with shady walks, lots of red clay tennis courts, restaurants, ping-pong halls and a beautiful outdoor pool. Most people here today lounge in chairs in the shade, or sit by the bar. Like always, a half-dozen slim Vietnamese and French girls in bikinis lie on the steps in the shallow end cooling their feet.

"Professionals," my mother hissed last time she was here.

After showing off our prowess on the diving board, Greg and I order a couple lemon-cokes. A very tanned Vietnamese man with a thin mustache and a large scar on his chest does a perfect dive and swims over to the girls. He grabs one of them by the ankles and tries to pull her in. She screams and kicks him.

"It's Bobby Ho," Greg says excitedly. "Hi, Bobby," he calls. Bobby waves and hoists himself out of the pool.

"Hey, guys," he says. "Which one of them should I screw tonight?" he asks nodding at the girls in the pool.

"I like the one in the yellow polka-dots," Greg suggests.

Bobby Ho is a helicopter pilot with the Vietnamese Air Force. He received his flight training in California, which is where he learned English.

"You guys still virgins?" Bobby asks. Greg and I look at one another and nod. "What are you waiting for?" asks Bobby. "You're missing all the fun."

Greg gets up the nerve to go over and talk to one of the girls in bikinis. I can't keep my eyes off of Bobby Ho's scar. "You get that in the war?" I ask.

"Where else?" He takes a swig of his 33 Export beer, his eyes lost behind aviator glasses.

"How's it going?"

He faces me. "The war?" His tone turns serious. "It's fucked up."

"Why?"

"Because our generals are assholes. They're either completely incompetent or corrupt."

"You think you could lose?" I ask.

Bobby Ho smiles slyly. "You Americans won't let us." He pokes his chin towards a tall, thickly built Vietnamese man in a white tennis outfit who sits near the bar. "There's one of our generals over there," he says. "Big Minh. A complete bullshitter. Dumb as a fucking brick. But he speaks English and knows how to kiss-ass with Americans."

Almost on clue, the big Vietnamese man says something and the three American men who are with him throw back their heads and laugh.

"I've seen him around the club before playing tennis," I say. I don't tell him that my father knows him.

"He'll go far," says Bobby finishing his beer and snapping his fingers to summon the waiter. He orders *cha gio*, which are small fried rolls made of rice paper stuffed with shredded pork, crab, shrimp mushrooms and vegetables. When they arrive, he dips them in *nuoc man* — a very smelly fish sauce. "Try one."

They taste like Chinese eggrolls, only crispier and more flavorful. In my right periphery I spot Patty Hunt and her younger sister dipping their smooth thighs into the pale blue water. I excuse myself.

"Good luck," says Bobby with a wink.

Patty's a sweet girl and seems happy to see me.

"I missed you," she says, shading her eyes with her hand.

"I missed you, too."

She doesn't want to swim. And she doesn't want to sit with Bobby and eat *cha gio* and drink lemon-cokes.

"Would you like to go for a walk?" I ask.

She nods, demurely. I never know what's going on in her head. We take a long stroll to the other side of the club and the ping-pong hall. Then stop and kiss under a tree with bright red blossoms.

Her lips are tender. She holds onto me. She's wearing a red bikini and a little silver chain around her ankle. Her hair, as always, is pulled back neatly into a ponytail. She smells good, too.

"I wish we were in the States," Patty says with a sigh.

"Why?"

Her blue eyes are dreamy. "I don't know," she answers. "There are more things to do."

I take her inside the ping-pong hall, which is lined with a dozen tables. Young Vietnamese and Chinese men wage furious games, their play punctuated by shouts of pain and triumph that echo off the walls. Some of them are stripped to the waist.

Patty, in her red bikini, feels out of place. "Is it okay for us to be here?" she asks.

"Sure." I hand her a paddle and we play gently back and forth. The players are too involved in their games to even notice how beautifully she moves or the way the light glances off her hair.

After two games to twenty-one, I walk Patty back to the pool and tell her that I like getting away from Americans and blending in with local people. We stop and kiss again.

"Thanks," she says. "That was nice."

"Yeah, it was. See you on the bus."

I see Greg's smiling face watching us from the entrance of the men's locker room.

"Good work," he says as I join him. He holds up the phone number of a French girl named Monique and tells me he's going to call her.

* * * * * *

Monday morning, on the bus, I notice the sad expression on Patty's face. "What's a matter?" I ask, as I take the seat beside her. She hands me a note. I unfold it and read the words that have been written carefully:

> "Dear Michael: I have to break up with you. I'm sorry. Very sorry. I told my mother that we went on a walk together at the club and played ping-

pong. She said that what you did was irresponsible. She said I am not allowed to be alone with you again. She said I could have been raped in the ping-pong hall and you shouldn't have taken me there. I told her it wasn't your fault. I told her it was my decision, but she wouldn't listen. I'm afraid I have to obey my parents. I think you're a great guy and I'll miss being with you. I'm sorry. Love, Patty."

I fold up the letter and turn to her. She looks out the window past the protective screens to the bicycles on the street. I take her hand and squeeze it. She starts to cry.

When I get home, my mother's in her room. Our maid, Ti Moui, the one with crisscrossed eyes, says, "Your mother, no dis-turd."

"What?"

Ti Moui holds out a hand to stop me. "No dis-turd."

"Is she sick?" I ask, lowering my voice to a whisper.

"What the matter?" she asks back. "You no understand Ti Moui English?"

I would laugh if I weren't feeling bad about Patty. "No, I don't understand Ti Moui English."

Ti Moui's previous employer was a US Army captain, who she says taught her "perfectly English." She has a lot of pride, even though her name, *Moui*, means tenth, which in Vietnam is bad luck.

She screws up her mouth and crunches her teeth. Then she spits out the words excitedly, pumping her arms up and down like a chicken trying to take flight, "No bother. No bother! Your mother rest. She rest, okay? You got outside and play."

I get the message. The only air-conditioned rooms in our house are the bedrooms. I don't feel like going into my room and reading history. I don't have enough piasters to go to the Cercle Sportif or visit Greg and can't get any without disturbing my mother.

So I go outside where it's hot and steamy and the air is perfectly still. The only sign of life in Norodom compound are two skinny Vietnamese boys trying to fly a kite. They're on the empty football field just beyond the other row of houses. I arrive just as they're rolling up the string. The tallest kid shrugs. I know what he means. It's impossible to fly a kite today.

"*Vous voulez?*" I ask, miming kicking a soccer ball.

They look at one another and exchange some Vietnamese words that slur up and down like horses on a carousel. They both wear white shorts. The shorter kid has a long, serious face and hair that sticks straight up. His shorts are cleaner, finer. He wears a matching white shirt. I believe he lives in the big, white house, the second story of which peeks over the back of the Norodom fence.

"Not to-day," he answers in English, although the last syllable gets stuck in his throat.

"*Chou anh,*" I say.

"*Chou anh,*" they echo back. The taller boy stops, looks back at me and grins. I've seen him in front of the white house sweeping the driveway with a big rice-straw broom.

They disappear into the shade of a huge flowering tree where someone has pushed down the barbwire atop the brick fence and placed a cinderblock on each side so that it's easy to climb over. One day I want to explore their world.

My feet take me out the gate, past the sleeping guards, down Norodom Boulevard, left on Tu Duc Street. Practically all the shops are closed and only a few men sit reading newspapers at the sidewalk cafes. As I approach the Cathedral I see Father McDaniel standing in a doorway dressed in a long, white gown. He waves.

The cool dark entrance invites me. I enter even though I'm wary of Father McDaniel and all his questions. "What brings you here?" he asks. "Where are your parents?"

Always the same. I explain that my father is at work and my mother is resting.

"I'd like to meet them some time," he says, motioning for me to follow him to the rectory. "Shouldn't you be in school?"

I tell him again that our school lets out before lunch because of security and that usually I'm back home by 1 o'clock.

"Would you like something to drink?"

We're in the wood paneled rectory. He settles into a stuffed high-back chair and puts up his sandaled feet. I sit across from him on an ottoman. He rings a bell and a very old Vietnamese woman appears.

"I'll have a lemonade, please," I say.

He gives the white-haired woman instructions in French. She nods without looking up. "You look sad today, Michael. What's wrong?"

It bothers me that my feelings are written so nakedly on my face. As he sips red wine and I drink lemonade (which is much too tart), I tell him about what happened with Patty Hunt. He listens carefully.

There's something moving in his eyes like they're looking for an opportunity to trap me. I didn't come to play cat and mouse.

"Do you think it's okay for a boy your age to start having a physical relationship with a girl?" He almost spits the last word out with disgust.

I look for the right words to explain that I feel this yearning to be close to girls, to spend time with them, to talk intimately, because girls are all about feelings and boys are different. I end with, "I'm not sure I can explain."

He leans forward and clasps his hairy hands together. "Let's talk honestly, Michael."

"Okay."

"Aren't you really yearning for a physical relationship?"

I examine my conscience. I want to be perfectly honest.

59

"Yes and no. I mean that's not all I want."

Father McDaniel looks disappointed in me. He thinks he knows better.

His voice rises as he talks about temptation and sin. He stops to ring the bell again to ask the little old lady to bring more wine. That's when I remember the poem I wrote about Mr. Tu.

"How is Mr. Tu?" I ask. "I wrote a poem about him for English composition."

Father McDaniel stops, removes his glasses and cleans them on his robe. "Mr. Tu?" he asks. "Who is Mr. Tu?"

"I'm sorry, I meant Mr. Nhu, the man you introduced me to the first day I arrived in Saigon."

"Yes, Mr. Nhu. The president's brother," he says. His eyes and face brighten as though a cloud has lifted.

"I wrote him a poem," I say.

"Bring it to me," says Father McDaniel. "And I'll show it to him."

"I will."

* * * * * *

At home, I sit down to dinner with my brother and sister. Ti Moui comes to inform me that my father wants to see me in his room. He stands in his underwear pulling a white shirt out of the armoire. Seeing me, he points to a pair of shoes on the floor. "They need a little polish," he says.

I find the little wooden box at the bottom of the armoire and give his shoes a shine. My father says, "I spoke to Sy. He said he'll meet you tomorrow at the entrance to your school at 12:30."

"Okay."

As I put away the box, I ask, "Dad, what's a strategic hamlet?"

"Not now," he groans, undoing his tie and knotting it

again. I intuit that he and my mother are getting ready to go to a reception. He waits until I'm on my way out of the room to add, "A strategic hamlet is a program that was started to protect South Vietnamese civilians from the Vietcong."

I stop and pivot back to him. "Why?"

"In the late '50s the Vietcong guerillas started targeting village leaders. They would go to them and say... 'Cooperate with us or we'll kill you.' Those who didn't join the Vietcong were assassinated. It was savage... but effective. Someone in the US government came up with the idea of gathering peasants together into strategic hamlets that could be protected from the Vietcong."

"Do they work?" I ask.

"The jury is still out," he answers. "Now get lost."

* * * * * *

The next morning, when I get on the bus, Patty sits with friends looking out the window and chewing her lip. I catch up with her as she walks to class with her books clutched in front of her and her eyes cast down.

"Hi, Patty," I say.

She lifts her head just enough so that her blue eyes shine over her bangs and says, "Hi, Michael."

After school, I find Sy waiting at the front gate wearing sunglasses with metal frames and a plaid short-sleeved shirt that looks like it's been slept in. He leads me to a black American pick-up where a dark-skinned man sits behind the wheel. "Meet Mohammed," Sy says.

"Hi."

As soon as our eyes meet, I know we'll be friends. Mohammed's in his thirties, 5' 9", looks like he's from India and has smallpox scars on his face.

"Mohammed is our supervisor," Sy explains. "He goes from job to job and makes sure these lazy bastards are doing the work we pay them for."

Although Sy's words sound harsh, he smiles to let me know that he doesn't take himself seriously and doesn't expect me to, either. He lights a Winston and hangs his elbow out the open window. I sit in the middle. The Chevy truck rattles. I turn and see two cans of paint and a load of bricks in back.

"After we stop at the Neuhart's place, you can leave me off at the Embassy," Sy says to Mohammed.

At the Neuhart place, we're greeted by a maid in black silk pajamas. "Is the Madame in?" Sy asks.

"She try to sleep now," the Vietnamese maid answers, muttering more words we can't understand and pointing upstairs. We pass a sweeping white stucco stairway with red tiles and are greeted by muffled pounding from the back of the house.

"What do ya know," Sy says with a smirk. "They're working."

The moment we enter the kitchen, the pace of hammers hitting concrete doubles. The narrow room fills with dust.

"We're putting in all new cabinets, a new sink, the whole works," shouts Sy over the racket.

I make out six Vietnamese workers. Two squat on the concrete counter and beat at it with hammers. Four more attack it from the floor. "Where are the goddamn sledgehammers we gave them?" shouts Sy over the noise.

Mohammed addresses the men in Vietnamese. The work stops. Half of them have cigarettes clenched between their teeth. All wear shorts. Only a few of them have bothered with shirts. One is wearing something that looks like a diaper.

"Why not use a fucking ice pick?" Sy asks the man in the diaper who doesn't understand English. "It would be just as effective."

Seeing a sledgehammer propped in the corner, Sy lifts it and brings it down to the counter with force. The Vietnamese men scatter. Dust and bits of concrete fly everywhere. Sy grabs his wrist. "Fuck!"

"You okay?" asks Mohammed. The man in the diaper grins.

"You son-of-a-bitch, I saw that," says Sy grimacing.

Mohammed takes the sledgehammer and goes to work on the counter. Within minutes it lies in ruins. Then he offers the sledgehammer to me and points to a short partition that separates the counter from the space for the stove. It takes me ten swings to reduce it to rubble.

Mohammed pats me on the back and says, "Good work."

"It would have taken these knuckleheads a week to do that," Sy growls. "No, not a week. A goddamn month."

When Mrs. Neuhart appears, Sy tells her how beautiful her new kitchen is going to look with a brand-new pink refrigerator and matching stove.

"When?" she keeps asking. "When?"

Mohammed draws a sketch on a clean patch of wall outlining how the whole job will be done: where the pipes will run, how the cabinets they're making in the shop will be hung.

"We've got a week with that dame," Sy explains as we climb back into the truck. "One week to finish before all hell breaks loose."

"Okay, boss," Mohammed replies with a grin.

"Good work," Sy says as we near the Embassy.

He hops out, slaps the truck and we continue.

After stopping at the shop to see how the Neuhart's cabinets are coming, Mohammed and I visit two more jobs. At the Ruppert house a crew of Vietnamese workers is taking down the roof; at a house down the street from the Ambassador's residence six men splatter the walls with white paint mixed with sand.

Suddenly my life has become more interesting. I'm no longer thinking so much about Patty and the other girls in my class. I'm not worrying about which friends will meet me after school. I'm not thinking about how to avoid the nasty French kids at the Cercle Sportif. I'm not thinking about my mother and the long spells of silence in her room. I'm not as worried about my father and what kind of mood he'll be in when he gets home.

I'm doing something useful and making new friends. Besides Mohammed and Sy, I get to know Huang, the man who runs the Embassy motorpool, which is housed in a warehouse next to the shop. Huang has a clean, open face and shiny black hair that he combs back with brilliantine. He's thin with regular features, even teeth and a ready smile. He also speaks perfect English.

I pepper him with questions about life in Vietnam. Do people here believe in God? (Yes.) What is of primary importance to most people? (Family.) Before God and country? (Yes.) What kind of religion do people follow? (For most it's a combination of Confucianism, Taoism and Buddhism.) I didn't know Confucianism was a religion. (It really isn't. It's more like a set of principles for dealing with the temporal world, but people here are very practical.) Do people here like art? (They worship beauty in all its forms, especially poetry.) Poetry? (Yes, poetry.) Who's your favorite Vietnamese poet? (Tan Ba.)

We go on like this for hours and take turns. I ask my questions, and then he asks me about "the American approach." Whenever Mohammed stops at the shop to talk to Sy or Mr. Bowers, I seek Huang out.

Every night at six, Mohammed drives me home on his motorbike. I hold onto the metal rails of the rear seat rack as he weaves through trucks, cars, taxis, mopeds, buses, cyclos and carts. At the intersections —most of which are unpoliced and have no working signals — traffic comes at us from all directions. Each vehicle moves anticipating the path of the others. They flow in curves and fits and starts like schools of fish.

We pass white and pastel facades of French colonial

buildings. Large trees, painted white at their trunks, line the road like sentries. Sidewalk kitchens serve *pho* noodles and fresh and fried spring rolls. A snake handler pulls up alongside us on a moped with a cage of live vipers. The meat is considered a delicacy and drinking the blood is thought to be good for your virility.

Mohammed steers the motorbike into the Norodom compound and I get off. The sun peeks through the trees behind him, causing me to cover my eyes.

"Thanks, Mohammed. See you tomorrow."

"Good work today, Michael. Goodnight."

CHAPTER
SIX

At home, I find Corey and Maggie in the dining area eating sloppy joes. My father appears, standing stiff and looking impatient in a blue seersucker suit. "Where's your mother?" he asks even though he knows the answer. "We're going to be late."

"Mohammed says that we have to replace all the supporting beams in the Ruppert house before we fix the roof."

"How come?" he asks.

"Because they're rotted out. When Mr. Ruppert came by today and saw his house without a roof, he almost had a heart attack."

"I don't blame him," says my father checking his tie in the reflection off the cabinet glass.

"Remember that man I met who I said was Mr. Tu," I continue. "Well, I found out from Father McDaniel that he's someone else."

"Who?"

"You'll never guess who he really is."

"I don't have time to play games," he growls, turning to my mother who breezes in on a cloud of perfume wearing her glamorous movie-star face.

She's so lost in her world that she doesn't even notice me sitting at the table. She says to my sister and brother, "When Michael comes home tell him that we're going to a reception at the Ambassador's residence."

"Hi, Mom," I say.

"Oh, you're here. Ti Moui will put the kids to bed."

"You look beautiful, Mommy," gushes my sister. "Can I try some of your perfume?"

My mother removes a small metallic vial from her beaded purse and spritzes perfume behind my sister's ear.

"Thanks," Maggie purrs.

I remind my mother and father that Leroy is picking me up at seven to take me to Pershing Field for the playoff game.

"Have fun," she says gaily. She's like a different person when she goes out.

Her happiness is contagious, because now my father announces that we'll soon be moving to our permanent house. "It's very nice," he says with a smile. "You're going to like it," he says, looking at our mother to make sure she agrees.

She gushes: "It's so big and grand."

He also tells us that next week is the beginning of Tet, which is the Chinese New Year, and all the families in the Norodom Compound are hosting a party. "We'll have a big barbecue and dragon dances. Everyone from the Embassy is invited."

* * * * * *

At ten past seven I wait for Leroy at the gate. The setting sun creates magnificent pinks and shades of orange framed by dark gray clouds. The whole city seems to sigh. Outside the gate, a Vietnamese soldier squats in a little guard hut and eats from a bowl of noodles. Another soldier stands outside smoking a cigarette with his carbine slung across his back. Beyond them three barefoot boys toss one-piaster coins against a wall.

"*Bac co khoe khong?*" I ask.

Binh thuong," the soldier says back. When he smiles his silver front teeth glow gold from the reflection of the sky.

I'm wearing my blue and white Special Forces t-shirt and cap.

Wondering if Leroy forgot me, I return to our house, which is third in the first row of residences— the one farthest from the gate. Chico barks as I push in the screen door. "Did anyone call me?" I ask Maggie who is lying on the tile floor drawing pictures. Corey looks up from the house he's building out of blocks. Armed Forces radio plays *Mack the Knife* by Bobby Darin.

"Did anyone call?" I ask again, trying to think of the words in French so that I can ask Ti Moui and make sure she understands.

Maggie looks up. "I thought you were going to the game."

"I am," I answer. I go to my room — the one I share with Corey — and count the money on my dresser. Only fifty piasters, which is probably not enough to cover the cab fare to Pershing Field. I'm trying to calculate how close the fifty piasters will get me, when I hear Ti Moui call my name: "Michele."

"*Oui?*"

"Someone's here to see you," says Maggie as I enter. Coop stands at the door his nose beet red and his ears sticking out farther than before.

"You ready?" he asks.

"Yeah."

"Quick. We've got to hurry."

The clock in the kitchen reads 7:35. The game starts at eight.

"Where's Leroy?" I ask Coop as we climb into the backseat of the taxi that's waiting outside.

Coop gives the driver instructions in terrible French and adds: "*Vite! Vite!*" to tell the driver to go fast.

"Leroy had to go pick up the equipment from Starcom," Coop answers looking at his watch. "We lent it to them for a picnic and they never brought it back."

"I thought Leroy was going to Pleiku," I say.

Coop grins and says: "He got his orders changed so he could make the game."

The driver bites an unlit cigarette as he weaves through a nest of bicycles, cyclo-pousses, buses, motorbikes and motor scooters. A Lambretta pulls alongside us with a young Vietnamese girl wearing a *bao dai* on the back. She clutches her elegant straw hat with one hand and holds onto her boyfriend's waist with the other.

"*Beaucoup vite!*" shouts Coop to the driver.

The little Renault we're in rattles at full speed. "You think this thing will hold together?" Coop asks.

I'm not sure. The traffic thins as we approach the American School. The road to Pershing Field is to the right.

Coop screams: "*A droite! A droite!*" over the din of the engine.

At the entrance to the field, I see an American standing and holding a flashlight. At first, I think he's directing traffic for the big playoff game. Then he holds up his arms to stop us. The cab driver has to slam on the breaks.

The man with the flashlight has a panicked look in his eyes. His mouth is slack as though someone just punched him in the face.

Coop is out and talking to him in the glow of the headlights. The man gestures wildly and points in the direction of the ballfield. I see the dark outline of men walking towards us from the field. They appear to be carrying something.

Coop shoves a 100-piaster note into my hand and shouts: "Michael, pay the driver! Pay the driver! Wait for me here!"

I hand over the 100 piasters without thinking about the change. My eyes are focused on the figures emerging from the field. Two big American men are helping a third man between them. The man in the middle has blood streaming down his face and wears a Special Forces t-shirt just like mine.

"Bonner!" The bottom part of his right leg is missing below his knee.

Oh, God! I almost faint. Two weeks ago Bonner was teasing me that the hamburgers we were eating at Brodard's were made of dogmeat.

"Bonner!" I try to shout, but my voice is barely a whisper.

"Hold that taxi!" the man with the flashlight screams. I keep the back door open repeating "Bonner, Bonner, Bonner" over and over, but no sound comes out. The two men set him on the back seat. Bonner looks up at me and tries to smile.

Please, God!

"No game tonight, kid," he says. His eyes are big and dull like they're stuck on a moment in the past.

"Bonner. Oh, Bonner." My eyes drift to his shredded leg, which one of the men has covered with a shirt. "Bonner, I'm so sorry."

The door closes and the taxi backs away sending up a cloud of red dust.

"What happened?" I ask the man with the flashlight, who is frantically trying to look in front and behind him at the same time.

"Help me," he says like he's pleading. I try to stay calm, but I'm really in shock.

"Help you, how? What happened?" I ask him again trying to act like I'm John Wayne on Omaha Beach.

He has trouble getting out the word: "B-b-b-bombs."

"What bombs?"

The Vietcong have bombed the softball field! The Vietcong have bombed the softball field! The answer from my brain flashes over and over in my head.

I'm very concerned about Leroy and my friends. I want to find them. The man with the flashlight grabs me by the front of my shirt.

"Help me," he pleads again. He presses the flashlight in my hand and points to Cong Ly highway. "Take this!"

"Why?"

He points to the highway, then back at the dirt road leading to Pershing Field. The sirens inch closer. "Help show them... the way in," he stammers.

I get it. He wants me to direct traffic. He's going to stand in the highway and stop the stream of cars and bicycles, while I direct vehicles in and out of the dirt road leading to Pershing Field.

"Okay. Okay!"

Time speeds up and warps. I'm focused on the stream of headlights — Red Cross vehicles and ambulances entering; cars and trucks leaving the ball field, all engulfed in big clouds of dust and smoke.

The road is choked with people stumbling out — dazed, confused, shouting, bleeding. People holding bloody limbs. People with shirts tied around their faces to stop the blood. One man carries a hand wrapped in a white handkerchief. I can see the blood-stained fingers sticking out.

A part of me wants to run far away and hide. But I'm needed.

Using the flashlight, I direct the injured onto a practice field on the right. There's room for some of them to sit or lie on picnic benches.

"Over there," I shout, my voice cracking. "Get out of the road. Let the trucks and the medics in. They're here to help you!"

"Back!" shouts a tall MP who appears behind me.

"Let the trucks in!" I yell. "Let them in so they can help the injured." My throat is wide open because it has to be, in spite of the dust that gathers in my mouth, in spite of the tremendous ball of emotions I somehow manage to hold back.

The MP says to me, "You can handle this. I'm going up ahead," like I'm his equal.

Intermittently, I'm aware of my nostrils clogging with dust, my eyes burning, headlights, vehicles and flashing lights. My mind blocks out the rest.

Streams and streams of cars, ambulances, trucks. In the background, men scramble, scream for help, shout orders, call for their mothers. There's no way to describe the chaos and pain.

Through the collective will of the medics and rescuers, order is restored. The injured are removed. The dead are covered with blankets and loaded into trucks. The dust settles. The pain passes and a dull emptiness comes over me.

There's something huge that I have to digest. I head back to the road carrying my body. I wish I could shed it like my clothes.

It feels as though days have passed, centuries, but it's less than an hour since Coop and I arrived. Where the road meets the highway, a group of MPs have taken charge with flares and flashing lights that cast monster-like shadows against the backdrop of trees and buildings. Wooden barricades hold back hundreds of Vietnamese civilians who have come to gawk — bare-chested boys in shorts, men puffing on cigarettes, women chewing betelnut, girls selling rice cakes.

"Good work," shouts an MP slapping me on the back. "We did it!"

"Did what?" I ask back.

"Everybody's been cleared out."

I've suddenly grown into a man, and I don't like it.

He stares hard into my eyes, as though he's leaving his

body and traveling deep into mine. "You're a kid," he says surprised. "What the hell are <u>you</u> doing here?"

I don't have the energy to answer, or the courage to explain. I point to my blue and white "Special Forces Softball" jersey.

"Oh..."

"What happened?" I ask again.

He takes my shoulders in his hands and says gently, "The VC placed a half-dozen bombs in the stands, which were detonated electronically, possibly using a telephone."

I feel myself drifting off, pulled by the breeze. I hear a man say, "We've got a rough count of three dead, fifty to sixty injured; twenty-five seriously."

I'm sitting on the rear bumper of a jeep, holding my head in my hands, waiting for my friends, my family, someone who knows me. The man with the flashlight hands me a can of beer. "Here, kid."

It tastes slightly bitter, but washes away the dust in my mouth. Without realizing what's happening, I lean back against the seat and fall asleep.

When I awake, I'm back at Norodom – the gate, the low ranch-style houses, the huge tamarind tree. Coop helps me out of the jeep. Ti Muoi stands at the door.

I turn to Coop and start reeling off player's names.

"Wag?" I ask.

"Wag?"

"Yeah, Wag," I insist.

"He's fine."

"Sarg?"

"Slightly injured. Nothing serious."

"White?"

"Okay."

"Scott?"

"Caught a piece of shrapnel in his leg."

"Rolands?"

"I didn't see Rolands."

"Smithy?"

"Clean."

"Richie?"

"A cut on the head. No big deal."

"Adams?"

"He's on leave. Wasn't there."

"Leroy?"

Coop doesn't answer. We're inside the house now. My eyes are growing heavy again.

"Coop, what happened to Leroy?"

He shakes his head.

"Hurt?" I ask. "Was he injured?"

"I don't think he made it," he says.

"You mean he didn't make it to the field or...."

Coop's chest heaves and his eyes tear up, revealing the answer before he says: "Leroy won't be playing ball again..."

That's all I can take. I retreat to bed, weep, and dream of great clouds of dust and headlights. I direct huge waves of cars and trucks, people and more people. I'm trying to keep order where there is none. Chaos and more people and trucks. They're determined to overwhelm me. I keep trying until I can't anymore and give up!

* * * * * *

In the morning my father sits across me at the dining room table as I stare down at a bowl of cornflakes with powdered milk. I have no appetite, no desire to do anything except return to bed.

"Eat," he orders.

"I can't."

"Yes, you can!"

"Dad—"

"Don't feel sorry for yourself."

"But, Dad—"

"Eat!"

I pick up the spoon. It feels heavy.

"I heard you had a rough time last night," he offers.

I nod.

"Sorry you had to witness that," he says lowering his voice. "Life isn't always pretty."

After breakfast I walk slowly to the Cathedral and sit in the back pew like a leper. I don't want to be seen or disturbed while I pray for the dead and injured. When I return home I crawl back into bed and fall asleep.

* * * * * *

Monday morning I'm back in school. Greg comes up to me at recess with our friend Alain. They want to talk about wizards and the Knights of the Roundtable, but I'm far away in another place.

"What happened with Patty?" Greg asks when we're alone.

"That's old news."

"What happened?"

"We broke up."

"Did you break up with her or did she dump you?"

I look into his wide, friendly face. He means no harm.

After school, I ask Greg and a heavy kid named Bill if they want to walk with me across the highway to inspect Pershing Field.

My heart quivers in my throat as we pass through the entrance, past the practice field, around the bend to the field, which is empty. Even the ghosts have departed. Everything is still.

"We'll never play here again," I say out-loud to no one.

The wooden stands have shattered in places.

Bill says that he heard a Marine's head was blown off and landed in a woman's lap. I don't tell them I was here shortly after the bombing, directing traffic. I don't want them to treat me differently or know that I've changed.

I wait as my friends search for souvenirs — pieces of shrapnel, discarded softballs, a woman's white high heel shoe, a bloodstained t-shirt. From the pitcher's mound, I count the craters where the bombs were buried. One at home plate, three big ones in the stands that are studded with sharp shards of metal. A long one like a trench at third. A deep, round one in front of the home team's dugout, right where I used to put our bats.

I kick the dust and want to cry, but nothing comes out. I keep imagining Leroy standing at first base, his bright smile, the way he tilted his head as he stood in the batter's box. I keep thinking about Sarg coaching third base shouting, "Come on, Leroy, get something started!"

CHAPTER
SEVEN

"Is Bruno coming?" My mother asks for the third time.

"Who's Bruno?" I ask my father.

"Don't you remember Mr. Gelbart?" he asks back. "Remember when we were living in Mexico and he came to stay with us? A tall man who is missing two fingers on his left hand. He brought your mother some records he'd picked up in Italy."

Yes. I remember that he struck me as someone who couldn't be trusted. He brought my mother a record of the song "Volare" that she played over and over until we couldn't stand hearing it anymore.

It's the first week of February and the first day of Tet Nguyen Dan, which I've learned from Huang is the most important holiday in Vietnam— a combination of Chinese New Year and a celebration of spring. We're entering the Year of the Hare 1963, the year that Mr. Nhu foretold would bring great political change to Vietnam.

Over the last couple of days I've seen people all over the city sweeping, scrubbing, cleaning and painting. Houses have been decorated with New Year's trees called *cay neu* – which are bamboo poles stripped bare of leaves except for a tuft at top. The pole is then decorated with red paper. It's supposed to ward off evil spirits during the absence of the Spirit of the Hearth (Ong Tao).

According to legend, Ong Tao is privy to all the intimate secrets of the family and leaves the house at the end of the year to report to the Jade Emperor. After making his report, Ong Tao travels back on either a bird with great wings or a golden carp. Paper images of these are sold everywhere. Vendors also sell live fish in little plastic bags that people then release into rivers and ponds.

I see golden yellow *mai* apricot branches everywhere – in houses, shops, restaurants, hotel lobbies. Also, miniature kumquat trees.

Huang explains that the kumquat trees should be about three feet tall and should be thick with dark green leaves and have little ripe orange fruit as well as green fruit that will ripen later. They should also have some light green sprouts. The leaves and fruit symbolize different generations of the family and the tree signifies good luck.

According to a Vietnamese saying, "Trees have roots; water has a source; when drinking from the spring, one must remember the source." It means that one should never forget one's ancestors.

Tet is a time for family reunions and exchanging gifts. People believe that the first person to visit their house on the first morning of Tet is very important. They also believe that the first day will determine their fortunes for the rest of the year.

The first person to visit our house is Bruno, who stops by with flowers and a box of French chocolates for my mother. He's a big man, over six feet tall, with a large square head and short sandy hair. His real name is Pierre Gelbart, but he likes to be called Bruno for some reason.

"You look more beautiful than ever!" he gushes as he takes my mother's hand. His wife is a thin French woman named

Simone, who hides in his big shadow. His two daughters, Claire and Danielle, look formal in plaid skirts and white blouses with their hair pulled back. They speak little English and attend the Lycée Français.

A big crowd has gathered on the football field that's part of Norodom Compound. The Relafords are there, along with the Bowers and all the other Embassy families. Butlers dressed in white hand out trays of gin and tonics, mint juleps and daiquiris. Hired cooks with red sweatbands tied around their foreheads cook steaks, hamburgers and hot dogs on grills made from oil drums that have been cut in half.

Tables are filled with potato chips, dips, coolers of American beer, coolers of Shasta soda and salads.

"It's a real American picnic!" Mrs. Relaford announces.

She doesn't see the irony of having an American picnic on an important Vietnamese holiday.

Samantha's inside our house with Bruno's daughters and my sister. Outside under the overcast sky, Brad Jr. rides his bike round and round the perimeter of the field chased by my brother Corey and other kids. I spot our two Vietnamese neighbors watching from the tree in their backyard. When I wave they duck their heads and disappear out of view.

Strings of firecrackers snap in the distance. For the first time I can remember, I don't hear the sing-song shouts of vendors who usually pass on the street peddling rice, soup, vegetables, live chickens, ducks, crabs and snakes.

Guests fill their plates and retreat to long tables in the shade where they sit and eat. I look for Sy, Mohammed, Greg, Huang and my other friends.

When lunch is over, three trucks drive onto the field and energetic Vietnamese men unload big drums and a colorful dragon costume with huge bulging eyes. A gong sounds. People gather 'round. The gong sounds again and a dragon dance begins with great drumming and shouting. We Americans look on with curiosity and take pictures.

The Vietnamese men shout and jump with great enthusiasm, but their ritual is just a show to us. I learned from Huang that the dragon dance is supposed to ward off evil and bring good luck while Ong Tao is away.

I see my mother standing with Mrs. Relaford and Mrs. Gelbart. They're holding pink daiquiris with long yellow straws.

She says: "Charming, isn't it?" in a detached and condescending way.

Mrs. Gelbart nods politely. Her face looks pinched. Mrs. Relaford covers her ears and shouts: "Why do they to make so much noise?"

I spot Sy leaning against a table, sipping a Tiger beer.

"Hi, Sy," I say.

He looks like he just woke up and didn't have time to shave. I know that if my mother and Mrs. Relaford see him, they won't approve.

"Some show," he grunts, pointing at the crowd of Americans and lighting a cigarette. "If you see your Dad and Bowers, tell them I stopped by. Okay?"

"I will, Sy."

He turns and walks towards the gate shuffling from side to side.

"Where are Mohammed and Huang?" I ask as I follow him.

"The powers that be decided not to invite locals since we're having our own party at the shop on Monday," he sneers. "We're catering a Chinese banquet. There's going to be a huge spread. You're invited. Monday after work." He flashes his quirky little smile and exits.

When I see Mr. Bowers who is mopping sweat off his forehead with a white handkerchief, I tell him that Sy was here but had to leave.

"I wonder why?" he asks, barely masking his disgust. "To visit one of his barmaid girlfriends?"

Mrs. Bowers shakes her head.

Mohammed told me that they're Jehovah's Witnesses, but I'm not sure what that means.

I escape with Brad Jr. and some other kids and organize a game of monopoly in my room. When that ends we bust out my toy soldiers and wage war.

Mr. Relaford and Bruno stick their heads in. Mr. Relaford asks, "Who's winning?" His wavy hair falls over his forehead and his cheeks are flushed.

"We are!" Brad Jr. exclaims, pushing a metal tank forward into the pretend battlefield.

"No, we are!" shouts my brother Corey wiping his nose with the back of his hand.

"You sound just like the Vietnamese," comments Bruno with a cigar clutched between his teeth.

* * * * * *

By 4 PM the party starts to break up, but the Gelbarts and the Relafords remain on the porch with my parents, laughing, drinking cocktails and having fun. Bruno tells a story about how he once crossed the border into communist Hungary disguised as a woman. He gets up to show how he walked in high heels and the others howl. That's when Mr. Relaford spots me and whispers something to my father.

My father grabs me and says, "You'd better go inside."

"Why, Dad?"

His expression turns into a glare. "This is no time for explanations," he says shoving me away.

Later, when it turns dark and our parents are still laughing gaily on the porch, Brad Jr. and I slip outside.

Brad Jr. complains that his parents never let him leave the house. "I go to school; I go home. It's like living in a prison. They won't even let my sister visit her friends."

He's two years younger than me with short hair that sticks up at odds angles like hay and medium blue eyes. "My parents are always going to parties," he continues. "Nice for them. At home, it's me and my sister, the maids and those stupid monkeys my father bought. My mother got a bird. A macaw! All it does is make a lot of noise and shit."

We run and chase shadows, pretending that we're in the jungle. Then we stop and catch our breath under the big tamarind tree. Gongs, drums and fireworks echo off the walls. Stars tease us from behind long black clouds.

"Listen," Brad Jr says. He suddenly takes off, tearing between the houses and back onto the field. There's no moon tonight. I follow his dark shape across the field until it dissolves into darkness near the wall.

"Over here," I hear him call. He's crouching near the ground like a tiger and breaks a limb off a fallen branch. "I wish I brought my b-b gun," he announces.

I'm about to ask him what he would do with it but decide to change the subject and ask him if he knows Bruno.

"Bruno's a neat guy," he says. "He's killed people. He and my Dad are friends."

"He's killed people?" I ask. "He told you that?"

"He tells me all kinds of things," Brad Jr. answers. "My Dad says he likes to tell stories."

"You believe them...? You believe the part about him killing people?"

Brad Jr. runs off across the field, holding the stick in his hand like a club. I follow him with my eyes until I lose him in the dark. Near the tree where the long tables are still set up I see something move. I make out two figures in white shorts. They're bending and picking up things off the ground.

"Brad?" I whisper. There's no response. I whisper his name again, but my voice is drowned out by the stirring leaves.

"Brad?" I ask louder.

I hear a shout like from a movie: "Charge!"

I watch Brad Jr.'s thick figure charge from right to left,

straight at the two figures by the wall. They freeze in a half-bend, hands on the ground, heads up. Brad, Jr. closes in and crashes into them. Bodies spill; a table falls over. Brad Jr attacks them with his stick.

"Stop!" I shout. "Brad, what are you going? Stop!" I run as fast as my legs will take me. In the dark I make out the faces of the Vietnamese boys who live on the other side of the wall. The taller one, the one I've seen sweeping the drive, holds a hand over his right eye. A dark stream of blood drips past his nose to his chin. The better-dressed boy with the long face is on the ground grappling with Brad Jr. and punching the back of his head. Brad Jr. reaches back and grabs the boy by the hair.

I try to get between them but can't. Then, I pull the Vietnamese boy until he lets go and we both stumble back onto the grass. Like a spider, he's on top of me, fists ready, prepared to slug me in the face. When he recognizes me, he stops.

Brad Jr.'s dark figure looms behind him.

"Don't, Brad!" I shout.

The Vietnamese boy turns just in time to fend off Brad Jr.'s blow. The one bleeding from the eye, steps into the light, delivering a sharp left that catches the side of Brad Jr.'s nose.

Crunch! There's a moment of silence. Then Brad Jr. lets out a scream that ricochets off the walls and trees. The Vietnamese boys quickly scramble up the wall and disappear.

I hold Brad Jr., who bleeds all over his shirt. "My nose! My nose!" he shouts. "I think they broke it!"

I peel off my shirt and use it to try to stop the blood. That's when I see what the boys were picking up from the ground, because there's a pile of them gathered in a discarded plastic tablecloth next to one of the tables — plastic knives, forks and spoons.

I want to shake Brad Jr. I want to take him by the shoulders and ask, "What did you think you were doing attacking them like that?"

Holding my shirt to his nose, I help him to our house.

When his mother sees us, she doesn't scream at the sight of the blood. Instead, she asks me in a scolding tone, "What did you do now?"

Their gaiety stops on a dime. Mr. Relaford calls the military hospital. My father brings the Mercedes around to the front. My mother fetches a clean towel and water. Soon my father and Mr. Relaford whisk Brad Jr. off in the car. My mother orders Ti Muoi to clean up the blood; Mrs. Relaford and Mrs. Gelbart gather the children. Bruno pulls me aside.

"What the hell happened?" he asks, squeezing my arm until it hurts.

I explain again that Brad Jr. ran into a tree.

"You're lying," Bruno says roughly. "I know you're lying." He glares down at me, trying to peer into my head with eyes with points like daggers.

"I was on the other side of the field," I say. "That's what I saw."

He yanks me by the arm out the screen door and onto the field. The flashlight in his other hand cuts a path across the lawn. "Show me," he growls. "Show me where it happened."

I lead him to the back corner of the compound. "There." I say, pointing at a tree near the wall.

He examines the tree like a detective, measuring where Brad Jr. might have run from and what he might have been running to. Then he notices the plastic tableware wrapped in the plastic tablecloth. His eyes travel up the wall to the spot where the barbed wire has been pushed down. Then he focuses on the ground and the trail of blood.

He shines the beam in my eyes. "How do you explain this?" he asks pointing to spots of blood on the wall.

"I don't know." I answer. I point to another tree five feet away. "He hit his nose over there."

Bruno scratches the back of his head. "Did <u>you</u> hit him?" he asks.

"No."
"You kids get into a fight?"
"I didn't get into a fight with anyone."

* * * * * *

When I wake, I find myself curled up on the porch sofa. The lights are on inside the house. I hear my mother through the window explaining something to my sister. The clock on the wall behind her reads 9:45. I've been asleep for something like forty-five minutes, even though it feels like I've slept through the night.

I step past Chico who is curled up on the floor and leave the porch. I hurry to the wall where I wrap the plastic tableware in the plastic tablecloth, then exit Norodom compound, take a left and another left at the corner. I stop in front of a big white French colonial house. Shiny banana leaves poke through the iron fence. A stately old Citroen rests on the front drive. I ring the bell at the gate.

A man in black pajamas pants and a t-shirt saunters out and lets me in. He points to the front door. It's open; soft French music pours out. I stop. The man waves me vigorously forward. "*Entrée!*" he says.

Inside it smells of orchids and perfume. A pink light spills out of the room to my left. A half-dozen people sit in the dark watching an elegant Vietnamese man and woman sway gently to the music. They both dance with their eyes closed.

A delicately boned middle-aged man rises, pushes his hair back and walks towards me. Behind him follows a lady in a blue gown with a big red flower in her hair. The man adjusts his glasses and extends a hand. "*Bon soir.*"

I explain in rudimentary French that I live in one of the houses in the compound behind them and I've come to see his son.

The man calls inside, "Gerard!"

While I wait, the woman scolds her husband in Vietnamese.

Gerard, the boy with the long face and the hair that sticks up straight, takes my hand and without saying a word, leads me inside past an altar featuring a picture of Jesus holding his heart, framed photographs of relatives, incense, flowers, square rice cakes and fruit to a big room with old stuffed furniture, a large Phillips radio and ceiling fans that slowly stir the air.

Another boy, who looks to be French, sits in the corner before a beautiful carved ivory chess set. Gerard introduces him to me as Victor.

"*Ou et votre amis?*" I ask pointing to my eye.

"That is why you have come, of course." Gerard says in broken English.

I nod.

"Follow me."

We pass through other rooms to the back of the house, then through a small backyard crowded with plants, papaya trees and flowers to the maid's quarters. The heavy, rancid smell of *nouc baum* mixed with peanut cooking oil and fetid water assaults my nostrils. There are no pretensions here. Just skinny cats, half-naked children, bare light bulbs and rows of laundry hanging up to dry.

Gerard leads me to the last door on the left. A sad, gray dog looks up from the ground. Framed in the open window stands an old woman bent over an ironing board with a cigarette clenched in her rotting teeth. Upon seeing Gerard, she grunts and points her chin inside, then gives me the once over.

Inside it's dark and crowded with pots, bicycles, cots and a small shrine with burning incense that smells like jasmine. In the back room three boys lie on cots. Two young ones sleep in their underpants. The older one has his back turned to us.

Gerard whispers, "Duc?"

The boy turns; he has a comic book in his hand and a big white patch over his right eye. I start to turn away. But the Vietnamese boy's face is relaxed and inquiring. He asks Gerard something in Vietnamese that I can't understand. My mind is tangled with confusion and guilt.

I say to Gerard, "Tell him I'm sorry. I'm very, very sorry." I'm still carrying the tablecloth with the plastic tableware wrapped inside, which I now hand to Duc. "This is for you."

As Gerard translates, Duc stretches his mouth into a smile. Then, just as quickly, his smile disappears and his eyes grow dark.

"He wants to know what happened to other boy," Gerard says in broken English. "Was he your friend?"

I explain that Brad Jr. is my friend and the son of someone who works with my father. That I was shocked by his behavior. That I tried to stop him as soon as I realized what he was doing.

My explanation is interrupted by a shouting from Duc's mother. Doc calls back to her, then addresses me.

"Your friend, okay?" he asks in broken English. "Your friend, okay now?"

"Yes," I answer into his good eye as though I'm entering it taking my shame, confusion and anger with me. I even carry the pain of what happened at Pershing Field.

I stand wondering: *How do I fill the gap between Duc's battered eye and Brad Jr's frustration? How can I explain why my father is here when I don't really understand it myself?*

I want to blame it all on Mr. Relaford and Bruno and men like them, but that doesn't seem fair.

I stand paralyzed. My mind snarled. Duc and Gerard see my distress.

Gerard says gently, "Sit. Please."

Duc clears a place on the cot next to him. His mother enters with a tray with three cold bottles of Coca-Cola. Duc clicks his bottle into mine; Gerard does the same. Then we drink.

The next thing I know we're outside, all four of us — Gerard, Duc, me and Gerard's friend Victor — shooting marbles in the grass under the lights from the porch. It's Gerard and Victor against me and Duc, and we're winning.

Ping! I knock a small cat's eye out of the crude circle. *Ping!*

"You are good," Gerard says.

Our friendship flows naturally until Duc's mother calls and Gerard has to excuse himself and run inside the house.

Victor stands and bows. *"Excusé moi. Mons peres depart."*

"Oui," I say. We shake like the gentlemen we hope to become.

Duc shows me to the place where they climb the wall. He hoists me up, then climbs up himself and watches from the top as I hurry across the field towards our house. My heart feels lighter.

I stop and wave back to him. *"Au revoir, Duc."*

"Au revoir, Michele."

Since the incident at Pershing Field I've had to rock myself back and forth to sleep. But not tonight.

* * * * * *

My father wakes me in the morning as a sharp shaft of sunlight reaches across my bed. "Get up," he says roughly. The alarm clock nearby the bed reads seven.

I pull on shorts and a clean shirt and shuffle into the dining room. My father scowls from the table as my mother serves him coffee. They're both wrapped in bathrobes and wear serious expressions.

"Michael, what the hell happened last night?" my father asks.

I repeat the same story that I told Bruno about Brad Jr. running into a tree.

"I don't believe that bullshit and neither does Bruno," my father responds practically spitting the words in my face. I turn to my mother, but her disapproving look tells me that I can't expect any help from her.

She says, "Brad Jr. has a broken nose. He broke his nose, Michael!"

"Will he be... okay?" I ask trying to comprehend the seriousness of his injury and why it is so important.

"He's got a broken nose!" my father shouts as he pounds the table. "And your stories aren't the same! He says that some Vietnamese boys jumped him and beat him up."

"I... I didn't see that," I say turning from my mother to my father, back to my mother.

"One of you is lying," my father snarls.

"What did you think you were doing out there in the first place?" asks my mother in a high-handed way.

"Brad Jr. and I wanted to explore," I explain. "It was dark. We couldn't see where we were going. I kind of lost him. Then I heard him hit something. When I ran over to see what happened he was bleeding and holding his nose."

They look like they half-believe me, which is appropriate since what I've said is half-true.

"Well, none of that was smart," declares my mother.

"No, it wasn't very smart at all," adds my father. "Go to your room."

I turn to leave.

"And stay there!" my father shouts at my back.

CHAPTER
EIGHT

Monday morning my mother wakes up to find her right eye is swollen shut. Our maid, Ti Muoi, claims that my mother has been cursed. In fact, she swears to it and advises my father to set up a small altar with offerings in front of our house.

But my father will have none of it. "Nonsense," he says as Ti Muoi recites a list of things we need to purchase from the central market including a dog's tail and canary eggs.

"We'll handle it our way," he says in a scolding kind of way.

"You hope," she mutters under her breath, continuing on about "bad omens" and "spirits."

I try to remember what Mohammed told me about karma and how it works. Meanwhile, my father calls the Embassy doctor, Dr. Silverman, who tells him that he will prescribe special drops for my mother's eye.

When I cross to the side gate to wait for the Marines to escort us to school, Ti Muoi is still talking to herself. "This is bad," she tells me. "This is black magic!"

Black magic? The same kind of black magic my friend Alain talks about all the time in his fascination with wizards, the Holy Grail and numerology? I corner him at recess and tell him about my mother. He leans into me with a twinkle in his eye and says that black magic in the wrong hands is very dangerous and hard to resist.

"Look at Hitler," he says raising an eyebrow, excited by the concept of power. "He mesmerized so many people that he almost conquered the world!"

"I'm not talking about Hitler, Alain, I'm asking about my mother's eye."

Throughout my Medieval History and Algebra classes I'm trying to trace the link between the injury to Duc and my mom. *Is it just a strange coincidence? Is there a connection between them?* But as much as I try to connect the dots, I can't.

* * * * * *

At 12:30 I see Mohammed's smiling face waiting for me outside the school gate. "We've got a lot to do today," he announces.

I'm glad to hear it. Working with him is my refuge from the violence, my father's anxiety and my parents' almost constant disapproval.

Mohammed and I are friends. Even though he's a thirty-five-year-old man from Malaysia, who worships the Muslim religion, is the father of two sons (his oldest son is from his first marriage) and a daughter, and I'm a thirteen-year-old kid from the States, we trust each other on a deep level.

He's a good-hearted man with intelligent eyes and a quick sense of humor who enjoys life and likes people.

We work together as a team. When we arrive at a job site, he inspects the workers while I unload the truck or help out. Depending on what's needed I might do some painting, or knock down a wall, or nail new plywood into wooden studs. When Mohammed's finished, we meet in the truck and compare notes as we make our way to the next job.

There are always at least half a dozen jobs going on at once. A house needs painting; at another house a bathroom is being refitted with modern fixtures; at a third one a wall is being taken out to open up the living room; at a fourth the roof is being replaced.

Sy reluctantly shows up at the important ones. He's always funny. Today he's at the Neuharts', hands on his hips, fuming and taking the last drag of a cigarette and angrily crushing it out.

"Look at that son-of-a-bitch," he says pointing at an emaciated Vietnamese painter standing on a paint can. "Do you see what he's doing?"

Sy refers to the fact that the painter is using a two-inch brush to apply paint a wide expanse of ceiling. It's one of his pet peeves.

"You ever hear of a goddamn roller?" Sy asks the man directly.

But the painter doesn't speak English. And the painters on our crew are proud men who think of themselves as craftsmen. They don't like to be told what to do, or how to do it. This doesn't stop Sy, who is soon on a ladder with a roller and a pan of paint showing them how to do it efficiently.

The painter protests to Mohammed, explaining in Vietnamese that he doesn't use rollers because they splatter paint all over everything. He points to the little white speckles that appear on the floor when Sy uses the roller. Sy descends from the ladder and wipes more specks of paint off his forehead. The painter smiles.

"What is this idiot grinning at?" Sy asks.

"He says that rollers waste paint," Mohammed answers carefully.

"I don't care if they waste paint," Sy fires back. "They're a hell of a lot faster and do a better job!"

The painter doesn't agree. He grumbles and kicks an empty can to express his displeasure. Sy tells me to show him how it's done. I start by filling the pan, dipping the roller, rolling it so that the paint is even. After a few long strokes across the ceiling, the painter's pride takes over. He takes the roller from me and continues. Mohammed and I move on.

As the afternoon sun spreads glare through the sky, we return to the Embassy shop where workers are setting tables and chairs for "the end of Tet" party. Mohammed and I help them and soon Sy appears. He's pissed off again. This time he's complaining that Mr. Bowers doesn't want liquor served at the party.

"That goddamn holier-than-thou dip-shit can kiss my hairy ass," Sy steams. "It's a party, isn't it? A celebration. What's wrong with serving a little booze?"

He's arguing with himself, because no one disagrees, not even Mohammed who doesn't touch liquor because of his religion.

"If he doesn't want to drink that's his goddamn business," Sy says. "I hate people who are always telling other people how to live their lives."

Sy's bowed legs carry him to the front of the shop, where trucks have arrived bearing wooden crates filled with glasses and silverware. As I help unload the crates and carry them to the tables, Sy's last thought lingers in my head. "Live and let live," strikes me as a reasonable motto.

Mohammed counts and recounts the place settings and comes up with eighty-five.

"Will that be enough?" I ask.

Mohammed purses his dark lips and quickly calculates in his head. Then, nodding at me, he instructs the carpenters to set up two more tables out of sawhorses and sheets of plywood. That's when Mr. Bowers arrives with his hands thrust in his pockets, which gets our attention because Mr. Bowers rarely ventures outside of his air-conditioned office.

He's wearing the same thing he wears every other day — white short-sleeved shirt, black pants, shiny black shoes and a blue tie.

"What do you think?" Mohammed asks grinning.

Mr. Bowers crosses his arms across his chest and nods. His mind seems to be somewhere else. Craning his head in my direction, he tugs at my shirt, "Michael, come with me."

I follow his wide back to his office, where he closes the door and says, "Sy and Mohammed tell me that you're a big, big help around here. I appreciate that."

"Thanks." He picks up his black telephone and dials a number from memory. Then, he says, "Mr. Relaford wants to talk to you."

I'm completely taken aback. "Mr. Relaford? Now?" I wonder if he's still mad about the incident with Brad Jr.

"Michael?" Mr. Relaford's voice sounds deeper and more self-important than usual.

"Hi, Mr. Relaford," I say. "How's Brad Jr.? Is he feeling better?"

"He's healing quite nicely," he answers as though that's not of interest. There's a pause during which I calculate the big gulf between us. He's my father's boss. I'm a kid who helps out around the shop.

"Michael," he continues in a serious tone. "I understand you've been helping out with Sy and Mohammed."

"Yes, sir," I say, trying to anticipate where this is going.

"Good," he continues. "And I understand that you've been invited to the party tonight. The one at the shop."

"Yes, I have."

He pauses again. "Michael, that's a problem for a whole host of reasons that I don't have time to get into now. The long and short of it is that I don't want you to go to that party. I'm sure you understand."

"Why?" It's the only word I can squeeze out. "Why?" I ask again trying to contain the emotion gathering in my chest.

"Because you don't belong there," he answers in a snide tone of voice. "Now let me talk to Bowers."

Wide-eyed, my breathing irregular, I hand him the phone. My face, my hands, my chest are on fire. Mr. Bowers doesn't take his eyes off me, as he listens and nods his round head.

"Yes, Mr. Relaford.... I understand. Yes, sir."

I don't wait for the conversation to end. I leave the shop and duck outside, where the afternoon heat quickly envelops me. I could unburden myself to Huang two doors down in the motorpool. I could talk to Mohammed.

But this feels like something I have to face alone. My parents and the Relafords treat me the same way they treat the Vietnamese – with high-handedness and insensitivity. *Why do they feel the need to put us in our place?*

Is this Mr. Relaford's way of getting back at me for what happened to his son?

I want to scream until my anger rings off the walls and ricochets off the river.

Instead, I sit in the shade on the bumper of Mohammed's truck and wait for my emotion to subside. Birds arrive and fight over discarded fish heads. Sampans float by on the canal. Vendors' sing chants related to rice, mangos, live chickens and fish.

I don't know how long I've been sitting here when I hear Sy's voice behind me, "There you are!"

Without pity or condescension, he sits beside me and lights a cigarette.

"Can you tell me why that self-important asshole cares why you're invited to our party?" he asks, releasing a long stream of smoke that disappears into the warm, wet air. "Can you tell me why he cares?"

I appreciate his directness. We both wait for an answer, which doesn't come.

"I called Relaford and spoke to him myself," Sy says. "He told me it was none of my goddamn business. I told him to go fuck himself."

"You didn't have to do that, Sy," I say, my voice starting to tremble. Even though I'm a kid, I realize how rare and special it is to have someone stand up for you. And, Mr. Relaford is Sy's boss.

He lays a hand on my shoulder. "We'll miss you tonight, Michael. It won't be the same."

After assuring Mohammed about two dozen times that I'll be okay and I want him to enjoy the party, Sy drives me home. I peer out the window at the passing trees with their trunks painted white. My head feels swollen. Sy has a lot on his mind, too.

At the intersection of Tu Duc and Norodom he slaps the wheel. "I don't understand your father," he says. "I told him the other day that we should be paying you, even if it's a little something. Hell, you contribute just as much as the other men. And they appreciate you. They do. But your Dad won't budge.'"

"I don't care about the money, Sy."

I carry frustration with me into the house, past Chico's pink tongue, past Ti Moui who takes my lunchbox and mutters something under her breath. My father is home, sitting on the porch sipping a gin and tonic with my mother as though nothing important has happened. He looks at me over his shoulder without saying a word.

After washing my face, I find the poem I wrote for Mr. Nhu, stuff it in my pocket and slip outside. The sun sets gently, casting an invisible curtain over the city. This is a time of ease; my favorite part of the day. It's a time when spirits and ghosts enter our world to greet us and push us gently on our way. I feel them accompany me along the avenue to the Cathedral.

I don't feel like facing Father McDaniel today with his probing questions and quotes from the Gospels. I believe in God and the message of Jesus but understand that religion is tricky and I don't want to get caught up in it.

My spirit needs to be free of dogma and rules. It needs time to grow wings so it can fly on its own.

I see a young French priest with a soft, angelic face setting fresh lilies on the altar. I hand him the poem and ask him to deliver it to Father McDaniel. He gazes with soulful eyes like a portrait my aunt once showed me of Saint John the Baptist by her favorite artist Leonardo Da Vinci.

I approach the river, which is surrounded by activity, and repeat the poem in my head:

> Two rivers:
> One old and gentle
> Slowed by the finest silt:
> Culture, the sap of human kindness,
> Grace in all its guises
> History;
> One new, fast on its feet, sure
> Like a shiny Oldsmobile.
> They meet in a torrent
> And before they can ask why
> Or scream
> Between thunderclaps
> They are changed forever.
>
> The old river is pulled quicker than before
> So fast that it must shed
> Lyrical traditions
> And gentle trails of silk
> Grasping for a comfortable rhythm
> It looks in the mirror of the moon
> For a new face
> Only to see an image that is harsh,
> Unformed and hurried.
>
> The new river is slowed by
> Ancestors, sighs
> Complicated manners
> And a woman's long caress.

Without the luxury of speed
It's not sure anymore
And this new insecurity
Breeds impatience and anger.

Sharing a new destiny
Suspicious of one another
Partners in ways they can't begin to fathom
They stare at one another in their strangeness
Across the gap of mutual acceptance
And fill it with horror, recriminations, self-hate
And deadly blame.

Life along the Saigon River unfolds like a real-life movie. This evening, military equipment is being unloaded from gray ships by old and very young people with thin wiry bodies that have been pushed beyond the point of exhaustion.

The stronger, more vital men in the army zigzag through adjoining streets on Hondas. They're spared the more physical work because of their role in society.

It's a complicated story that never stops, day or night. Along the piers wait trucks to load the heavy sacks of cement to carry off. To one side wizened women squat, sew torn sacks and spit betel juice from mouths that look like gaping wounds. Others refill the spilt cement using paper funnels. Tubercular old men lean on crates of US military hardware, savoring a few last puffs from hand-rolled cigarettes before they return to work. Young boys tease each other, then wash the white paste from their faces.

You can almost smell the chaos. The future colliding with the past; the West imposing itself on the East. Tonight, I feel like the only American witness – me, with my uncertainty and curious brown eyes.

My poem feels insignificant. I consider tossing it in the river, boarding one of the nearby ships and leaving for some far-away place. Maybe my new adventures will help define who I am and make me strong. Maybe my disappearance will shake my parents out of the spell of their beliefs.

I imagine my grandfather scolding them and the confused looks on the faces of my brother and sister. I imagine how my disappearance will affect Mr. Relaford, Brad Jr. and Samantha.

I remember the party that's taking place in the shop. The little colored lights I strung with Mohammed. The smell of sweet and sour pork. Huang and the others asking for me and Sy's angry explanation, a beer can clutched in his hand.

It would be easy to run away, especially from my father, whom I know I have to face and try to solve. He's still sitting on the porch when I return, reading *the New York Times* and sipping his second or third gin and tonic. I sit across from him and tell him exactly what happened with Mr. Relaford, straight and without emotion. As he listens, his jaw tightens.

"So?" he asks looking up at me like a bully who has stolen my marbles and has no intention of giving them back. Chico patrols the other side of the screen, waiting for something to pounce on.

"What right does Mr. Relaford have to tell me what to do?" I ask into his little eyes.

"He has every right," he shoots back. "He has authority over the running of the Embassy and everything connected to it, including you."

My mind raises questions about inalienable rights. My emotions rise. "Do you agree with what he did?" I ask.

My father screws up his mouth into a cruel smile. "Yes!"

"Why?" I ask him.

"Why?"

"Yes. Why?" I ask, standing my ground.

He looks like he might get up and punch me in the mouth. "I don't like the tone of your question," he snarls back.

When cornered or challenged, the bully always emerges to put me in my place. I say, "Dad, I'm your son. It doesn't seem fair. I'm trying to understand."

Narrowing his eyes, he looks at me hard. "Mr. Relaford told you not to go to the party. That's all you need to know."

I'm supposed to put my tail between my legs and leave. But if I do, I'll never learn. So I press on as gently and unemotionally as I can. "Will you please talk to Mr. Relaford? Will you ask him for an explanation?"

His answer is, "No, goddammit!" Like a quick slap to the face.

I stand staring at him in disbelief, thinking to myself: *He's a coward, a liar. He's not really my father.*

"You look at me like that and I'll kick your ass!" he growls, trying to pull himself up from the chair.

"Dad...."

Flailing his arms, he sends an ashtray flying across the floor so that it shatters against the wall. Gathering his hands beneath him, he makes another effort to pull himself up.

"I'll wring your scrawny little neck!"

I turn and leave. There's no point arguing. He's had several gin and tonics and I don't want him to hit me. Closing the door to my room I wait for my mother, but she never comes. Feeling betrayed, abandoned, wishing I'd stowed away on a ship, I rock myself to sleep.

* * * * * *

I dream that I'm driving out of the city with Mohammed, through dense jungle, until we reach the shore. Father McDaniel waits for us on the beach, his hands on his hips. Standing behind him are Sy, Mohammed's family and a whole group of friends. Time skips forward and we're playing tag on the beach, grilling shrimp, watching gulls swoop in wide circles. The sky turns dark and a loud mechanical noise attacks our ears.

Sy's the first one to point it out. A huge gray helicopter

descends from the clouds. It lands twenty feet from us with big claws, creating chaos with the sand. My father jumps out wearing military fatigues. He's carrying a rifle with a long bayonet. He grabs me by the shoulder and pointing to the helicopter, shouts: "Get in!"

My feet freeze. My legs harden into cement. My father pushes me. I fall down in the sand. I feel it enter my mouth. He grabs me by the collar, picks me up and pushes me, so that I stumble and fall again.

Sy is at my side, explaining to my father in low voice that I'm really a good kid and don't deserve to be treated like this. My father lifts the bayonet and stabs him in the chest.

The following afternoon at work, everyone is quiet. We're all pulled inside ourselves: me, Huang, Mr. Bowers, Sy, Mohammed and the others.

* * * * * *

Hours later, Sy, Mohammed and I stand on the second floor of the Ambassador's residence looking at paint samples, when the Ambassador walks in. Up until this moment I've only known him from his picture. In real life he's larger with the gentle, reassuring aura of a kind grandfather. Silver hair, roughly chiseled features on a wide face. He takes my hand and tells me that he's glad to meet me.

His eyes and voice are sincere. For the first time, I sense that there's an American here who understands and appreciates the Vietnamese people, which gives me hope. Together we pick out a heathered yellow color for the upstairs sitting room.

Afterwards, Sy takes me in the black pick-up to a narrow street called Ham Nghi, directly behind the Embassy. I follow his lurching side-to-side walk into a dark place called the Milk Bar which has walls the color of dried blood. We ease into a booth that smells of mildew. Sy orders a Coke for me and a

333 beer for himself.

"We missed you," he says. "You talk to your Dad?'

I give him a quick capsule of our conversation.

He orders another beer and says, "I don't know what it is about this fucking country. Maybe it's the beauty, the sensuousness of the place... Men like your Dad and Mr. Relaford think they've got to possess it, like they gotta make it their goddamn mistress."

His face is creased with a depth of concern that I've never seen in him before. He pushes the sparse hair back over his head. In the back a tableful of men sings loudly in English, over the drone of the air conditioner.

"Do you think the Ambassador understands what's going on here?" I ask.

"I think so," Sy answers, "I just hope he's strong enough to get his way."

The men in the back sing to the tune of "My Bonnie Lies Over the Ocean," but the words are different. Something like:

My mother's a Montagnard sergeant,
She draws jump pay and quarters to boot,
She lives in Saigon on per diem,
And always has plenty of loot.

Stay here, stay here,
Oh, don't let the program go down, go down.
Stay here, stay here,
'Cause Saigon's a real swinging town.

My father's a part-time guerilla,
He gives all the ARVN a fit,
By selling for twenty piasters
A do-it-yourself ambush kit.

The song ends with an eruption of laughter and cheers. I

notice a wide figure emerge from the smoky gloom in back. It's Bruno clutching a glass and smiling from ear to ear. He lists to one side, then rights himself against a large fish tank along the wall. His eyes light up when he spots me sitting with Sy.

Leaning over the table, he pokes a finger in my chest, "Who let this young pup in this bar?"

"I did," replies Sy looking into his Bau Muoi Ba bottle and finding it empty.

Bruno burps and covers his mouth. "What are you two planning?" he asks. Then turning to the bartender, shouts, "Where's the waitress? The service in this place stinks!"

The slim waitress moves like liquid. She's used to the gruff manners of Americans who drink too much. "What you want, mister?"

"What do I want?" Bruno rolls his eyes. "What do I want?"

"What you drinking?" she asks, her voice sliding higher.

Bruno smells the glass. "It's Bacardi rum. Not that cheap crap you usually serve. Bacardi!"

"One rum coming up," she sings, slinking off.

Bruno slides in next to Sy and says over his shoulder. "Give me a cherry with that, sweetheart," winking at me like I'm supposed to understand.

"What's new, Bruno?" Sy asks trying to maintain some space between himself, the wall and Bruno's big shoulders.

"We're holding our weekly meeting of the Cosmos Tabernacle Choir," Bruno answers. "What did you think of the song?"

"Nice."

"Nice?" Bruno bellows back as the waitress slides the rum in front of him and squirts out of reach.

"I wasn't really listening," Sy explains.

I try to not to eavesdrop either, but can't help it, as the two men discuss gossip at the Embassy, politics and the military situation.

At one point, Bruno says, "They're Asian, goddammit. The Asian mind never faces anything straight on. If we want it to go our way, we've got to do it ourselves."

His approach is different from my Dad's. My father takes pride in being precise and backing up his reasons with hard facts. Bruno enjoys taking large leaps that propel him forward into uncharted territory. He's bold like an explorer. And like most explorers he has no compunction about killing a few natives or cutting down a few trees.

He references his experiences in Corsica, Greece, Korea, France, the Congo, and Iran. And he leans on his understanding of individual personalities and idiosyncrasies, which is something my father doesn't trust.

I like Bruno, even though he's killed people according to Brad Jr.

"Did I ever tell you that I knew Uncle Ho when he was a skinny graduate student fresh out of Paris?" he asks.

"No," says Sy shaking his head.

"True," Bruno boasts. Then in confidence, "If you ask me, we picked the wrong side."

My father, Mr. Relaford and other Embassy officers would consider this heresy, but Sy doesn't bat an eye.

"I thought he was a communist and you don't like communists" Sy remarks.

Bruno waves his arms like he's breaking free from invisible strings. "Communists, nationalists, socialists, fascists... They're all the same game." He slaps his palm flat down on the table rattling the glasses. "They all want power! Control. All I care about is: Are they on our side or playing footsie with the bad guys?"

Sy slowly swirls his beer and waits for the implications to sink in. "You're a cynic," he says. "A Machiavellian."

"I'm a realist," Bruno pokes back. "I speak from experience. You think we're goodie two-shoes? You naïve enough to believe that crap? Hell, I've been running ops against the North since this boy here was in diapers," he says, downing his rum, then holding up his glass and shouting: "One more!"

"I lost count of the number of sap teams I sent above the 42nd parallel. Into North Vietnam! You know what a sap team does, kid? We assassinate local officials, cut their balls off, blow up bridges, sabotage factories, drop propaganda and generally fuck with their minds."

He's got another rum now and throws his head back and downs it. Then, he lets out another big sigh and seems to relax like a switch is his head has been shut off. Sy waves at the waitress, indicating that he wants the check.

Bruno suddenly springs to life again. "I keep telling people at the Embassy that the Vietnamese aren't like us. They don't cling to life with the same kind of desperation that we do. They're superstitious. I mean they believe in dragon spirits, for christsakes..." He turns to me and asks, "You believe in magic?"

I don't have to think about it. "Yes."

His eyes drift far away. Sy signals with his thumb that it's time to go.

Before we have a chance to say goodbye, Bruno grabs my arm and speaks in a low voice, "I was five fucking years old. Five! We were visiting my mother's family in the south of France. We were in a car, driving through a forest near the Spanish border. I'd never been there before. My father turned around a bend and I yelled: 'STOP!' My father hit the brakes. I got out and ran into the woods. I stopped at a certain tree I recognized and started digging with my hands. My family caught up with me. They watched me dig with my bare hands about a foot or two into the ground until I found a little leather bag. I pulled it out and opened it. The bag contained several dozen gold coins. They helped my Dad start a business and later paid my way through college. Explain that!"

We are already on our feet.

Bruno looks up at us with bloodshot eyes and says like he's confiding a secret, "Sometimes you just know things, right? Like I know that that President Diem will never fucking win this war and this kid is trouble."

CHAPTER
NINE

The house we've moved into was built on a grand scale by the Emperor Bao Dai for one of his favorite mistresses. It's hidden behind a high wall on a busy street called Phan Thanh Gian. About a half-mile north, over a bridge, Phan Thanh Gian turns into the highway to the town of Ben Hua.

It's interesting because Bao Dai's house is on Phan Thanh Gian Street and both men – Bao Dai and Phan Than Gian – campaigned for Vietnamese independence. I know this because our history teacher recently explained how the two of them served as bookends to the French occupation. Phan Than Gian was a mandarin and ambassador, who after failing to convince Emperor Tu Duc to wage a nationwide resistance against the French, took poison on August 4, 1867 and died after a thirteen-day hunger strike.

Bao Dai was the last emperor of Vietnam. Even though he had a reputation for being a weak, corruptible playboy, he refused to give into the French ambition to restore Vietnam as a colony after World War II.

Our new house boasts a beautiful garden, a screened front

porch with large square white and black tiles, a living room the size of a small football field with a built-in mahogany bar and an enormous marble staircase. The bedrooms are on the second floor. The kitchen and maid's quarters are in the back and stand separate from the main house.

Many gifts have arrived to welcome us, most of them from Chinese merchants who do business with the Embassy – including exotic teas, boxes of mangoes and mangosteens, ginger jars, lacquer paintings of tigers and elephants, carved pieces of ivory and a beautiful kumquat tree that my mother has placed on the bar.

Our cross-eyed maid, Ti Muoi, has left, in part because she kept insisting that my mother consult a spiritualist to help cure the problem with her eye. In her place, my parents have hired a new maid named Ti Ba, a butler named Dong, a cook, a gardener, and a new chauffeur to replace Mr. Fu.

Ti Ba and Dong do all the shopping, so that my mother rarely has to leave the house. She only ventures out at night, when she and my father go out to one of their "functions" — dinners, formal receptions, cocktail parties — which they do approximately five nights a week. My father says that it's part of his job to socialize with Vietnamese officials so that he and the Embassy can gain a clearer understanding of what's going on.

We've never lived in such grandeur before. Prior to Vietnam, we rented a small three-bedroom apartment in Arlington, Virginia. The only other time we lived abroad, in Mexico, our house was modest, although my mother did have a maid to help with the cleaning.

My parents seem to enjoy the new luxury. My father likes having Dong wait to open the front gate when he drives home after work. He approves of the cocktails Dong mixes for him and my mother, and the way he serves them in the living room with hors d'oerves prepared by the cook. And he likes the fact that Ti Ba cleans his dark green Mercedes every morning before he leaves for work.

But my mother still complains. Last night when the Relafords stopped at our house for a drink on their way to a reception at the Ambassador's house, I heard her say, "I hate having all these people in my house. I feel like I have no privacy. I can do all of it better myself."

The thing she seems to enjoy the most is dressing up at night and going out. But she complains about that, too. I've heard her tell people that the favorite part of her life is raising her children. But she rarely spends time with us and when she does, seems distracted and sad.

When I gently ask my father why she is that way she is, he says, "You're very lucky to have such a wonderful mother. If she needs time to herself, just leave her alone."

I draw her pictures, bake pastries and cakes and tell her stories. But her interest wears off quickly and the dark clouds creep over her again.

Is she still thinking about her brother? Is that why she's never silly and rarely smiles? Is she hiding something even more terrible?

A couple of nights ago she came into my room as I was falling asleep and sat on the edge of my bed.

"Mom, is something wrong?" I asked.

"Not really," she said.

I could tell there was something on her mind. She reached out and took my hands.

"What is it, Mom?"

She said, "You get along well with your father."

"I try."

"I know it isn't easy."

"Mom, is something wrong?"

"You're growing up so fast," she said with sadness in her voice.

I reminded her that when I was sick in bed as a little boy she used to make me soup with tiny meatballs and read me stories.

I wish I knew how to chase her regrets away.

She's calm when we're alone together. Not nervous the way she is around other people. She tells me that she loves me the most; that I'm the only person who understands her; that I'm the only one she can talk to. She says that it's hard for her to treat me as a son because I remind her of her brother.

When I ask her how I can make her feel more comfortable here in Vietnam, she calls me "her angel" and tears well up in her eyes. But she doesn't tell me what she wants.

Does she want to escape her life altogether? Does life disappoint her in some fundamental way?

When I discuss her with my father, which I have to do in a very indirect way, he says, "Women are a mystery." Or, "Your mother had a difficult childhood." But that doesn't answer my questions. In the end, he makes me feel guilty for prying when I'm just trying to understand.

My parents' disinterest affects my sister and brother, too. My Dad is busy with work and not really interested in anyone who can't discuss the things he wants to talk about in an intelligent way.

When they're not in school, Maggie and Corey are home. Sometimes they play together until Maggie insults my brother, and Corey tells her "to go to hell." It would help if they had friends who came over. But that rarely happens, because we live on the edge of town and most Americans don't like to travel far from their homes.

Sometimes I think I'm the only one who's happy here, because I have a full life with friends and work with Mohammed.

Since we moved into our new house, I've started to feel acquisitive and I don't know why. It began when I discovered the little brick guardhouse hidden under the thick foliage by the front fence.

I told Mohammed that I wanted to convert it into a

workshop. I swept it out and scrubbed the mildew off the walls. Mohammed had carpenters at the shop construct a small worktable with a drawer for tools and a stool to sit on. Then Mohammed gave me some tools — a saw fixed an at angle with a handle on top like the ones the Vietnamese workers use, an old vise that I clamped to the table, a hammer and a chisel. I asked my father for money to buy nails and screwdrivers. When he said "no" I asked Mohammed if he could find some for me at the shop.

It happened one evening after he dropped me off on his motorbike. We stood in my moldy little workshop while Chico sniffed around. There wasn't any judgment in Mohammed's black sparkling eyes, just a kind of curiosity. He didn't ask if I'd asked my father first. He just nodded as though he understood my need.

I felt bad. I felt even worse the next afternoon when we went to the Ambassador's house and a picture fell out of Mohammed's shirt pocket. When I bent down to pick it up I saw that it was a photograph of his family — a young girl, a younger boy and an older boy with a scowl on his face.

Back in the truck, I asked Mohammed about his sons and daughter. He told me that his youngest daughter wasn't feeling well and had developed a cough that wouldn't go away.

I felt ashamed of myself – as though I'd taken advantage of his friendship. Here was a man with real problems and I had been asking him for nails.

* * * * * *

That night my father returned home while I was feeding my tropical fish in two large aquariums under the stairs. He looked preoccupied the way he usually does after work and started climbing the steps without saying "hello."

"Hi, Dad," I said. "I've got to talk to you about something."

"Later," he said gruffly.

"It's important."

He paused halfway up and frowned down at me. "Wait till I come down and have my drink."

Dong was already behind the bar mixing a gin and tonic and cutting a wedge of lime. He watched me from behind the kumquat tree with his hangdog eyes. A lock of straight hair fell across his forehead. He smiled enigmatically like he understood my dilemma with my father.

Maggie and Corey were already sitting down to dinner, squabbling about the rules to Clue, when my father returned. He'd changed his shirt and was knotting a striped tie. His eyes looked tired. He said, "Would you tell those two to please shut up, before I have to shut them up myself?"

I warned my brother and sister, then hurried to the porch where Dong served the gin and tonic with a bowl of cashews on the duck basket that my mother had made into a table with a glass top.

"Shouldn't you be eating dinner?" my father asked, his eyes wandering to Chico, now fully-grown – a strongly muscled mixture of pit bull and hound mostly white with brown splotches, patrolling the front lawn.

"He's turned into a good guard dog," my father said picking up a *Time* magazine with a picture of Jacqueline Kennedy on the cover.

"Dad," I started.

"Leave me alone," he groaned between sips of his drink.

"Dad, Mohammed's daughter has a bad cough that won't go away. He's taken her to a doctor, but she isn't improving."

My father took another long drink and continued leafing through the magazine.

"I was wondering if the Embassy doctor, Dr. Silverman, could take a look at her," I continued.

"Can't you see I'm trying to read?" growled my father.

"Dad—"

We were interrupted by growls and high-pitched squeals

from the yard. Chico was fighting with what looked like a ball of red and brown feathers. Then the feathers jumped up out of his paws and took flight, and Chico raised himself on his back legs and tried to swat the chicken or rooster out of the air.

"I'd better stop him," I said, taking a step towards the door.

"Leave him alone!" barked my father.

The chicken pumped it wings wildly, skipping across the lawn, trying to get aloft. Chico pounced and beat the bird against the ground, flinging its head from side to side, until the chicken stopped moving and Chico's mouth and nose were covered with bright red blood.

"Powerful mutt," my father said proudly. Then he called for Dong to fix him another drink.

I'd lost my appetite for dinner. The next day, Saturday, I went to see Father McDaniel at the Cathedral. He listened to me with hands folded in his lap as a chorus practiced "hallelujahs" behind us.

When I finished my confession, he said, "You've been covetous, Michael."

"Yes. I have, Father."

"Take what God has given you and use it. But don't covet things that you don't need."

In my room listening to "Wipe Out" by The Ventures on the radio, I remembered that I had met the Embassy doctor, Dr. Silverman, when my father took me to his house. Dr. Silverman, who is a bachelor, wanted to see the electric racecars I'd gotten for Christmas.

My father and I entered his living room to find two-dozen grown men racing cars on a track that snaked through Dr. Silverman's house. They were betting, cursing and smoking cigars. As we left, after testing my cars on the track, my father called Dr. Silverman "a weird duck."

* * * * * *

It's Monday afternoon and Mohammed and I are on the way back to the shop. We're carrying an old porcelain bathtub and bidet in the bed of the Chevy pickup. I ask him to stop at the Embassy and wait a minute while I go inside.

The Marine Guard at the desk is a big guy with a wide neck named Hughie. He's also the catcher for the Embassy softball team. I tell him that I'm here to see to Dr. Silverman.

He directs me to the second floor where I find Dr. Silverman at a desk reading a Pogo comic book. He wears a white coat with a stethoscope around his neck.

"Michael, what brings you here?" he asks.

I tell him about Mohammed's daughter, Gita, and her cough. He runs his hand over the bald spot on the back of his head and asks, "Where is she now?"

I tell Dr. Silverman that she's resting at home, which is somewhere west in Cholon. He looks up at the clock on the wall behind his desk and says. "I'm not supposed to do this, but... tell Mohammed to bring her here at say... six-thirty, seven."

"I'll do that. Thanks," I say, reaching in my pocket for the racecar that I brought with me.

"What's this for?" he asks.

"I thought you might want to borrow it."

His face lights up with excitement. "Thanks!"

Back in the truck, I convey the news to Mohammed, who listens quietly and nods. "I appreciate this very much," he says.

"It's nothing, Mohammed."

"I'll be sure to thank your father, too."

"No, Mohammed," I say. "You've got to promise you won't tell my father.

And one more thing... I don't want any more tools. I've got everything I need."

The next afternoon Mohammed informs me that Dr. Silverman found tuberculosis in his daughter's lung.

"Tuberculosis?" I repeat, thinking that it sounds serious,

wondering if his daughter is going to survive. But Mohammed seems calm. He wears a light blue cotton shirt that makes his skin look like it's made of dark chocolate.

"Is she going to be okay?" I ask.

"Dr. Silverman is taking care of everything," Mohammed says confidently. "He's a very clever doctor. He says we caught the disease in time."

Before we cross the bridge to the shop, Mohammed pulls over and parks under a tree bursting with orange blossoms. "Come," he says.

We sit in the shade on rickety folding chairs watching two barefoot boys push bicycle rims with a stick. Birds argue in the trees above. Mohammed orders a lime cooler. I've been told never to drink anything with ice or water, so I choose Coca-Cola in a bottle.

"My wife and I are very grateful," says Mohammed as he reaches into his pocket and produces a wristwatch on a silver chain.

He hands it to me and says, "You must take this as token of our appreciation."

"No, Mohammed. I can't take this. You've given me so much already..." I'm overcome with emotion. Mohammed takes my hand in his. Warmth spreads from my heart.

* * * * * *

Two weeks later, I'm in the big bedroom that I share with my younger brother, reading *A Tale of Two Cities* by Charles Dickens, listening to bats flutter in the attic, when I hear my mother scream.

Dropping the book, I rush into the upstairs parlor and find her at the window watching Dr. Silverman enter through the front gate.

"What's the matter?" I ask.

She points to the doctor walking to the house and says,

"Something awful must have happened to your father."

"No, Mom. It's something else."

Together we greet him in the living room where he gallantly kisses my mother's hand. "Good evening, Mrs. Sforza."

"Good evening, doctor," she says breathlessly.

He slowly reaches into his pocket. "Thanks," he says handing me the race car I lent him. "First class. It's got loads of pep and I like the way it handles the curves."

"You're welcome to borrow it anytime," I reply. "You can have it if you want."

"No, no." He winks at me and says, "The situation is under control." Then turning to my befuddled mother, asks, "Is everything okay with you, Mrs. Sforza? Your eye still looks inflamed."

"Yes, it is," she says.

"I want you to see a specialist at the military hospital," he says, writing out a name and address.

* * * * * *

After the English mass on Sunday, I tell Father McDaniel that I'm not feeling "covetous" anymore. He pats me on the shoulder and leads me into the rectory.

"We've got a couple of things to discuss," he says as one of the altar boys helps him lift a gold robe over his head. "First, it's time for you to start your catechism. I've talked to Father Ralston at St. Paul's who is starting a new class next week. It meets on Saturday morning, ten o' clock."

"Okay." St. Paul's is a new, very modern church that was built especially for the English-speaking community.

"Secondly, Mr. Nhu liked your poem and showed it to his brother. He wants to know if you received the gift he sent you."

"What gift?" I ask.

"He says he sent a very special kumquat tree that was cultivated by Buddhist monks to bring good luck."

"Oh, that," I say, remembering the tree full of little golden fruit that my mother placed on the bar. My parents didn't say that it was a gift for me.

"Also, he wants to invite you to the palace for dinner," Father McDaniel says stopping what he's doing to gauge my reaction.

"Really?" I can hardly believe what I'm hearing.

"Yes, and he invited me, too."

I've never been to a palace before. The closest I've come is a tour of the White House with my fourth-grade class.

I don't tell my parents, because they won't believe me until they see the invitation. Every evening when I get home, I ask Mr. Dong if any mail has come for me. He looks at me slyly, smiling out the side of his mouth as though he thinks I've got a secret girlfriend that I'm hiding from my parents.

I'd be happy to tell him that the object of my affection is Samantha Relaford. Samantha's friends tell my friends that she likes me, too. She wrote in a slam book circulating through the eighth grade that I'm "very nice and interesting" with "gorgeous brown eyes" and I'm the person she would most like to be shipwrecked on a deserted island with. I wrote back that I want to be shipwrecked with her, too.

It's difficult for Samantha and me to be alone together because our parents are close friends. I see her at school. She has a way of smiling at me in the private space between her bangs and the books she carries over her chest.

She's shy and discreet. She told my sister that her parents won't permit her to date boys until she's fifteen. When our families get together, which happens every other week or so, she usually plays with my sister and I do things with Brad Jr.

Tonight, I'm seeing her at a birthday party for our classmate, Alain Perry, who's turning thirteen. I arrive at his house by taxi with Greg Hecht. Alain greets us at the door and tells us that his parents aren't home.

"Great," says Greg. "We'll have an orgy!"

"What's an orgy?" asks Bill Rydell who is the fattest and nicest kid in class.

"An orgy is a wild sexual free-for-all," answers Sally Forsythe, looking over black-framed glasses. She's at the record player leafing through Alan's 45s.

Sally is one of those girls who act as though they're not shocked by anything and think boys are immature. At the age of thirteen she affects the air of a jaded bohemian who spends her free time sipping espressos in French cafés and flirting with dangerous men.

"What's wrong with you, Alain?" she protests. "You don't have the Kingston Trio."

"Who are the Kingston Trio?" I ask.

Sally turns to me and groans, throwing her long brown hair over her shoulder. The truth is that I know very little about music, and don't have 45s. My parents own the only music that's played in our house — show tunes from *My Fair Lady*, *The Sound of Music* and *South Pacific*, an Eartha Kitt album and the Tijuana Brass.

More kids arrive. Debby who is tall and serious, Matt who draws the funniest dirty cartoons, C.J. who is pretty but very, very skinny, and Samantha who hides behind Debby and C.J. She says a general "hi" to the entire room, spots me and casts her eyes down to the floor. She wears her long amber hair pulled back in a braid with a cluster of little white flowers. Her dress is blue and white with no sleeves.

We're gathered in two rows on the floor with the boys on one side and the girls on the other. Alain's maid serves cokes, shrimp chips and hamburgers. I'm drawn to the music — Jan & Dean, the Beach Boys and the Searchers — which is ripe with yearning and exuberance.

The talk is about school, which teachers are nice and which ones are mean and give too much homework. Sally and

Alain are arguing about whether French cigarettes are superior to American cigarettes when a beautiful song starts: "Venus, oh my love...." It's the song that Coop played at the Brodard before Leroy died. Emotion starts to rise into my throat. I catch Samantha watching me. She smiles warmly and looks away.

Greg and Sally are trying to get the others to play Spin the Bottle, but Debbie and C.J. protest. "My parents will kill me if they find out," Debbie says.

"Who's going to tell?" Sally asks.

"Anybody could!" Debbie exclaims, throwing up her arms and leaving the room. C.J. and Sally follow. Kevin and Alan have gone inside to look at the rubbers in Alain's father's bedroom drawer.

I'm so entranced by the music that I don't realize that Samantha and I are alone except for Greg who's curled on the sofa reading comic books. A new song comes on. A male voice sings: "Listen to the rhythm of the falling rain, pitter patter, pitter patter...."

I move closer to Samantha and say, "I like this song."

"Me, too," she responds.

"I really like this music. I've never heard it before."

She smiles sweetly. "Sometimes they play it on Armed Forces radio."

"Really?" I ask.

"Yeah." She tugs at her bottom lip. Everything about her — the way she smells, the brightness of her skin, her smile, the sparkle in her eyes — is wonderful to me.

My whole body trembles. I feel like I have to say something, so I ask, "Do you like to swim?"

"I love it," she answers.

"Would you like to go to the Cercle Sportif with me some day after school?"

"When?" she asks.

"Monday?"

"I can't," she answers.

My disappointment freezes everything. I don't know if I have the confidence to continue.

"How about Tuesday?" I ask, trying again.

She rests her chin in her palm as she considers. "Is next Wednesday okay?" she asks.

"Sure!" I decide I'll tell Mohammed that I'm taking the afternoon off.

A frown of concern crosses her face. "But don't pick me up," she warns. "I'll meet you there."

"Okay. How about we meet at say one-thirty?"

"Fine."

I have to retreat outside, because my pulse is jumping and my face is on fire. The sky sparkles with an infinity of stars and planets. The wind tickles my nose. A high, plaintive Vietnamese voice sings beyond the tall walls. Even though I can't understand the words, it seems to be a call for love.

Greg appears rubbing his eyes. "I've been looking for you," he says. "What's going on?"

"I'm just getting some fresh air."

He looks at me quizzically as though he can read the thoughts cascading through my brain. "I saw you talking to Sam," he whispers. "What did she say?"

"We just talked."

He winks and pokes me with his elbow. "Get out."

* * * * * *

Back home in bed, artillery rumbles in the distance — a reminder of the danger that could reach us at any time. In the morning, Greg and I meet in church for the first day of catechism. Father Ralston is a tall man with a thin, sallow face. About a dozen kids sit before him in the front pews. Light spills in from skylights. The modern, colored glass windows cast kaleidoscope patterns on the floor.

Father Ralston tells us about the Holy Trinity. Greg passes a note that says: "No one is listening!"

I nod and Father Ralston shoots me a look. He's bathed in green from the eyes up and gold from the nose down. "Any questions?" he asks.

I raise my hand. "Father, you said that the Holy Ghost is not separate from Jesus, but acts and speaks through him. Could you explain?"

Greg coughs and says, "Excuse me, Holy Father." Then, ducking his head behind the pew, he grins at me like a monkey and mimes laughing out loud.

"Which one are you?" ask Father Ralston, pointing a long, bony finger at me.

"Michael Sforza."

"Mr. Sforza..." He repeats as someone snores behind us. Greg finds this very funny, covers his mouth and coughs again.

"Perhaps you need a glass of water," Father Ralston says to Greg.

"Thank you, your holiness."

The Father points to a door to the right of the altar. "In there."

Greg walks solemnly. When he reaches the door behind Father Ralston, he turns back to me, smiles and waves. I have to struggle to keep a straight face.

Father Ralston says: "The Holy Ghost is not something that I can hand to you like a piece of chewing gum, Mr. Sforza. It's not something you can touch or taste. The Holy Ghost is something you must accept on faith."

CHAPTER
TEN

"I'm giving you this assignment, and I don't want you to screw it up." Those were my father's instructions at breakfast.

They echo in my head as I crouch on the concrete floor of the maintenance shop in front of a large wooden crate. I have a hammer in one hand and a crowbar in the other, and don't know where to start.

The wooden crate stands as tall as I am and is nearly as wide as it is high. The stenciled address says that it was sent from Rome, Italy. I've heard that it's laden with delicious things that my parents, the Relafords and Gelbarts ordered months ago. My job is to separate the goods and deliver them safely to their respective buyers.

Seeing that there are screws and bolts to contend with, I exchange the hammer for a screwdriver, socket wrench and ladder and get to work. I wonder about Mohammed, who has taken the week off to be with his family. Huang, my friend in motorpool, heard that his daughter's health is improving.

My father explained that Bruno (Mr. Gelbart) is the one

who sent in the order to Italy. He told me to address any questions I have to him. My goal is to complete the assignment without calling Bruno.

Once I unscrew the top, I carefully remove the two side panels with the help of Chung, a carpenter. All the goods are packed neatly and wrapped in clear plastic. I carefully remove green and white boxes of pasta, large cans of plum tomatoes from Salerno, round provolone cheeses, wheels of parmesan cheese. The smells take me back to another place and time.

I'm in the kitchen of my grandparents' apartment in the Bronx, watching my grandmother create a crater in a mountain of flour, fill it with fresh eggs and start to knead the dough. Behind me braciole and pork simmer in tomato sauce, filling the air with a sweet aroma, sharpened and complemented by the parmesan cheese my grandfather is grating as he sips a glass of Scotch.

My soul travels through the memories and back. I stare at two cases of orange soda at the bottom of the crate and realize there's a problem. During shipment from Rome to Saigon about half of the bottles broke. Since they were at the bottom, the spilled soda did little damage to other contents of the crate.

I work and sweat, taking a break for a peanut butter and jelly sandwich and Shasta soda. It takes most of the day to separate everything and check the items against the manifest, and then compare them to the list Mrs. Relaford gave me with different columns for the three different families. I separate them into piles, then load the piles into boxes.

Sy wanders over and asks, "Having fun?"

No, I'm trying not to "screw it up," which is why I'm carefully double and triple-checking the list. I didn't notice at first that the Perugina chocolates came in two different flavors — milk and dark.

Satisfied that I've got everything sorted correctly, I walk to motorpool in the next warehouse. Teams of Vietnamese men who quit at four are already leaving the shop on an assortment of motorbikes and bicycles. Huang provides me with a truck and driver.

It feels like I've never been given so much responsibility, which is silly. But since these things belong to the Gelbarts and the Relafords who are my parents' closest friends and they're delicacies from halfway around the world, I want to show them I'm a person who can be trusted.

My first stop is the Gelbarts. They live in a group of houses set off from the main street by a gate. Three Vietnamese soldiers in khaki uniforms with white belts, spats and helmets wave me in.

The truck winds through carefully manicured lawns and foliage. A petite and neatly groomed Mrs. Gelbart waits at the door in a blue sweater even though the sun is hot.

Inside, the house is cool. Everything about Mrs. Gelbart is delicate — her hands, the way she holds her tea, the way she purses her lips, the little flowers on her dress. "I miss France," she says, which surprises me because Saigon was a French colony and the French influence is strong and much in evidence.

"Sometimes proximity makes one's longing deeper," she explains. She talks proudly of the architecture of Paris, the art, the museums and the way people dress. "Everything is done with care," she says, "with a certain flair, you know. It's not like that here."

I want to defend Saigon but let her enjoy her moment of nostalgia. All transplanted people are entitled to that. When she's finished, she turns her head to me like a hawk.

"How is your mother?" she asks sharply.

"Fine," I answer, wondering what she means by the question, which hangs in the air between us.

"I haven't seen or heard from her in awhile," she says, setting down her teacup and picking up a slice of fig. "Your father is so full of spirit and good will. But your mother is much harder to get to know."

She watches me as she chews, which makes me feel uncomfortable. Up until now, I wasn't aware that other people noticed that my mother is so withdrawn.

"She's a very lovely woman. Beautiful," Mrs. Gelbart says. "I'm sure she's different when you get to know her, n'est pas?"

I leave thinking about Mrs. Gelbart's remarks. I imagine her discussing my family with her husband, Bruno, and the two of them picking us apart and her filtering us through her judgments about Americans. I'm sure we come out flawed and clumsy.

It's a relief to arrive at the Relafords, where I know that my parents are warmly accepted and liked. Except Mrs. Relaford doesn't invite me in. Nor do I get to catch a glimpse of Samantha who I'm told is in her room doing homework. Instead, the driver and I help their gardener unload the boxes and place them in the kitchen.

My mother's long face waits for me when I get home. Before I can even say "hello", she says, "Mrs. Relaford just called and talked to your father. She's very upset with you."

"Why?" I ask.

There's no answer, just a dark disapproving look.

My father waits on the porch cradling a gin and tonic, petting Chico who lies at his feet surveying the yard for another bird or cat to pounce on.

"I thought I asked you to be careful," my father snarls.

"I was," I answer, wondering if I delivered the dark Perugina chocolates to the Relafords instead of the milk chocolate ones by mistake.

"Then what happened to Mrs. Relaford's two cases of Orangina?" he asks.

"What's Orangina?"

"Don't be a wiseguy!" he snaps.

"I'm not."

"Weren't there two cases of orange soda in the crate?" he asks, sipping his cocktail and narrowing his eyes.

"Yes," I answer.

"Then how come only one crate made it to the Relafords?"

"Because a lot of the bottles were broken. The crate was packed with the sodas on the bottom. Maybe it was dropped or something. I don't know...."

"You don't?" he asks, looking at me like I'm a stranger who can't be trusted.

My mouth turns dry, but I manage to say, "I guess you take your chances when you ship two cases of soda halfway around the world."

"Don't be a fucking smart-ass!" he growls.

His words sting. I want to tell him that I'm not trying to be smart, that I'm telling the truth, and that I expected thanks not disapproval for the work I've done. But the arguments in my head travel faster than my ability to summon the words. I look over his head into the yard and ask, "Is that all?"

My father sips his drink again, then fills his mouth with nuts. "You know what Mrs. Relaford thinks?" he asks.

I shake my head.

"She thinks that you and Mohammed and some of your friends opened one case and treated yourselves to her soda."

"That's a lie!" I say gritting my teeth.

My father reaches out, grabs the front of my shirt and pulls me towards him. "Don't you ever call Mrs. Relaford a liar! You hear me?"

I hate him for treating me like a criminal. It's wrong.

* * * * * *

My sister Maggie overheard everything from the dining room and can't stop grinning. "What happened?" she asks, her lips turned up at the corners, her big brown eyes past the point of teasing into something crueler. She's trying to egg me on. I know that if I complain to her, she'll turn around and report everything to my mother, who will then repeat it to my father, who will punish me. But not before my mother sits me down for a talk. That's when she'll tell me that she knows my father is difficult, but that it's my job to try to get along. She'll want me to cry, so she can hold me. And in return for that, she'll tell my father anyway, who will call me "a sissy" or a "cry baby" when he gets the chance.

And I'll just end up feeling further humiliated. I bow my head and stare at the breaded fish and string beans on my plate.

"I hate it when Dad gets like that," my sister says, trying to goad me. I bite into the fish instead. My brother Corey hides his head, trying to pretend he doesn't know what's going on.

My sister asks, "Why does Mrs. Relaford need orange soda from Italy when you can get it here?"

"Good question," I answer.

Behind her, my mother approaches from the living room. She's the next to last person I want to see. She stops and stares at me like I'm a stranger who has just fallen through the roof. Her face is made up with red lips and high cheekbones and she's wearing a green silk dress.

"When you're finished, your father wants to talk to you," she says. "He's upstairs in his room, getting dressed."

When my mother's out of sight, my sister adds, "He must really be mad."

I could run away and sleep in the Cathedral. I could hide in my shop. But sooner or later I'll have to confront him. If I try to avoid him he'll call me a coward. That's the way he is – always challenging me to "face things straight on," which is hard to do since he's so severe.

I climb the winding marble stairs and knock on his door.

"Come in!" He's standing in his boxer shorts and t-shirt, reaching for a clean dress shirt. He points to a pair of brown shoes lined up next to the blond wood shoebox kit. "They need a shine."

I get down on the floor and apply polish. I brush, buff and

shine. He looks the oxfords over, then tosses me a compliment. "Good job." Then, "Sit down."

I plop on the corner of their queen-sized bed. He twists up his mouth as though what he's got to tell is difficult to say.

"I've been invited to an official dinner," he starts. "It's a stag dinner, men only. I thought you might like to attend."

"Who's hosting the dinner?" I ask surprised by this gesture of good will.

"That doesn't matter," he answers. "You've got to promise to be on your very best behavior. And dress up. Your mother will select your clothes."

"When is the dinner?" I ask.

"A week from this Friday."

* * * * * *

That night I fall asleep with artillery shells falling in the distance and rattling the windows.

I dream I'm in a large green bathroom combing my hair in the mirror, when my father walks in. He grabs me by the arm and points to the green towels. "Look!" he says. His hands have been replaced by long knives that protrude from his wrists.

He asks, "Is that the way you leave a towel?"

I turn back the mirror and note the amused expression on my face. Then I feel a blade against the back of my neck.

"You're useless!" he screams. "You're a goddamn screw-up!"

He shouts the last sentence over and over, and I cover my ears and wait for him to exhaust himself. He pants hard and holds himself up against the wall.

I ask calmly, "What's wrong with you? Do you ever listen to yourself? Did you hear yourself just now raving about towels? Do you know how ridiculous you sound?"

Soon I'm screaming just like him. The words get stuck in

my throat. In frustration I stop and pound his chest with my fists. He slashes back with the knives. I fight through the pain and keep pounding until he falls to his knees and is finally silent and still.

When I look up, I see my mother and my sister watching in the doorway. Their bodies are slack and lifeless, their faces paralyzed with fear.

Then I travel forward in time, and I'm a grown man on a train, looking out a window. Bare trees fly by. The landscape and sky are gray. I look down at a brown briefcase in my lap. I wear a long tweed coat. A felt hat rests on my head.

In the blink of an eye, I'm being ushered into a railway station. A fire is burning in the corner. A man extends his hand, "It's an honor, Mr. Russick."

I hear hooves outside on cobblestones, then see a carriage with four magnificent brown horses.

"Are you ready, Mr. Russick?" the man asks.

"Of course," The men around me smile at my absent-mindedness. My briefcase is heavy. My head is full of diagrams and figures.

I gaze out the carriage window at slick streets and flickering gas lamps.

A man in a blue coat ushers me down a slate walk. "This way, Mr. Russick. Watch your step." The walkway is dark and wet. A door opens omitting a sick, yellow light. A woman who reminds me of an older version of my sister Maggie waits at the door.

"Finally, you're here," she says. "We've been waiting so long."

She takes my coat. A log cracks in the fireplace. A teenage girl and boy stand on the stairs. They look sad and defensive like they think that I've forgotten them. I struggle to remember their names.

"Hello," I say. The girl, who is the older of the two, looks at her brother, and the two of them hurry up the stairs without saying a word. They remind me of younger versions of my mother and father.

As I step into the living room, a strange energy surrounds me. "Welcome home," the woman says behind me. I remember that she's my wife.

The four of us sit at a table eating soup with little squares of venison and potato. The broth is thin. They look at me with expectation.

"What's wrong?" my wife asks me. "You look tired."

"I am tired," I say, knowing that if I don't get out of this house soon, I'm going to die. The atmosphere is suffocating. I'm an inventor, a man of ideas. I like to travel. My wife treats me like I'm sick and helpless, maybe even crazy. My son is condescending and angry. My daughter is constantly telling me how much she misses me to make me feel guilty.

She's talking to me now in a soft voice, trying to seduce me with her eyes. She's telling me that my wife, her mother, talks badly about me behind my back. She tells the neighbors that I'm brilliant, but helpless without her, that I cheat on her with other women, forget the names of my children and lose my hat, gloves and money.

My daughter is leading me upstairs where she runs a bath. "You relax, father," she says. "You need to relax." I sense something is wrong as steam wraps me in its warm embrace.

Her cold hands are on my skin. She unbuttons my shirt, unbuckles my belt.

I'm standing on the cold tiles looking down at my feet. The girl is on her knees, testing the water. She beckons me to the bath with her finger: "Come."

I turn and see my wife and son standing in the doorway. The word "disgusting" forms on my wife's lips. My son, the one who reminds me of my father and looks to be about fourteen, holds a knife. His thin lips tremble.

"Get in," he snarls. "Get in, father."

I want to run away. My wife is grinning. "Get in," she says

smugly.

"Why?"

"You haven't treated us well," she says.

I'm overwhelmed with sadness.

"Come," says my daughter, who helps me into the warm water. Together the three of them push my head under. I struggle for a moment, asking myself how I allowed myself to get in this situation, then decide to succumb.

* * * * * *

I awake with a gasp. The room is dark. My brother's dark head lies face down on the pillow. A shaft of moonlight casts a blue triangle on the wall in front of me. Chico growls downstairs.

Did I live another life with my family where I was the father, my sister the mother and my parents were my children? Am I sick in the head?

A deep shiver runs through my body. Chico growls again. This time it's followed by the sound of furniture scraping against the floor downstairs.

I hurry through the sitting room. "Chico?" I call from the landing. The living room is dark and the big mahogany doors that separate the porch from the rest of the house are open. Did Dong forget to lock them?

I descend halfway. Through the space between the open doors, I see Chico's dark silhouette on the porch. He appears to be struggling with something. Maybe he caught a rat.

"Chico," I whisper, gliding across the cool living room floor through the half-opened doors to the front porch. There's something on the floor that doesn't belong there. It's Chico fighting with a thin, short Vietnamese man in black pants. Chico has him by the arm.

"Chico!" I shout. He turns and looks at me with blood dripping from his mouth and releases the man's arm.

The very thin man springs away, climbs through a hole in

the screen and dashes across the yard toward the front gate.

Chico spots him and gives chase. "Chico!" I shout. "NO!!""

He skids to a stop on the white gravel driveway. I grab him and hug him. "Chico, you saved us! Good boy."

In the narrow pantry behind the living room, I fill his bowl with his favorite food as my heart bounces in my chest.

The next morning at breakfast, my sister talks excitedly before a bowl of Rice Krispies. "A robber tried to break in," she says. "He cut himself climbing through a hole in the screen porch. Daddy found the trail of blood this morning. When the robber got to the big door, Chico started barking and scared the robber away."

"Not exactly," I say.

"What do you mean, not exactly?" she asks.

"I was there. I saw it happen," I say, reaching for the powdered milk.

"You saw it happen?... I bet."

When I tell my mother, she doesn't believe me, either. "How did the burglar get through the big doors?" she asks.

"Maybe they were left open," I answer. "Maybe he picked the lock."

"Oh, Michael," she says, pursing her lips.

Every time I tell her about something that happened, she acts like I made it up.

* * * * * *

Hearing the bus honk outside, I run with a paper bag containing my towel and bathing suit clutched under my arm. A Marine with a submachine gun escorts my sister, brother and me through the side gate. When we get to the Relaford's house, a maid comes out and tells the driver that Samantha and Brad Jr. won't be taking the bus today.

That's not surprising because sometimes they ride to school with their father's chauffeur. At least that's what I'm hoping since today is the day Samantha and I arranged to meet at the Cercle Sportif.

Yesterday afternoon I told Sy to tell Mohammed not to pick me up after school. Sy asked if I was meeting a girl. When I didn't answer, he grinned like he knew.

Today our class splits into different groups — some like me take advanced math and algebra, some including Greg take logic and others like Samantha have chemistry lab. The clock above Mrs. McClure's head reads 11:22 as she writes an equation on the blackboard. I raise my hand.

"Yes, Michael?"

"Can I be excused to use the bathroom?"

"Of course, you can."

Past the boy's room, around the corner, I stop outside the chemistry lab where Samantha stands next to her best friend, Niki Clifford, pouring blue liquid into a beaker. They both wear white lab coats. Waving from the door, I get Niki's attention. She nudges Sam who looks up. I mouth the words: "See you later."

Samantha nods.

I'm light and happy until twelve, when Greg Hecht stops me in the hall.

"Want to catch a movie this Saturday?" he asks.

"Yeah."

We walk together towards the front gate. "What's in the bag?" he asks.

I'd rather not tell him, but he's my friend, so I do.

"Where you going swimming?" he asks.

"The Cercle Sportif."

"No, you're not," Greg says with a grin that almost splits his face.

"What do you mean?"

He says, "The Cercle Sportif is closed on Wednesday."

"It is?" It takes a moment for me to realize that I've never been to the Cercle Sportif on Wednesday.

I have to find Samantha. I leave Greg and run ahead to the parking lot. Our bus, the #4, has already left.

When Greg catches up with me, he suggests that I go with him to his house, grab a snack and call Samantha from there.

"What time were you supposed to meet her?" he asks.

"One-thirty."

"You've got an hour," he says. "Plenty of time."

In his kitchen we feast on Shasta sodas and potato chips. Then I call. Brad Jr. answers.

"Hey, Brad, it's Michael. Your sister home?"

"She's not here," he answers.

"No... When's she getting back?"

"Later."

"Much later, or like twenty minutes from now?" I ask.

"She'll be home for dinner," he answers. "She's over at a friend's house."

"Which friend?"

"Beats me."

Greg and I confer again. Now the situation's even more difficult. We can't decide if (one) Samantha knew all along that the Cercle Sportif was going to be closed today, or (two) she found out at the last minute like I did and went home with a friend.

Then the question is: What am I going to do? Greg's going to be picked up in ten minutes and taken to his piano lesson. I decide to head to the bowling alley where I hope to run into some friends.

It just happens that the avenue is clogged with traffic, so the driver takes a route that passes in front of the Cercle Sportif. I tell the driver to take the next right (*a droit*) at the next corner when out of the corner of my eye I see Samantha standing at the gate looking worried.

Arrete! I shout.

The driver pulls over and stops. I hand him some piasters and run across the street to Samantha, who smiles. She's wearing a pretty blue sleeveless dress with yellow flowers and carrying a wicker bag, which probably contains her towel and bathing suit.

"It's closed," she says pointing at the gate.

"I know. I'm sorry. I just found out from Greg."

"I didn't know, either."

"What should we do?" she asks, shrugging.

"Would you like to go bowling?" I ask.

"Yes!"

The bowling alley is only a couple blocks east, so we walk. She's wearing shoes with little, stacked heels that emphasize her long, sleek legs.

"I haven't really bowled before," she says, hiding her blue eyes, tossing her long braid over her shoulder, seeming delicate and rare.

"That's okay," I say. "It'll be fun."

We round the block past noodle vendors and kids hawking newspapers. It's a residential part of the city with big houses behind high walls topped with shards of glass. Everything is fine until we reach a stretch of sidewalk in front of an abandoned house that is being used as a human toilet.

"Sorry," I say as we step around the feces. She smiles her little secret smile and doesn't protest.

I hold open the glass doors of the bowling alley and we pass an American MP who stares ahead into space. It's modern with six sleek AMC alleys with automatic pinsetters, a jukebox, soda machine and kitchen that serves hamburgers and French fries.

I order two lemon sodas and bowling shoes for both of us. She's trying out a green ball. I show her how to hold it, where to put her fingers. Her wrist is almost rectangular with pale, soft skin, little blond hairs and freckles.

"I'm going to embarrass you," she says after she throws two balls in succession into the gutter.

"No, you won't," I answer.

I show Samantha how to throw the ball and she rests against me so that our bodies touch. This time her ball heads down the middle of the alley and knocks down eight pins.

"Look!" she squeals, throwing her arms around me even though she's got an 8-10 split.

The bowling alley is nearly empty. The only people there are a group of older American men in short-sleeved white shirts and short hair and three women who look like military wives.

I wonder if Samantha can tell how much I enjoy watching her. Away from her family she's happy and carefree. To me she's the most beautiful girl in the world.

After the game, we sit at a little round Formica table, sip our sodas and talk. Neither one of us wants the afternoon to end.

"I don't want to be close-minded," Samantha says. "I want to accept things. To have fun, to welcome other people who are not like me."

She explains that her mother thinks she knows exactly what is wrong with Vietnam – that the Vietnamese have very little regard for life, that their babies aren't healthy, that the gap between rich and poor is too severe and that the government is rotten and needs to be fixed by the United States.

Everything about Samantha seems light and fresh.

"You're smiling," she says.

"I know," I say, "I'm sorry."

"Don't be sorry." She tilts her head towards mine and brushes my hand. Instinctively, I take hers in mine.

The thrill of her soft skin, her pulse beating with mine, her brilliant eyes, the light through her hair, the way her tongue caresses her words, is completely intoxicating. I'm fighting to keep control of myself, so I don't drool, or faint.

"Do you think it's inevitable that we'll end up like our parents?" she asks.

"I hope not," I say, trying to come up with a thoughtful answer that will distinguish me in her eyes. "I don't want to close myself off from new experiences, either," I add, thinking that anyone who feels as wonderful as I do at this moment would never do that.

"I don't want to, either," she purrs.

"Right now I feel so... open."

"Me, too."

When the clock on the wall reads 4:30 she stands and, looking worried, starts to gather her things. As she's changing out of her bowling shoes, she says, "I have to call my mother to send our driver. Where should I tell him to meet me?"

I give her directions to the bowling alley and the address. Then, offer, "I can take you home."

She balances herself on my arm. "No," she says, biting her lip. "But you can drop me off at the gate to the Cercle Sportif."

The ride in the back seat of the taxi is short. I barely have time to admire the way she sits with her back straight and holds up her chin.

"Here we are!" she exclaims.

I instruct the driver to pull over. He smiles back through the cracked rearview mirror, a lock of black hair forming a comma on his forehead.

Before I realize what's happening, Samantha turns to me so we face each other and our lips meet in a kiss. I feel her aura; her magnetic field surrounds me, taking me in deeper, deeper. I let myself go.

"Wow..." She sighs deeply. "That was nice."

I feel my face turn red. My body blazes from the inside, indifferent to the heat of the taxi. She's out now, talking to me through the open window. The Relafords' black Mercedes waits nearby.

"Thanks," she says. "I really had a wonderful time."

I look at her helplessly, drinking in her beauty, trying to comprehend what she's saying, what she means.

"Let's do it again," I manage to squeeze out as the taxi starts to pull away.

"Yes."

She waves through the oval-shaped back window. It feels like a dream.

* * * * * *

When I get home Mohammed stands waiting with my mother near the bar. I wonder if Sy forgot to tell him that I wasn't going to work today.

"Where have you been?" my mother asks, her face pinched and dark.

"I was at the bowling alley with a friend."

Mohammed stands at an odd angle looking at the floor. I sense something is wrong.

"Mohammed's here to see you," says my mother.

She turns and leaves, so that he and I are alone.

"What's wrong, Mohammed?" I ask.

He's still for half a minute, then lifts his head slowly. "My son's dead," he says in a little voice, sounding as though he's far away.

"Your son?... Dead?" I can't believe what I'm hearing. I thought it was his daughter who was sick with tuberculosis, but the last I heard she'd fully recovered.

I look around for help. "Your son, Mohammed? Something happened to your son?"

He nods his noble head. "Yes. My oldest son. Rami."

"Rami..." I summon his image in my mind —a tall, thin boy of seventeen, dark skin, but not as dark as his father's, light brown eyes, good-looking, dressed like his father in a cotton shirt and khaki pants. "Rami?"

"Yes." Mohammed leans a hand against my shoulder to hold himself up. He uses the other to cover his eyes.

"Oh, Mohammed... " I feel something clutch in my chest.

"What happened?" I ask. "When?"

"Barely an hour ago. He... he was riding... his bicycle on the Ben Hoa highway. He was riding his bicycle... alongside the road."

I picture the new, black asphalt two-lane road with the paved shoulder that's usually busy with bicycles and ox-drawn carts in my head.

"He was riding in the right lane, when he...was hit. He was hit...by a truck."

I imagine Rami on his bike. I see a truck swerve to avoid something approaching in the other lane. I see the truck knock Rami's bicycle into a concrete pole. I see the bicycle crumple. I see Rami thrown over the handlebars and landing on his head.

"Oh... Oh, God..." I don't know how many times I repeat it, or tell Mohammed "I'm so sorry."

He remains leaning on me with one hand and other covering his eyes with the other.

It's impossible for me to imagine how he feels. I don't know what it's like to have a son, let alone to lose one. "Oh, my God..."

"Only seventeen..."

"Mohammed... Mohammed... What can I do?"

He shakes his head. Ti Ba arrives with lemonades. I help him into a chair and hand him a glass. He sits with head down and doesn't move.

When he leaves an hour later, I'm so tired that I can hardly make it up the steps and into bed. The following day at school, I have trouble concentrating while Mrs. Fischer traces the roots of the French Revolution.

I hear her say, "It was the anger and frustration of generations of peasants, who were forced to not only support but witness the unsurpassed splendor and frivolity of the idle rich."

After class, my feet carry me automatically to the front gate. Niki Clifford hurries beside me and hands me a folded piece of paper. "It's from Samantha," she says. I nod and stuff it in my pocket. "Read it."

Sy stands by the black pick-up, his face gray, dark circles under his eyes. We drive in silence to the Ambassador's residence. It starts to rain. As we get out, he says, "The funeral is tomorrow. Mohammed wants you to come."

"Okay."

That night after dinner while I'm feeding the tropical fish, my father calls me to the porch.

"I heard about Mohammed's son," he says between sips of gin and tonic. "A terrible tragedy."

"He was seventeen years old."

"You knew him?"

"I met him... once," Without waiting to be dismissed, I turn to leave, then stop. "I'm going to the funeral tomorrow."

"I don't think that's a good idea," my father says. I'm already on the steps, climbing to my room.

He calls after me: "Michael... Michael..."

I remove my pants and lay them across the chair so they keep their pleat, then remember the note Niki gave me.

Samantha's letters are round and carefully formed. "Dear Michael," it reads. "I had a great time with you yesterday. It was so much fun, bowling with you and talking. I feel like we are very special friends and you're a very special person. I feel lucky to know you. But I don't think my parents should know about us. I'm afraid they won't understand. So, please, don't tell anybody about us (even Greg). With love, your friend, Samantha."

CHAPTER ELEVEN

I sit next to Sy on the front seat of the Chevy pickup. He looks strange in a dark blue blazer, black pants, white shirt and blue tie. We're driving west on Cy Long highway past Ton San Nuit airport. The rainy season's a month away, but the sky today is the color of wet cement and turning darker by the minute.

We pass a team of huge white oxen pulling a cart filled with red bricks. The land's flat and lush with cool green rice paddies in the distance.

I close my eyes as the first drops pelt the windshield and bolt awake when the truck jerks to a stop.

"We're here," Sy announces as he reaches behind the seat for a black umbrella. Rain falls in a steady silver sheet. Mustard-colored mud oozes over the tops of my brown loafers as I step on the ground.

We join the procession down a narrow path led by a drummer who beats a steady, heavy rhythm that causes our hearts to tremble. Another instrument that sounds like a clarinet plays sour notes that make me wince. Between the black umbrellas, the hats and the sheets of rain, it's impossible to distinguish one person from another.

We move like a long black snake. Women wail, children

mumble prayers in Vietnamese. When we gather around the gravesite, the music stops. My view's blocked by a mound of mud and wreathes of red, white and yellow flowers. The rain hisses angrily through the air.

The moment is so sad and heavy it feels like we're sinking into the ground. A man with a white beard recites prayers in a language I don't understand. He bows his head. Then a girl sings in Vietnamese, "Wind is heaven's broom and rain its silk robe."

The man raises his arms. People shout in anguish and cry. It's heartbreaking.

When the ceremony is over, we leave together, our heads bowed, our eyes cast to the muddy ground.

"Did you see Mohammed?" I ask Sy who walks beside me.

"No," he mutters as he wipes his eyes with a handkerchief.

In the parking lot, we see Mohammed leaning against an old black car, greeting friends and relatives. Suddenly, it looks as though he's levitating as men lift him onto the running board of the car. His sorrowful eyes meet mine. I wave. He nods his head and shrugs as if to say, "What can we do?"

* * * * * *

A week later I wait in the front yard for my father. The sky's clear, the air soft, the light is fading. Mohammed hasn't returned to work. I've filled the last few days working with Sy thinking about Rami and my friend Leroy from the Special Forces softball team.

My father emerges from the front porch and strides to the green Mercedes. Chimes tickle my ears. From beyond the gate I hear the muffled song of the ice cream vendor.

"Let's see how you're dressed," my father says squinting, holding me at arm's length. I wear a white shirt, red and blue striped tie and my best gray dress pants. "Where's your jacket?" he asks.

"I don't have a jacket that fits me," I answer, getting ready to remind him that I've grown three inches in the last year.

Without warning, he shouts, "Jesus Christ!" and runs his long hand over the roof of the car. Lights from the porch illuminate a dozen palm-sized dimples in the metal. "How the hell did this happen?"

"I don't know."

I remember seeing Ti Ba early in the morning squatting on the roof cleaning his car with a feather duster.

"Who the hell did this?" he asks, his anger rising. I know Ti Ba didn't mean to dent the roof.

"I don't know, Dad," I say. I make a mental note to alert Ti Ba as soon as we get back.

He curses as he weaves through traffic. "Goddamn car isn't even a year old! You been throwing things at the roof?"

"No," I answer.

I look out the window at the tall modern statue of the Trung Sisters on an island in the boulevard, thinking how my father acts as though he's managing a huge load of responsibility. He's clearly under a lot of pressure at work.

"Keep your mouth shut tonight," he snaps. "Be on your best behavior. If a question is addressed to you, think before you answer. Use your head."

He still hasn't disclosed the name of our host or our destination. We approach a roadblock and I see Gia Long Palace ahead.

My father seems nervous; his manner is gruff. This isn't the right time to ask him if the invitation came from Mr. Nhu (the president's brother) and if it was addressed to me.

A policeman in white uniform and white gloves directs us through a high iron gate. After we park another man in a black silk tunic with matching pants ushers us through a big portico, past armed guards at attention and flags. Our footsteps echo up pink marble steps, then we continue along a courtyard with rows of flowers and white peacocks to a second stairway.

After passing down a hallway decorated with tapestries and paintings, we enter a large parlor where we're greeted by waiters, who ask us in English what we'd like to drink.

Despite the elegant setting, the smell is bad. My father turns to me and whispers: "The sewer must have backed up."

The other men assembled don't seem to notice as they help themselves to shrimp and fresh pork rolls offered by waiters dressed immaculately in white.

After fifteen minutes spent watching my father circulate among the men, a gong sounds and we're ushered into a formal dining room – completely white from the walls, to billowing curtains, plates, tablecloth, chairs and flowers.

I find my name on a card directly right of the head of the table. My father whispers: "Sit over there," and points to another place halfway down the table. We stand behind the white chairs until our host, Mr. Nhu, enters.

Mr. Nhu is dressed in a long white cotton shirt and white pants. He frowns slightly at the sight of my father at the place to the right of him. Seeing me further down the table, he grins. Then holding up his arms, he says: "*S'il vous plait, messieurs.*" We all sit.

I count sixteen men. The majority of them appear to be Vietnamese. Six are French. My father and I are the only Americans. The chair to Mr. Nhu's left is empty. He summons the headwaiter and pointing to the empty chair, says something in French. When the waiter returns, he escorts Father McDaniel to the empty chair. As he sits, he nods in my direction.

I nod back.

A second waiter places a small bowl in front of each of us, and Mr. Nhu rises and gives a short speech in French, which ends with: "Bon appetite."

Inside the bowl is a dark glutinous substance with what looks like a chicken or duck embryo in the middle. I watch the man next to me pick the whole thing up with a wide ceramic spoon, sprinkle the embryo with salt and spices and wash it down with rice wine. Summoning my courage, I do the same, except I wash mine down with Coca-Cola.

Between the strange taste and the smell, my stomach turns queasy. The next dish goes down easier — chunks of broiled tuna covered with lemongrass, chili, spring onions and coriander. Next comes a banana blossom salad, then shrimp grilled with lime and salt, crab cakes, a huge fish covered with grilled slices of mango. On and on, the delicacies continue. The only thing I have trouble with is the abalone, which is thick and impossible to chew.

After what seems like three quarters of an hour, the table is cleared and the men stand and toast our host with rice wine poured from individual white ceramic flasks. Father McDaniel speaks first. He recites a poem by a man named Tan Da.

> Sure there are those
> better off than I,
> But I outdo all at poverty.
> My scenery includes
> mountains and rivers,
> hamlets and alleys,
> Houses without brick
> roofs, not even thatch.
> My literature's cheap,
> unwanted, looking at
> it is a bore,
> Fine living, passions,
> I find thinking of
> them bland.
> In a former life, I
> remember being born
> during the summer rain era,
> When it rained gold
> three days, so I'm
> bored with spending coins.

Mr. Nhu raises his glass and thanks him. He looks pleased.

A tall Frenchman offers a proverb, "When the father eats food too salty, the child strongly risks being thirsty."

A Vietnamese man recites another, "Educate a child from birth. Correct a wife from the time she enters the family."

Another man says, "A frog at the bottom of the well sees the sky as a lid."

Mr. Nhu seems to particularly enjoy one offered by a Frenchman with long, gray hair, "It's by the trial of misfortune that one recognizes a faithful subject."

The poems and proverbs circle around the table counter-clockwise. A man at the far end of the table presents us with a riddle,

"I'm planted in the very center of the house.

If by chance someone touches me,

I will burst into tears.

What am I?"

The man to my left answers: "A waterfall."

Everybody drinks a toast. The man to my left has been filling my glass with rice wine, which makes my face hot.

It's my turn. Father McDaniel addresses me in English: "Do you have anything to contribute, Michael?" I glance at my father at the end of the table, who shakes his head. I stand.

I consider reciting the poem I wrote to Mr. Nhu and his brother, but it seems too long. Instead, I remember a quote from the ancient Chinese philosopher Lao Tse, who we studied in History, "When men lack a sense of awe there will be disaster." I repeat it in English, then Father McDaniel translates my words into French.

At the end, there's a pause, then, Mr. Nhu says, "Excellent, Michael! Very apropos." The men toast me and move on.

I can barely remember the rest, except my father who recites one of his favorite philosophers, Ralph Waldo Emerson, "God offers every mind its choice between truth and repose. Take which you please — you can never have both."

A gong sounds and dessert is served — bowls of a soupy, greenish kind of soup and star-shaped pineapple tarts. The foul smell that we noticed when we first walked in emanates from the bowls in front of us.

"What do you call this?" I ask the Frenchman to my right.

"I believe you call it breadfruit," he says in English. "In French we call it *fruit de durian*. Dreadful smelling when it's ripe, but I think you'll find the taste quite pleasing."

Despite the sewage-like smell, the fruit itself is mild and delicate. I find my father's face at the end of the table, point to my bowl and raise an eyebrow. He nods back.

The headwaiter announces that coffee will be served in the parlor. Mr. Nhu stands and the rest of us follow. As I enter, he takes my arm, "Why did you move your seat?"

Before I have a chance to answer, he addresses a second question to my father, "Can I borrow your son for a minute?"

My father hesitates, then looks down at his watch. "Yes, of course. But it's getting late."

I follow Father McDaniel and Mr. Nhu into a small passageway that leads to an open door and a large room that's mostly empty. There's a sofa, an oval rug, shelves filled with books, vases of red and yellow hibiscus flowers. At the end behind a modest desk, sits a man with a round face peering down at a book.

Mr. Nhu clears his throat. "Our visitors are here," he says in French. The man pushes himself up. He's short and round with short arms and a serene face that reminds me of Buddha.

"Michael, I want you to meet my brother, Mr. Diem," Mr. Nhu says proudly.

My knees start to tremble. The President says softly in English, "Welcome and please sit."

He points to a place on the sofa next to him. Father McDaniel and Mr. Nhu settle into chairs across from us.

Mr. Diem turns to me with unusually clear, bright eyes. He reminds me of a monk.

"Tell me about yourself, Michael," he says, pouring me a cup of tea that smells of jasmine, mint and lemongrass.

I tell him about my life in Saigon. When I get to the part about the bombs at Pershing Field and the death of Leroy, he takes my hand and says, "I'm sorry."

I reply, *Cam on*, which means "thank you" in Vietnamese.

"This is a very difficult time for all of us."

"Yes," says his brother.

"Do you believe in destiny?" President Diem asks in a smooth, high-pitched voice.

"I don't know yet," I answer honestly.

He tells me how he once wanted to become a priest and lived in a monastery in New Jersey. "But the problems of my country seemed to beckon me. They almost insisted that I play a part. It's not something I necessarily wanted. But here I am. If I have to die for my country, I will."

I imagine my grandmother saying in her simple, direct way, "He's a good man."

He doesn't live like a president. I notice a stack of *National Geographic* magazines in the corner.

President Diem offers me a thick, round cookie from a plate decorated with an enamel dragon. It dissolves in my mouth and tastes of almond and butter. Mr. Nhu stands, and bowing, asks to be excused.

"Your poem touched me, Michael," the President says.

Father McDaniel leans forward. "Michael is a sensitive young man and an acute observer."

Mr. Diem leans closer, "You sense things, don't you?"

I nod. "I... I love Vietnam and its people."

My head should be spinning. The President of South Vietnam sticks out his round chin and asks, "What do you see for us in the future?"

I hear the voices of my mother, my father, my grandfather, my grandmother all speaking in my head at once.

"Me?" I ask.

"Yes. Take your time."

"I don't know... I think the future will be... difficult. You have enemies... to the north. You have enemies... within. The United States wants to help you... But I know the kind of men who are here to help you. Maybe their intentions are good. They believe in democracy and helping people, but they don't know your country... and it's in their nature to want to tell people what to do. Your country and your people are different from ours. I don't think they realize how important that is. I think it could lead to... problems."

As soon as I finish, admonishing voices resound in my head.

President Diem nods. "Father McDonald is right. You are an acute observer."

"Thank you, Mr. President."

Father McDaniel puts down his cup. "We should be getting back," he says gently.

Mr. Diem offers his hand. "To friendship, Michael."

"To friendship."

His face shines with goodwill. "Thanks for coming to visit me. Please keep in touch and visit again."

"Thank you, Mr. President," I say. "I wish you and your country the very best."

Back in the tight space of the car, my father's mood is dark. "What was that all about?" he asks out of the side of his mouth.

"I got to meet the president."

At the stoplight, he looks at me with deep suspicion, then the light changes and we continue home.

As we turn onto Phan Tan Gian, I say, "He wanted to thank me for sending him a poem."

"You sent him a poem?" my father asks. "What kind of poem? Why?"

"Because... Because I thought he might be interested."

He honks twice at the gate for Mr. Dong who looks like a ghost in the glare of headlights. The Mercedes comes to rest on the gravel drive. The house is completely dark as we enter.

"Go to bed," my father says without asking to read the poem, or about what President Diem and I discussed.

* * * * * *

I lie in the dark with my eyes open tracing the shadows on the ceiling and summoning the image of Samantha walking with me through a park. A fountain flows. Pink blossoms fall from trees. Birds crisscross through the air and sing.

Two hours later, I wake with a start. Just as I glance at the clock that reads three minutes before 2AM, there's a big flash of light outside my window, followed by the sound of a huge explosion. The whole house shakes, then everything grows quiet. I rush into the sitting room and look out the window onto Phan Tan Gian Street. Several Vietnamese men are pointing down the street and running.

I tiptoe into my parent's room. "Dad?" I call. "Dad?"

He opens his eyes halfway but doesn't move. "What?"

"There was a big explosion down the street. It woke me up and shook the whole house. I wanted to let you know in case it's important."

He reaches for his glasses and stops. "Are your brother and sister awake?"

"I don't think so."

"Okay, then," he whispers. "Go back to sleep."

I return to my room but can't sleep. So I wander back into the sitting room. From there I see a light under my parent's door and hear my father speaking into one of the radios that he keeps by his bed. "Control two-four-two, this is red rooster five-zero. Come in. Some eggs have hatched. Repeat. Some eggs have hatched on Phan Than Gian about a half a mile west of bridge."

In the morning my father's big hand shakes me from side to side. "Get up," he says sharply.

"What?"

"I want you to clean out the hall closet," he says, "organize everything, then polish all my shoes. Do a first-class job."

He leaves at 6:43 carrying his golf cleats. Part of me wants to run after him and ask about the explosion last night.

I rise, dress and hurry downstairs. Halfway across the long living room, I hear a car honking and the side door slamming shut. I find Mr. Dong sweeping the walkway between the main house and servant's quarters with a long cane broom.

"Your father just left," Mr. Dong says in French with an unfiltered cigarette sticking to his bottom lip.

"Did you hear the explosion last night?" I ask.

He rests the broom on the side of the house, takes a long drag on his cigarette, drops it and crushes it with his bare foot. He wears an old spaghetti-strap t-shirt and white silk pajama pants. He hasn't combed his hair or shaved.

Holding up four fingers, he says: "Four American soldiers died. Young boys," he adds. "They were drinking in a bar."

"Which bar?" I ask.

"The Four Aces. On the other side of the street, down one block."

I've passed it many times – a narrow dark place with a long bar, a row of stools and a second row of stools along a long counter attached to a wall.

"Four young American soldiers," Dong says, picking up the broom and shaking his head. "Many more injured. Terrible. Blood, screams. Very, very bad."

In the evening, I'm helping Corey try to trap a lizard when my father calls from the porch.

"You do everything I asked you to?" he asks a sipping gin and tonic with my mother seated beside him.

"Yes."

"I hope you did a good job, now that you think you're a big shot."

I stop in my tracks. My mother leafs through a fashion

magazine and pretends not to be listening.

"I don't think I'm a big shot."

"Did you write any poems today?" my father asks highlighting the word "poems" as though it's silly or obscene.

"No. I was too busy cleaning the closet and polishing your shoes."

"Good."

* * * * * *

Sunday morning at twelve I attend the English mass at the Cathedral. I expect to see Father McDaniel, but for some reason he's not there. A French priest says he'll be back at two. I wander down Tu Duc Street to the river where I watch fish being unloaded from boats and sampans arriving packed with chickens in cages, mangoes, pineapples and bunches of bananas.

The cafés are empty as I make my way back up Tu Duc in the heat of the afternoon. I see Sy's head pop out of a shopping arcade ahead. He's as disheveled as usual and has his arm around a tall, beautiful Vietnamese girl in a *bao dai*.

"Sy!" I exclaim before thinking that maybe he doesn't want to be seen.

He greets me warmly. "Michael. Say hello to Chan."

She's poised and graceful with pretty dark eyes, pink lips and high cheekbones. Everything about her is long and thin. Sy tells me that she's studying geography at the university and wants to be a professor.

"It's a plea-sure to meet you Mi-chael," she says in broken English.

She keeps running her delicate fingers over Sy's bare forearm.

"Isn't she something?" Sy asks.

They snuggle and giggle completely unselfconsciously like kids frolicking in the water as we step around children with clubbed feet, amputees with missing legs, lepers, kids hawking lottery tickets and enter an old apothecary shop. The old man behind the counter has a mole on his chin with hairs growing out of it that reach his chest. The mahogany shelves behind him are lined with jars of dried plants, little bones, dried lizards and fantastic golden ginseng roots suspended in liquid.

Chan orders an herb for Sy's troubled stomach. She explains, "For us, disease is the result of an imbalance of vital energy at the level of certain organs, due to an excess or insufficiency."

I bid them goodbye at that Cathedral.

Sy protests, "Come with us. Chan thinks you're cute. She wants you to meet her younger sister."

I tell them I'd like to but can't.

In the back room of the rectory, I find Father McDaniel changing from street shoes to slippers. The room's dark and sticky. The old, hunched woman arrives and serves jasmine tea while Father McDaniel grumbles about the heat.

I tell him that I feel guilty about our meeting with the President.

"Why?" he asks, fixing glasses on his nose.

"I think I might have offended my father."

Father McDaniel pulls his chair close so our knees practically touch and says, "You aren't here on Earth to serve your father, Michael. Serve something higher. And always be true to yourself."

CHAPTER
TWELVE

This week in history class we're making charts that trace the connection between events. I could do the same with my life. From canned pineapple juice at the Majestic Hotel, to a chance meeting with Mr. Nhu at the Cathedral, to a poem about two rivers, to dinner with the President, to polishing my father's shoes.

No matter where I start, the chart leads back to my Dad. He's our captain. It's like the poem by Walt Whitman we're studying in English, "O Captain! My Captain! Our fearful trip is done..."

Today I'm sitting in the waiting room of the Military Hospital next to Dr. Silverman who's looking through a catalog filled with electric cars. The Military Hospital sits on the road to Cholon, which is the Chinese section of town. We're not far from the central market where a bomb went off yesterday killing a spice vendor and four other people.

My mother's inside, having her right eye examined by an Air Force doctor who has flown in from Okinawa at Dr. Silverman's request. I've accompanied her on orders from my father who said he couldn't get away from work. Maggie and Corey are back home playing hearts with friends.

"Copper pickups," Dr. Silverman says, pointing to a page of matchbox sized cars in the catalog. "Better conductivity. Produce more speed."

I want to say that the challenge with these electric cars isn't speed but keeping them on the track.

A man shuffles by slowly, held gently at the elbows by two Vietnamese nurses. His face is tomato red; his ears and neck wrapped in white gauze. Clear jelly covers his skin.

"Extreme sunburn," says Dr. Silverman as the man disappears through double doors. "From the look of it, I'd say he has the equivalent of third-degree burns."

A minute later, an American nurse in white, with a white mask over her face, emerges clutching a clipboard and whispers into Dr. Silverman's ear.

"Sure," he says without looking up. He follows her through the double doors just as a man emerges in a wheelchair with a bandage covering one side of his face and his right leg missing below the knee. Our eyes meet briefly. His plead: *Why did this happen to me?*

His young face is covered with orange freckles. I wonder if he's one of the soldiers who were injured by the bomb that went off in the Four Aces bar across the street.

The doors swing open again, and Dr. Silverman emerges with my mother, her right eye covered with white bandages and tape. She holds her chin high and her neck straight.

"The specialist confirmed my diagnosis," Dr. Silverman announces. "Viral conjunctivitis. Very rare. Very difficult to treat. He's prescribed a new medicine; we'll see how it works."

"How do you feel, Mom?" I ask in the car.

"Fine," she answers. "It's a little uncomfortable wearing this patch. When can I take it off?" she asks Dr. Silverman at the wheel.

"Not until your eye clears," the doctor answers.

He wants to talk about cars, but my mind is on Ti Muoi and what she said about the curse. "Do you believe in curses and black magic?" I ask him.

"Really, Michael!" my mother exclaims, throwing her head back and laughing.

If Dr. Silverman has anything to say about the subject, he keeps it to himself.

After he pulls the blue Impala up to our house and my mother gets out, he turns to me and says very seriously, "The healing process is critical. I'm concerned about scar tissue forming on the retina."

"Why?"

"Because if it doesn't heal properly, she could lose all vision in that eye."

"Blind?" I ask.

He nods. "Not completely. But blind in that eye."

* * * * * *

The sun's unrelenting. So hot it seems to draw everything out of us — energy, ambition, even intelligence. Yesterday it reached 105 degrees. I sit by the pool at the Cercle Sportif, thinking about my mother's beautiful brown eyes. I try to picture her in sunglasses like Ray Charles or sporting an eye patch like Sammy Davis, Jr.

When I repeated Dr. Silverman's warning to my Dad, he accused me of exaggerating.

"I spoke to him, too," he said lighting a Marlboro and blowing the smoke past my ear, "but he never mentioned any danger of going blind in that eye."

"Did he tell you the part about the scar tissue on the retina?" I asked.

"He said it could impair her vision. She might have to wear glasses. That's not the same as completely losing her sight."

Bobby Ho stands at the far end of the pool, waving his arms at my friends Greg and Alain. He's trying to explain the technique for performing swan dives without doing one himself. He can't because of the cast on his right arm, which is held up by a brilliant yellow sling.

Alain climbs on the diving board and gets in position. A group of French kids have gathered in the deep end and are taunting him. Bobby Ho shouts instructions, then throws his cap in the pool to show Alain where to land.

Alain bounces high on the board and thrusts his chest out, but as he starts to descend, crumples into a belly flop. The French kids laugh and applaud. Greg shakes his fist. Bobby, exasperated, stomps to my patch of shade adjusting the aviator sunglasses that hide most of his face.

He ignores the two lovely Vietnamese women dipping their long legs in the water. He turns his chair away from Greg and Alain, slumps in it and crosses his arms across his chest.

"Bobby, do you believe in black magic?" I ask.

He's traveled far away. His expression is grim.

"Do you believe in black magic?" I ask again.

"Do you have hair on your balls?" he asks back.

Bobby points to a long piece of black stone that dangles from his neck on a gold chain and is carved into the shape of a dragon. Then, he gets up and leaves.

Later in the men's changing room, Alain asks Bobby Ho what he uses to keep hair slicked back. "Chicken shit," Bobby answers.

Greg wants to know what happened to his arm.

"I was shot out of a helicopter," Bobby growls back.

"You were shot out of a helicopter?" Greg asks back incredulously.

Bobby stares into his open locker and drifts off again. I'm starting to think that maybe the war has turned him *dinky dow* (crazy).

"Come on," Greg groans, nudging Bobby's shoulder. "Tell us the truth."

Bobby Ho grabs Greg by the neck and snarls, "I got shot by a fucking Vietcong, you dumb son-of-a-bitch, like a hot metal rod shoved up my ass. Things are getting *beaucoup* crazy, as you fucking Americans would say. But you'll never understand. Will you, kid? You might never see your friend Bobby again. Fuck you!"

He slams his locker shut and stomps out, leaving Greg, Alain and me stunned and speechless.

Things are getting *beaucoup* crazy.

My father says, "It's the pressure."

What pressure? The unrelenting heat, the war, the inability to penetrate the mystery of the situation we're in, or the inability to find an answer that's satisfying to everyone.

"What do you think he meant?" Alain asks as we change out of our bathing suits and walk towards the back fence, which is covered with thick foliage and has a hole cut in it. It's a short-cut to Greg's house.

I push the foliage aside and stop. Three Vietnamese men are in the process of climbing through the hole in the fence. They're dressed in khaki shorts and black t-shirts and look unfriendly.

Stepping around them, I say, "Excuse me" in Vietnamese.

One of the faces looks familiar. It belongs to Duc, the Vietnamese boy who lives behind Norodom – the kid Brad Jr. hit in the head, and whose mother served us cold Coca-Cola before we played marbles together in the yard and became friends.

"Duc?" I ask looking back at him.

He stops and turns but avoids my eyes. The moment is awkward and pregnant with implications.

"Good to see you, Duc," I say in French.

He manages only the meagerest grin, then turns his back to me and continues into the club.

"What was that all about?" Greg asks when we reach the street.

"I'm not sure."

* * * * * *

I'm thinking about Duc, Bobby and my mother's eye as I sit on the deck of the PT boat that's taking us up the Saigon River. My father, the Relafords, the Gelbarts and another couple are drinking mint juleps made by a Vietnamese sailor with three gold teeth.

My mother stayed behind with Corey who isn't feeling well. She said she wouldn't be able to enjoy the trip on account of her eye.

We're now twelve miles southeast of the city. The muddy Saigon River has shrunk in half. Impossibly dense foliage sticks out like flames from both shores.

"Brutal, isn't it?" Bruno asks as his cool shadow falls over me. I'm not sure if he's referring to the foliage or the heat.

I hold my breath as Samantha emerges from the galley, spreads a blanket on the forward deck and pulls a t-shirt over her head to reveal a slim body partially covered by a paisley bikini.

A luminous shield of air swirls around her. Even the half-asleep Vietnamese sailor cradling an M-1 rifle seems to notice how sweet and perfect she is — her shiny brown hair gathered in two braids, the trail of blond fuzz that travels the gentle curve of her back, the pink polish on her nails.

"A Navy PT-boat like this one was ambushed near here just a week ago," Bruno bellows over the engines.

His words disperse like the acrid smoke from the stack. He's trying to scare me. Like my father he wants me to know what it takes to be a real man.

"We're a perfect target," Bruno insists, swelling his chest.

My attention shifts from Samantha lying facedown on the towel to making a quick assessment. *The boat is made of metal, approximately forty feet long with two mounted machine guns; both unmanned. Besides the man at the wheel who has a .45 in his belt, there's a man serving drinks, a cook in the galley with another helper. Our only real protection are the two sailors clutching M-1 rifles who both appear to be nodding off in the heat.*

In case of emergency, I decide I'll dash below deck with the other kids and Samantha. We'll hide there until we're rescued. I'll use the radio to call for help.

I make these kinds of assessments every day. I've spent many long nights since the bombing at Pershing Field escaping men who were trying to kill me in my dreams.

Covered all over with a thin layer of sweat, I look up at Bruno's face which reminds me of a red potato.

"What are we really doing here in Vietnam?" I ask him as he drains a glass of glass rum.

"Why are we alive?" he asks back.

The man at the wheel stops the boat in the shade and we eat fried chicken and potato salad from paper plates.

Mrs. Relaford talks loudly, complaining about the quality of the local art and furniture. "I keep telling Brad that we simply have to make a trip to Hong Kong as soon as we can," she says. "If I have to look at another mediocre lacquer painting, I think I'll die!"

Brad Jr. sits at the stern tossing pieces of chicken in the water and watching them being devoured by large fish and long black snakes. Samantha lies on her stomach reading *Frannie and Zoe* by J.D. Salinger. The man with the gold teeth serves a steady stream of fresh mint juleps and beer to the grownups.

Bruno, Mr. Relaford and a third man are complaining about the Vietnamese army now (the ARVN).

"They're completely ineffective," the tall man says. "Corrupt, poorly trained and badly led. The only way we're going to win this war is if we take the leadership ourselves."

Mr. Relaford asks, "How can you tell an ARVN tank from a regular tank? It only goes in reverse." He smiles with a schoolboy pleasure as the others laugh.

I cross to the front of the boat where the Gelbart girls are listening to a transistor radio and reading comic books in French. When I go to the cabin to get some Shasta sodas, I pass Bruno talking to my father about the Corsican Mafia.

"Those sons-of-bitches know how to get things done," he says. "If they have an enemy, even if he's on the other side of the globe, they get him, they slash his throat. They're remarkably efficient. Did I tell you that they made me an honorary member for life?"

"When are we going back?" I overhear Samantha ask her mother when I'm back on deck.

The Beach Boys sing in the background, "She's so fine my 409; giddy up, giddy up 409..."

"When we're told," Mrs. Relaford answers.

A half-hour later a smaller boat pulls alongside ours and a middle-age Vietnamese man is helped aboard. He's short and strong with a wide, friendly face and wears a khaki short sleeve top with an orange ascot tied around his neck. Bruno introduces him to my father as General Don.

"He's the best they've got," I hear Bruno remark.

"The President won't let us fight," General Don complains.

My father's eyes warn me to retreat to the front of the boat.

The grown-ups are having what they call "a grand old time" — drinking, eating and talking in the shade of the tarp, while we kids suffer in the sun. The heat is almost unbearable. The wind isn't moving. The air is busy with bugs and mosquitoes; and there's very little to do.

We were told that we were going swimming, but the Vietnamese captain informed us that the currents are too strong in this part of the river. So we sit in the sun, playing cards, reading and waiting. The cabin is forbidden to us because Mrs. Relaford says that we'll get in the way.

Even after General Don bids goodbye and leaves in the same launch that he arrived in, our parents continue talking and drinking like there's no end in sight.

Samantha and I play war from a double deck of cards. On the periphery I hear Brad Jr. talk about a movie he saw in which a man's clothes caught on fire and how he rolled in the dirt to smother the flames. The Gelbart girls and my sister Maggie tease him the way they always do. My father, Bruno and Mr. Relaford laugh loudly in the distance. The guards and captain have disappeared into the cooler air below deck.

While studying the little flecks of brown in Samantha's blue eyes, I smell smoke. Brad Jr. has balled up a piece of newspaper and set it on fire. My sister and the Gelbart girls watch.

"Brad, what are you doing?" I ask over my right shoulder, half-dead from the heat.

"Ignore him," Samantha says. "He's just showing off."

I stand to get a better look and see Brad Jr. rolling back and forth over the burning paper, trying to put it out. He says to the kids watching, "This is how it works."

Samantha sees what he is doing and exclaims, "Brad, you jerk!" Her face clenches with frustration.

Brad Jr. rolls with more vigor. The flame from the newspaper appears to have been smothered. I see a little orange patch of fire on the back tail of his shirt.

I look around the deck for a bucket as Brad Jr. rocks furiously back and forth. The smoke grows thicker.

"Brad!" Samantha shouts. "Michael!"

I reach down and rip at his shirt, which comes off in two pieces. I try to throw them in the river, but they land on the rail instead. Brad Jr. lets out a scream that echoes off the water and points to his lower back.

Pandemonium breaks out. Parents lunge towards us. Mr. Relaford hits his head on a metal pole and falls backwards. Bruno pushes me roughly aside. My father grabs me by the throat and shouts, "What the hell happened? What did you do this time?"

The men crouch around Brad Jr. as the mothers continue to admonish their children in English and French.

I overhear "burns" and "looks bad." The smell of burnt flesh hovers around us. I glimpse Brad Jr.'s pained, tear-stained face.

The soldiers and Bruno lift him while my father gives directions, "Careful. Careful. Watch your heads."

They disappear with Brad Jr. below deck. I catch a glimpse of Mr. Relaford holding a towel filled with ice cubes to his forehead, his eyes askew.

The engine starts. The towel Mr. Relaford holds to his forehead is spotted with blood.

"How is he?" I ask.

"Quiet," Mrs. Relaford answers. "Get us to a hospital. Quick!"

I realize that she's talking to me. "Hurry!" she screams in my face. "Why are you standing there like a monkey? What are you waiting for?"

I don't know what I'm supposed to do. Samantha and the other girls on the forward deck cover their mouths and eyes.

Bruno grabs me roughly by the shoulder. "Come with me!"

He leads me to the cabin, barks orders to the captain in Vietnamese, then pushes him into the gallery. Bruno sets the speed, steers the boat into the middle of the river, then takes my hands and places them on the wheel. "Steer us back!" he shouts over the engine.

I'm not sure I understand.

"Steer!" he barks again. Then putting a hand on my shoulder, shouts, "You'll be fine!"

"Why me? Why not the captain?"

"Just steer!" He leaves.

The boat moves quickly, slicing through the thick greenish-brown water, sending up a wake that upsets trees and foliage along the shore. Brad Jr., the grownups and soldiers shuffle about in the galley below.

Over the engine, I hear Mr. Relaford shout into a radio, "Tell them to have an ambulance waiting! And a burn unit! We need a burn unit! Tell them at headquarters."

The engine whines louder. I hear my father behind me, asking the other kids to explain what happened. Bruno appears at my side. He blares the horn as we approach a sampan. I keep my eyes fixed on the channel ahead.

"You're going good!" he says to me.

Then he turns to my father who approaches behind me. "Not now," he says to him. "Leave him alone!"

I turn to catch a glimpse of my father's annoyed expression. I guide the boat around a bend where the river widens. The river ahead is shrouded in a grayish-brown haze.

Samantha stands beside me, her eyes focused on the water ahead. I feel her arm brush against mine. A ripple of energy curses through my body into my groin. Without saying a word, she takes my hand.

Her long hair whips in the wind as we approach the city. Men in little boats and sampans paddle furiously to avoid our wake. We're going fast, but I didn't set the speed and I'm not sure how to change it.

"Over there," says Samantha, pointing to a reddish, brown area of the river up ahead. Freckles have appeared on the tip of her nose. The remains of a whole variety of bugs dot the windshield.

"Yes," I say, nodding, realizing it's the same dock we left from. I look at her. We both feel grown up.

Magically, the boat, the river and the air seem to have changed — thicker with possibility and romance.

"You're doing fine, kid," Bruno shouts over my shoulder. "Slow down."

He takes my hand and puts it on the throttle. Together we ease it back.

"There! That's good."

The city comes into sharper focus. Through the haze, I

make out the Majestic Hotel and the steeples of the Cathedral. Familiar smells fill my nostrils. Naked children dive into the muddy water and attempt to swim towards us.

The cacophony of the city draws closer. I steer into the busiest part, past the Majestic Hotel where the docks are jammed with sampans and bigger military boats. The Vietnamese captain appears behind me, ready to take over. I'm happy to relinquish the wheel.

As soon as we climb into our green Mercedes, I fall asleep.

CHAPTER THIRTEEN

It took some effort on Mohammed's and my part but we found her. First, we went to MACV headquarters, where a US sergeant took us to see a captain, who escorted us into a major's office, who told us they had no Captain James Reynolds working for them. Then we went to the Air Force building, where we spent an hour watching a corporal look through logs and files, before announcing: "We have no Captain James Reynolds assigned to us." Then we went to the Navy station where a major invited us into his office while his subordinates searched their records. They had no record of a Captain James Reynolds working for them, either. We received the same response from Special Forces, Starcom, MAAG, 45th Transport, VAA and TVA.

Mohammed and I were almost convinced that Captain James Reynolds didn't exist. That Ti Muoi had left that name with my mother to save face. Then Sy told us he had a friend who lived next door to a Captain Reynolds on Tran Qui Gap Street. So we drove there to take a look.

It turns out that Captain James Reynolds lives in a baby blue house on Tran Qui Gap Street. So much for American military efficiency and order.

The person we've really come to talk to is Ti Muoi who

now stands in the front hall waving her arms and talking excitedly about "her captain."

Her captain wants her to buy him American coffee. Her captain wants her to iron his uniforms without using starch. Her captain likes his steaks grilled on the outside barbecue. Her captain asks her to scan the American newspapers and clip out articles that mention Alaska or Wyoming. Her captain shares his bed with many beautiful women, but the woman he can't live without is Ti Muoi.

"Ti Muoi," I say. "My mother's eye has gotten worse."

She covers her mouth. "I knew this!" Then unknitting her crossed eyes, says, "I tell you many time, this bery bad. The worst."

I explain to her that my mother had to be evacuated to Okinawa where they might perform surgery.

Ti Muoi shakes her finger. "They can no do this. No!"

She lectures me, telling me what I should tell the doctors, as though they would take her advice. If I wasn't so desperate, I'd laugh and Mohammed would laugh too, because Ti Muoi is number 10, and ten to the Vietnamese means bad luck.

"Listen," I tell her. "I came to ask you for help. You told me that someone put a curse on my mother and you know what to do."

She grows more excited and waves her arms again. With spit flying out of her mouth she explains that spirits animate everything — including stones, lakes, animals and trees. That mankind sits between father (heaven) and mother (earth). That there are good spirits and bad spirits. That some people have learned to manipulate the dark ones.

"Are you talking about black magic?" I ask.

"Yes!" she exclaims. "Yes! Yes! Ti Muoi know what to do!"

A whole torrent of words spews out of her, one on top of the other. Between the speed of her speech and her ragged English, I try to keep up. I think she says that man has three souls, which are called *hon*, and seven vital principles, *phach*.

The three souls command the superior functions of life like intelligence and perception. The seven principles are concerned with instinct and senses. Women have two additional vital principles because of the special responsibility for bearing children. In my mother's case, it is the *phach* having to do with the eyes and vision that has been attacked.

"How?" I ask.

She pauses to take a breath.

Thinking that she might be about to launch into another long explanation of how the spirits work, I tell her that time is of the essence. Ti Muoi nods and leads us inside to a bathroom, where she shows us that the drain from the sink is leaking through a cabinet onto the floor.

"You fix here," she says, "I fix there." She points at her eye.

It seems like a fair exchange. The drain takes nearly two hours of bending, sweating and grunting by me and Mohammed to repair.

As we're cleaning up, Ti Muoi rushes in, grabs us by the shirts and practically throws us out of the house.

"The Captain is coming! The Captain is coming!" she screams over and over. "I have to start barbecue! I have to cook his steak medium rare so he won't be mad!"

"What about my mother?" I ask.

"You go!" she yells. "Ti Muoi take care of everything! Go now!"

* * * * * *

Two days later, there's still no word from Ti Muoi. Mohammed knows that I'm worried.

As we're leaving a house that's being remodeled, he turns a corner and slams on the breaks. Suddenly we're in the middle of chaos — smoke, water and people running and screaming. Some of them hold signs in Vietnamese denouncing the government.

"It's a demonstration," Mohammed explains.

Young men and woman chant slogans and throw rocks at soldiers in riot gear. Soldiers fight back with sticks and shields. They throw tear gas canisters and shoot streams of water from water cannons into the crowd.

Mohammed instructs me to roll up the window. Bolts of water hit the demonstrators knocking them onto the pavement and into trees and fences.

As Mohammed backs up the truck, I ask, "What's this all about?"

"It has to do with the Buddhists."

"Why the Buddhists?" I ask.

"They're mad at the government."

I know that President Diem and his family are Roman Catholic, and many Vietnamese are Buddhist. We studied the life of Buddha in school. According to Mrs. Fisher, Buddha said that the pain we suffer in life is caused by our desire for happiness, riches and power. When desire is overcome, man becomes conscious of the existence of Buddha, who is present in every living thing. Through virtuous living and renouncing pleasures, man can also break the chains binding him to earthly existence.

* * * * * *

Mohammed lets me off near the side gate. Inside, I stop to admire the green papaya, which is growing from our backyard tree. Chico sniffs my shoes. Bells jingle from the street followed by the sing-song chant of a vendor. This one offers to sharpen knives and scissors.

Ti Ba with her plump face and long hair parted in the middle hands me a folded piece of paper. "From Ti Muoi," she says in French.

Behind her, holding a bicycle stands a beautiful Vietnamese girl of eighteen or nineteen. She wears a light green tunic and white pants and carries the same conical straw hat worn by all the women called a *non gai tho.*

"This is my daughter, Ti Hai," Ti Ba says. "Your mother has hired her to do the laundry."

Ti Hai bows her head. She smells of orchids and has a cascade of brilliant black hair that ends at her waist.

My father waits for me on the porch, where he's reading the newspaper and sipping his gin and tonic.

"Dong said you wanted to see me," I say. "Any word from Mom?"

He puts down the paper without answering my question. A knowing smile flickers on the corners of his mouth. "It looks like your friend, President Diem, has stepped in deep shit."

The malevolence in his voice stops me. Switching gears, I say, "I heard the Buddhists are angry with him. What did he do?"

My father thrusts a copy of yesterday's *New York Times* at me and points to an article on the front page. It describes how government soldiers broke up a demonstration by Buddhist protestors in the northern city of Hué killing one woman and eight children. The demonstrators had assembled, according to the article, to protest a government order prohibiting them from flying the Buddhist flag on the Buddha's 2527th birthday.

The article goes on to say that Buddhists and students are organizing more demonstrations against the Diem regime in other cities.

"So much for your man of peace and empathy," my father offers looking pleased.

I try to reconcile my impression of President Diem with the description of his soldiers firing into an unarmed crowd that included women and children.

"Something is wrong," I say. "Maybe this article doesn't tell the whole story."

"It's the *New York Times*, Michael!" my father declares, mockingly.

"What did President Diem say about this?"

"He hasn't said anything. His brother is blaming the demonstrations on the Vietcong."

"You don't think that's true?" I ask.

"Don't be naive," my father hisses. "Did you know that Diem's other brother, Ngo Dinh Truc, is the bishop of Hué?"

Even though I didn't know that, it doesn't answer the central question: Is President Diem prejudiced against the Buddhists? My father thinks he knows the answer. He's happy to see President Diem fail. He, like most Americans, consider him corrupt, arrogant, lazy and out of touch with his people. The only American that I know who defends him is Ambassador Sherwood.

I should leave, but instead say, "You don't like President Diem, do you?"

My father doesn't like these kinds of questions. He removes his glasses, wipes his eyes and looks up at me like I'm the enemy. "I don't even know him," he answers. "It's nothing personal. I judge a man by his actions and the way he conducts himself."

He looks at me critically to let me know that he's measuring me, too. It's his way of telling me that my conduct doesn't meet his standards.

He says, "I'd say your friend Diem is a pretty strange duck."

A number of comebacks pop into my head: *Is he a strange duck because he lives like a monk? Is he a strange duck because he doesn't let the United States tell him what to do?*

These questions would only provoke my father's anger, which is something I don't want to do.

I leave wondering if President Diem is really prejudiced against the Buddhists. I wonder if he realizes how badly this makes him look given the fact that he and his family are Roman Catholics and the majority of the population is Buddhist.

* * * * * *

I sit on the bed doing algebra. Bats flutter and squeak in the attic above. Tonight, the world doesn't conform to straight lines and numbers. I know a couple things: One, President Diem and his brother Mr. Nhu are not stupid. And, two, politics in Vietnam are very complex.

I wonder if my father has considered that they might be more complicated than he thinks they are. This raises two more questions: *What makes people rush to judgment? Why is it hard for grown-ups to keep an open mind?*

Shifting on the bed, I remember the note in my pocket from Ti Muoi. Unfolding the lined, white paper, I read: "Micael. I taked care of the ting we talk about. Stop your worry. Action is taked against the spell effeted your mother. Do not remove potions in you front yard and under your mother bed. In return for my action, I ask you one favor. I think it very fair. My Captain Reynold like to read the New York Time of Sunday. Bring it to this house every week when your father is finish for the pleasure on my Captain. Sincerely, Ti Muoi."

The next morning at breakfast, my father complains about a sour smell upstairs which I'm pretty certain comes from the potion Ti Muoi placed under his bed.

He won't be open to the possibility that Ti Muoi's way might work, so I tell him that the smell probably comes from the provolone cheeses from Italy that are hanging in front of the air conditioner in the upstairs sitting room.

"You're right," he says. He instructs me to move them to my sister's room.

A week later on Wednesday morning I sit in Mrs. Fisher's class listening to her talk about the Declaration of Independence. My friend, Greg Hecht, passes me a cartoon drawn by a quiet, white-haired kid named Matt. It shows Mrs. Fisher on her knees before a man who looks like Thomas Jefferson.

Jefferson has his pants down and his dick exposed, which he's in the process of pushing into Mrs. Fisher's mouth.

The bubble emerging from his mouth reads, "Here's my pursuit of happiness! Gag, you bitch!"

The skill of the drawing combined with its lewd audacity makes me laugh out loud. Mrs. Fisher stops and turns to me. Eyes bulging, nostrils flared, she asks, "Mr. Sforza, you have something you'd like to share with the rest of the class?"

"No, Mrs. Fisher. Sorry. I was starting to choke."

I pretend to chew on something.

"No gum in class!" she shouts. "Throw it out!"

Head cast down, blood rushing to my face, I pretend to deposit the non-existent gum in the trash. Turning back to my seat, I spy Greg's face hidden behind his hands, his eyes rolling with laughter.

After class, we meet in the hall. "You almost got us killed!" Greg exclaims.

"You're good," I tell Matt, who barely reaches my shoulder. "You should be drawing for *Playboy*."

Matt's so shy he can barely speak. The next morning on the bus, he shows me a black notebook full of drawings. It's a wild fantasia of sex. His imagination has captured every girl in our class and many of the older girls from school naked. He's drawn them taking showers together, changing in the locker room and getting cozy at slumber parties.

"Exceptional," I say, "and sick."

He flashes a lopsided grin.

Greg regales us with jokes. Behind us, an American soldier in camouflage patrols the high barbed wire fence. Girls and boys in cotton gingham pass unaware that we're talking about sex.

"This couple was invited to a masked Halloween Party," Greg starts. "The wife got a terrible headache and told her husband to go to the party alone. So, he took his costume and went. The wife, after sleeping for an hour, woke up feeling better so she decided to go to the party, too. Since her husband didn't know what her costume was, she thought she would have some fun by watching him to see how he acted when she wasn't with him. When she got to the party, she spotted her husband dancing with one pretty girl after the other. His wife went up to him and they started dancing. She let him run his hands all over her body. After awhile, he was so hot he asked her if she'd like to go outside and screw. She went and did the deed. Just before midnight, when everyone was supposed to take off his or her costumes, she went home, took off her costume and slipped into bed. She was sitting up reading when her husband came home. 'Did you have a good time?' she asked him. He said: 'Not really.' 'Did you dance?' she asked. 'Not even once,' he answered. 'I went in the den and played poker with some friends. But I'll tell you what, the guy I lent my costume to sure had a good time!'

On the way back to class, Greg says, "I've got to get to second base with Niki Clifford. I want to feel her up."

"Not Niki," I respond. "No way!"

After school, Greg pulls me aside. He has a plan, "We'll take Niki and Samantha to the movies on Saturday. We can sit in the back and touch their tits."

"Sure, Greg," I say sarcastically.

"I'm serious. Why not? Are you scared?"

It takes me a whole hour after dinner to get up the nerve to call Samantha.

"Hi, it's Michael. How's Brad Jr.?"

"He's doing better," she answers. "But he's still in the burn unit, so we're not allowed to visit. We're hoping he'll return home next week."

"I hope so, too."

She says, "He got your letter and the comic books you sent."

It's time to pop the question: "Sam, I was... I was wondering, if you'd like to go to the movies with me on

Saturday."

She doesn't hesitate. "Sure."

"Great."

"The matinee, right?"

My mouth is like a desert. "Y-y-yes. Niki and Greg are coming with us."

"Cool." Then lowering her voice, adds, "That makes it easier. I'll go with Niki and meet you there. Okay?"

"Okay."

It's set. But I feel funny. *What if the girls don't want us to feel them up? What if they're insulted and never want to talk to us again?*

There are other complications. The next morning my father announces that he might be flying to Okinawa this weekend to visit my mother. "If I go," he warns me, "I'm leaving you in charge of your sister and brother."

In English class, I get a note from Samantha. "Greg hasn't asked Niki yet. You said they're coming with us. Tell your friend Greg to get a move on."

Greg is evasive when I see him after class. "I don't know if I want to," he says looking past me. "What happens if she doesn't like the movie? What happens if the girls sit together and pay no attention to us?"

"But, Greg..." I practically have to chase him all over school.

Finally, as we're heading towards the front gate, he lays down his terms, "I'll ask Niki, if you come over to my house after the movie. I want to talk to you about Bobby Ho."

"Bobby Ho? What's Bobby Ho got to do with this?" I ask.

Greg flashes his enigmatic smile. "You'll see."

* * * * * *

Mohammed waits outside the school gate, smiling and looking relaxed. We glide into the city onto a street resplendent with flowering trees. To our right the gate to the multi-tiered Xa Loi pagoda's gate is shut and patrolled by soldiers. Hanging from the fence are signs scrawled on white sheets that proclaim in English: "Down with the Diems. Destroy the government."

This isn't the first time I've seen anti-government slogans painted on walls, but the first time I've seen them in English. "Why are they written in English?" I ask Mohammed.

He shrugs. "I don't know."

A Land Rover screeches to a stop along the curb in front of us. Two American men jump out with cameras and start taking pictures. They get within a few feet of the gate before they're waved away by the Vietnamese soldiers. Through the back window, I watch the American reporters argue with the men in camouflage, then retreat.

Imagining the pictures in *Time* or *Newsweek*, I say, "Now I know why."

"Why?" Mohammed asks turning a corner on our way to the Ambassador's residence.

I explain my theory.

When the truck comes to a rest in the driveway, he turns to me and says: "I worry about you, Michael. You see too much."

To my mind, I don't see enough. I wish I had a photographic memory like James Bond. How cool would it be to walk into a room and remember everything — the colors of the rugs, texture of the air, quality of the light, etc.?

Ambassador Sherwood stands in a striped blue and white shirt and tie, gray slacks studying the walls we painted. His gray hair is combed back. Dark circles frame his eyes.

We've moved the air conditioners in the upstairs study to slots above the windows and painted the walls a golden shade of yellow. He removes oval glasses perched on his nose and says, "Good job."

He shakes both our hands.

"I hear you met the President," he says directing me to a chair in front of a bookcase.

"Yes, sir. I think he has a difficult job."

"That's an understatement."

"Is he going to be alright?" I ask.

"Things are problematic right now," he says thoughtfully. "It's important to keep things in perspective. I've been talking to literally hundreds of Vietnamese, French and Brits... from government officials, to military men, to street vendors, to diplomats, to journalists and priests. Whether they President Diem and his brother or not, they all agree that he's made enormous progress since the dark days of 1954. Those who experienced them say you can't imagine the disorder, the fighting and the misery. They say that if you only see Saigon today you have no idea what it was like. It really is a miracle what President Diem and his brother have been able to achieve in less than a decade."

I'm wondering if my father has ever heard the Ambassador say this as Ambassador Sherwood picks up a letter from his desk.

"I want to read you something that President Diem asked me to send to President Kennedy," he says. "It's a quotation from Buddha. It goes: 'The Wise Man is the one who fares strenuously apart, who is unshaken in the midst of praise or blame, who is a leader of others, but is not led by others.'"

"Is President Diem against the Buddhists?" I ask point-blank.

"You've met him, Michael. What do you think?"

"No," I answer without hesitation.

The Ambassador smiles. "I don't think so, either. But when you've got enemies, they look for anything to use against you. Sometimes they provoke reactions that make you look bad."

I've seen the same strategy used on the playground.

"At the very least President Diem needs to understand that his enemies are making him look bad," the Ambassador adds.

* * * * * *

When I get home, my father has news that makes the president look even worse. He delivers it to me as he sits on his bed, tapping his foot as he tries to get Mr. Relaford on the phone.

"Bruno and I were at the intersection of Le Van Duyet and Hong Thap Tu," he starts. "This crowd had assembled... students with big banners denouncing the government. This Renault stopped and several Buddhist monks got out. They were wearing saffron robes. One of the monks, an older man, sat down in the road and crossed his legs. Two other monks doused him with gasoline that they were holding in a plastic bag. Another monk ignited the gas with a lighter. A huge orange flame went up. The monk on fire held his hands together in prayer. People prostrated themselves on the ground and screamed. Traffic stopped. Photographers snapped pictures. The monk burned without saying a word. He burned to a crisp, like a barbecued chicken. Then his burnt body tipped over to one side."

"Oh, God!"

"He sacrificed himself in protest without saying a word," continues my father.

Like him, I realize that something important has happened, but I can't begin to understand the consequences.

"What were you doing there?" I ask. "I mean, how come you and Bruno were there when the monk set himself on fire?"

For a brief moment, my father looks embarrassed. "That's none of your goddamn business!" he snaps. Then squaring his jaw, he waves me out because Brad Relaford is on the line.

I try to imagine what it would take to set myself on fire. I can't.

* * * * * *

"Let's make a spaceship," Corey says when I enter our bedroom. He kneels on top of one of the tall dark mahogany armoires that line the far wall.

"Mission to Jupiter!" I say. "Prepare for blast-off!"

"Yee-hee!" Six-year-old Corey jumps from the armoire and lands hard on his bed.

We push our beds together and use brooms to create a tent. Inside we improvise a control room out of pillows with wheels from his erector set for dials.

"You can be the captain," Corey says, raising thick black eyebrows that make him look like a very young Peter Lawford.

"Ready?" I ask.

"Ready, Captain!"

"Rocket ignition!"

"ROCKET IGNITION!" Corey screams. "ROCKET IGNI-TION!" he screams again, imitating the roar of a rocket blasting off. His eyes beam with excitement.

"Mission to Jupiter!"

The door to our room flies open and crashes into the wall. Our father stands square in the doorway.

"What the fuck is going on in here?" he asks angrily.

Inside our spaceship, Corey shakes with fear. I lay a hand on his chest to reassure him, then stick out my head out and say in my most reasonable voice: "We're playing spaceship, Dad. We'll put everything back when we're finished."

My father looks confused. Hands on his hips, he shakes his head, disgustedly. "Keep your damn voices down, or I'll kick your butts."

"Yes, sir."

"Yes, sir," mimics Corey from under the sheets.

"Ssh!" I hiss.

My father stops in his tracks. "Is Corey in there?" he asks. "I want to talk to Corey."

Corey's eyes are bright circles of mischief. His mouth curls into an impish smile.

I've seen my brother use this face before to provoke my father to the point that he removed his belt and hit Corey in anger.

"Dad, we'll play quietly," I say, trying to sound responsible. "We won't disturb you. We're just playing a game."

My father grunts, "Okay, fine."

He doesn't lose his temper this time. Maybe my mother spoke to him. Maybe he realizes that Corey is just a mischievous little boy.

"Come on," Corey says, pulling me. "Let's play."

We do, quietly, for another fifteen minutes. We're checking our systems, readying the spaceship for takeoff when my father sticks his head in again.

"Michael, I have to go out for a couple of hours," he announces. "I'm leaving you in charge. No fooling around and make sure you're all in bed when I return."

"Yes, sir."

The release of tension adds energy to our game, which we elaborate with flashlights, cushions from the parlor chairs and Ti Ba's feather duster, which we use as an antenna. We perform space walks that take us to the top of the armoires and battle aliens with pieces of rolled up paper shot from rubber bands. Afterwards we return to the spaceship to make more plans.

It's hot under the sheets and blankets, so we strip down to our underpants. "Surprising heat from the moons of Jupiter," I announce. "I'd better adjust the reflective panels."

This task takes me back to the top of the armoires. I pretend to lose my balance and fall onto the bed, making sure to avoid the broomsticks and other obstacles. Corey roars with laughter.

"Aliens! Watch out!" he screams excitedly as he points behind me. I pick up a vacuum cleaner hose that I use as a ray gun. I'm wildly flinging it from side to side as Corey aims the machine gun and fires, "Rat-ta-ta-tat!"

We're interrupted by light knocking on the door. Corey says, "Enter at your own risk."

It's Ti Hai, Ti Ba's daughter — the one who does the laundry. She looks at me, starts to say something in Vietnamese, then blushes and gazes down at her feet.

"Look," Corey says. He's pointing at the front of my underpants, which stand out straight. In my excitement, I got an erection.

"God, Michael! What's going on?" My sister Maggie asks, pushing past Ti Hai and entering. Then pointing at my underpants, she screams, "Gross!"

I cover myself with a towel and, then, step aside so that Ti Hai can enter.

"She's looking for the feather duster," my sister announces.

"We're using it!" Corey protests.

"No you're not!" Maggie says, snatching it from the top of our spaceship.

Corey jumps down and grabs it away. My sister, Maggie, gives chase past Ti Hai, out the door and into the sitting room. All the time she's screaming over and over: "Dad is going to kill you. He's going to kill you guys when he finds out!"

Clutching the towel in front of me, I run to Corey's rescue. He yells, "Michael, help!"

Just an inch out of Maggie's reach, he tosses the duster to me. I turn and run.

Maggie grabs the edge of the towel and screams, "I got you!"

Desperate to save the duster, I let go of the towel and fly into the room, straight into Ti Hai. We both fall to the ground. I land practically on top of her but cushion the fall with my arms.

I'm immediately aware of two things. The alarmed look on Ti Hai's face and the sensation of my boner pushing into her flesh.

In a panic, I run to the bathroom, but not before the pressure releases and I spurt all over the front of my pants.

This isn't the first time this has happened. Ashamed beyond belief, I rinse out my underwear and wait.

Hours later, I open the door to find Corey snoring gently. I slip on my pajamas and get into bed. I wonder if Ti Hai is insulted. *What if she tells my father?*

I try willing myself to sleep, humming songs and rocking back and forth. The clock reads midnight. I go to the sitting room window and look out. My father's Mercedes still isn't back. Artillery pounds in the distance.

I descend the stairs, past Chico curled on the floor, through the pantry and out the back door. Light peeks from under the doors of the maid's quarters. I make out Dong's silhouette in a hammock by a window. There's a light on in the bathroom, all the way to the left. After a few seconds, it shuts off and a figure emerges and walks delicately along the concrete path. It's Ti Hai wearing a bathrobe, holding a towel on her head.

She enters the first room. I let several minutes pass, then whisper at the door, "Ti Hai, it's Michael." It's dark inside. "Ti Hai," I whisper again.

No answer. A siren whines down Phan Tan Gian Street. A gentle breeze tickles the trees. I hear a low voice calling me.

"Ti Hai?" I ask, approaching the open window on bare feet. It takes my eyes a few seconds to adjust to the darkness. Ti Hai lies on a low bed along the wall, her face hidden by the towel and her long, black hair.

As I turn to leave, I hear a moan.

"Ti Hai, are you okay?" I ask in French. "I came to tell you I'm sorry."

She shifts from her side to her back. The light from the house creates a triangle on her torso, which is covered by the shiny white robe.

My eyes run across her smooth legs and childlike feet. I hear another moan and this time I notice her right arm moving slowly between her legs.

As a frog croaks behind me, Ti Hai shifts farther onto her back so that the robe opens wider and I see her hand. It covers her privates, which she massages up and down.

I shouldn't be watching but can't move. Ti Hai raises her hands up to her head and pulls away the towel. The crack between her legs glistens like porcelain decorated with only a few wisps of black hair.

The robe has opened to reveal a flat, smooth stomach and the round knobs of her pelvis. She replaces her hand between her legs and sighs.

My heart beats low and deep in my chest as one long finger disappears inside her. In and out, twisting. When she removes it, the finger glistens. She dips it in again, then stops.

Suddenly she looks up straight into my eyes and I freeze. But her eyes aren't accusing. They're soft and inviting.

Her hand moves quickly over the smooth mound, parting the lips, which turn pink. One finger, then two slip inside.

Blood rushes into my crotch, stirring, swirling. My dick sticks straight out, creating a tent in my pajamas.

Our eyes are locked. The frog croaks again. I hear someone stirring in Dong's room. I step inside the doorway so I can't be seen. But this causes me to block the light. So I take one step farther inside and rest my back against the wall.

Her hand moves faster, making circles and playing with the swollen lips. Her eyes turn heavy, dreamy, like they want to rock back into her head. She raises her left arm so it points at me, cutting the roughly four feet between us in half.

I'm afraid of saying anything that might break the dreamlike spell between us. Electricity cleaves the air. Her eyes never leave mine. She points at my pajama bottoms and moans.

When I touch the elastic waistband, she bites her bottom lip.

I whisper, "You want me to take them off?"

She nods. I take a deep breath and pull them down. My dick stands naked, throbbing, tremendously swollen as though it's going to burst. This seems to excite her. Because her right hand moves faster. She points at my right arm that hangs limply by my side.

I reach out to touch my penis, pumping it slowly up and down. This makes her eyes grow bigger. Her little mouth quivers. She bites her bottom lip hard.

My head swims as I rub myself and watch the muscles in her legs tighten, and her body quiver with tremors that seem to start from her pelvis.

A little cry of ecstasy escapes from her mouth. Then I let go, too, in long spurts that splatter her smooth stomach and cascade across the floor.

Minutes pass. Next time I open my eyes, I'm crouched on the floor with my pants at my ankles. Ti Hai sleeps gently. In the darkness, I gather myself and return to my room.

When I wake the next morning, the episode with Ti Hai seems like a dream.

Will she feel ashamed? Should I? When I pass her at the bottom of the stairs on the way to breakfast, she looks up and smiles. Everything's okay.

My world is transformed.

CHAPTER FOURTEEN

By Saturday morning, the plans are set. Greg and I will meet Samantha and Niki outside the Kinh Do Theater at 12:30. The movie starts at one. The only problem is that I still don't know if my father's flying to Okinawa to visit my mother. If he does, I'll have to stay home with my brother and sister.

At breakfast his mood is surprisingly light. He reads the *New York Times* and hums the tune to "Old Man River," his favorite song. My brother and sister are still asleep.

"Did you see this?" he says, pointing to an article about the monk who sacrificed himself, Quang Doc. He was sixty-two and had entered the Buddhist monastery at fifteen. According to his fellow monks, his last words were a "respectful plea to President Diem to show compassion for all religions."

The article goes on to say that two other monks volunteered for self-immolation, but Quang was given precedence because of his seniority. According to the monks his body burned completely except for his heart, which they found intact. They tried to set it on fire two more times, but Quang's heart wouldn't burn.

In the article Mr. Nhu is portrayed as a "brilliant and eccentric right-hand man to President Diem" who controls the secret police and an "elaborate intelligence network." Mr.

Nhu, the article says, is at war not only with the communists, but with all critics of the regime.

"I don't know if I agree with this part about Mr. Nhu," I tell my father.

"Then you should see this," my father says, handing me the front page of the *Times of Saigon*. Underneath a picture of Madame Nhu, Mr. Nhu's wife, is an interview in which she says, "What have the Buddhists done... The only thing they have done, they have barbecued one of their monks whom they have intoxicated, whom they have abused the confidence, and even that barbecuing was done not even with self-sufficient means because they used imported gasoline."

"How stupid," I blurt out.

"She's going to get them killed," my father says casually, sipping his coffee.

I've completely forgotten to ask my father whether or not he's going to Okinawa. So I'm taken by surprise when Maggie and Corey sit at the table and he announces that our mother is returning tomorrow.

The three of us together send up a cheer, "Hooray!"

"Is her eye all better?" Corey asks.

"Improved," my father answers, lighting a cigarette and blowing smoke rings. "Improved enough that she won't need surgery."

"That's great news!" I exclaim remembering the potion Ti Muoi put under the bed.

"She's not out of the woods yet," adds my father. "But the signs are good."

Before he gets up from the table, he tells us that our mother is scheduled to arrive tomorrow at noon and we're expected at the Relaford's at 2 PM for lunch. "Brad Jr. will be there, too," he says. "It will be like a homecoming party."

Showering, dressing and taking a cab, I arrive at Greg's house as the noontime siren sounds from the police compound behind his house. As soon as I arrive, he starts to regale me with another dirty joke.

"There was this woman who was pregnant with triplets," he says. "One day she went into a bank. The bank was held up. She got shot three times in her stomach!! Luckily she lived. The doctor told her that her babies would live and one day the bullets would come out. Thirteen years later, one of the triplets, a girl, ran out of the bathroom and said: 'Mommy. Mommy. I was going to the bathroom and a bullet came out.' So the mother told her the story. The next day the second daughter comes out and says the same thing, 'Mommy. Mommy, I was going to the bathroom and a bullet came out.' So she tells her the story. The next day the son comes out and says 'Mom! Mom!' she goes, 'let me guess, you were going to the bathroom and a bullet came out?" He said: 'No, I was jerking off and I shot the dog!'"

We both laugh. With his rosy cheeks, freshly ironed white shirt and dress pants, Greg looks like an altar boy.

"Why'd you get all dressed up?" I ask.

"Girls like a man who's well turned out and neatly groomed," he says smoothing back his hair and admiring his image in the hallway mirror.

It sounds like a line from *Playboy*. "So what's going on with Bobby Ho?"

Greg holds up a finger, pulls me into his room and closes the door. "You know what a whorehouse is?"

"Of course." We all do. There are so-called "houses of pleasure" on practically every block of the city. Some feature scantily clad girls waving from the windows or balconies, trying to lure men inside.

Greg lowers his voice. "You ever been to a whorehouse?"

"No. Have you?" I ask back.

He shakes his head. "No. But Bobby Ho has, and he knows a lot about sex."

"So?"

"So... I told him about us. I told him that we're... like...

virgins."

"We are virgins."

"I asked him if he'd educate us about sex. And he said, the best way to teach us is to take us to a whorehouse."

Maybe I'm chicken or too much of a romantic, but the idea of paying some woman I don't know for sex doesn't sound good.

"Alain says he's been like twenty times," Greg says.

"You believe him?"

"Last time he went, he took that goofy guy Don Posner and Don got his thing in the girl and didn't know what to do. So he peed in her and the girl starting screaming. Don is such a jerk."

"So?" I ask, "Are you going?"

"I don't know, answers Greg. "I'm kind of worried about VD."

Horrifying pictures of pustules and oozing sores from a movie we were shown in Health class flash in my head.

"I've heard that even if you wear a rubber you can still get the clap," adds Greg.

On the way to the theater, he fidgets like crazy and asks all kinds of questions: What are we going to do if the girls don't like the movie and want to leave? What are we going to do if they want to sit together? What are we going to do if a friend of our parents sees us? What are we going to do if Samantha and Niki don't show up?

My answer to everything is, "We'll figure it out."

Greg doesn't like that answer. He snaps, "Michael, we've got to be prepared!"

Through the forest of cyclo drivers and bicycles, we spy the theater with Samantha and Niki standing out front. Greg grabs the driver's shoulder and directs him to turn at the corner, "*A droit! A droit!*"

The driver screeches right and we circle the block. "What'd you do that for?" I ask.

Greg winks and points at his forehead. "Psychology.

Psychology. It heightens the anticipation if they wait."

I don't read *Playboy* so I don't know all the moves. I do know the movie starts in ten minutes and I don't want to miss the short. "We'd better hit the gas," I say pointing at my watch.

"Five more minutes," Greg says like a military commander planning an ambush.

By the time we pull in front of the theater and pay the driver, the girls aren't there. "Good work, Greg," I say, rushing into the lobby and finding Samantha and Niki at the front of the concession stand buying snacks.

"You want some?" Samantha asks politely, holding a warm bag of popcorn.

Greg and I are both out of breath. It isn't the coolest of entrances. "That's okay," I answer. "Greg and I will buy the tickets."

Four tickets come to one dollar and forty cents. We enter the 200-seat theater as the lights dim. Greg elbows me and points to the back row. But Niki doesn't have her glasses, so she wants to sit in the front.

"Is this okay?" she asks, indicating the second row.

Greg mumbles, "It's terrible."

I answer, "Fine."

The girls slide in first but leave room for Greg and me to sit between them. It's Greg, Niki, me and Sam. The newsreel ends with a segment about our "brave military advisors in South Vietnam." The audience, which is made up mostly of GIs and their girlfriends, applauds.

We watch scenes of peasants constructing strategic hamlets. A US major with a thick Southern accent says, "I think here, lately, the program's going a lot better; I think we're beginning to win the people over; our operations are going better. We're actually getting VC."

It's the winning people over part that troubles me. *Are we here to win people over, or to help the country fight communism? Or both?* My father says the Vietnamese people want democracy. *If they want democracy, why do we have to win them over? And if the people don't want our form of government how are we going to win?*

I'm struggling with these questions, when the short starts. Roy Rodgers and Trigger and two of his compadres chase a band of bandits who have made off with an Indian squaw. They ride right into an ambush. The bad guys are hidden in some rocks. As Roy's partners cover him, he climbs up higher than the bad guys and shoots down at them until they surrender. The squaw is rescued, her tribe is grateful and Roy Rodgers sings, "Happy trails to you, until we meet again." Then he rides off into the sunset.

Samantha sighs next to me and offers me some popcorn. Her blue eyes glitter in the reflected light from the screen. As I reach over, I brush her hand. She looks up at me, smiling. Our fingers intertwine.

A warm rush runs through my body as the movie starts. It's *The Birds* by Alfred Hitchcock.

I whisper into Samantha's ear, "I saw another one of his movies before, *North by Northwest* with Cary Grant. I really liked it. I hope this one is as good."

She smells of orchids. Her pink lips stretch across her perfect teeth. I squeeze her hand, she squeezes back. She likes me even though I'm weak and still unformed. I want to be strong and brave like Roy Rodgers. I don't ever want to let her down.

During a section at the beginning of the movie where the screen goes dark, Samantha lays her head on my shoulder. When I turn to look at her, our lips meet and we kiss. It's short and awkward, but wonderful. I want to do it again. This time, after our lips meet, I feel her mouth open and our tongues touch.

I melt, transforming into something else. My body transmits all kinds of powerful signals that I've never felt before.

Finally, growing conscious that we're sitting in a theater filled with people, we break and watch the movie holding hands.

The story unfolds slowly, character by character. It's seems like a love triangle at first, but then the mood turns dark and creepy. About a third of the way in, Niki leans across me and whispers to Samantha.

Samantha says to me, "Excuse me. I'll be right back."

They stand and walk to the lady's room which is to the left of the screen. As soon as they're gone, Greg leans over and says, "What the heck are you doing, Michael? You're practically raping her. All the people behind us can see."

I don't care.

When Samantha returns, we kiss again. Then the movie gets real scary. Birds are going crazy. There's a scene when hundreds converge on a children's party. Samantha reaches over and grabs my thigh. She doesn't mean it in a sexual way, but immediately I get a boner and have to fight the urge to lose control.

The credits roll at the end of the movie and we sneak another kiss. When the lights come up we return to acting like friends. No kissing, no holding hands. As we pass through the lobby a woman with her husband shoots me a dirty look.

In the bright oppressive sunlight, Greg and I ask together, "You girls want to get a soda?"

Next thing we're across the street at the bowling alley, sipping cold Shastas. Niki hasn't said a word the whole time. I like her despite the fact that she consistently gets the best grades in class and sometimes acts like she's smarter than everybody else.

"Did you like the movie?" I ask.

She holds up her little nose and says, "It was interesting, but unsatisfying on an emotional level."

Greg smiles and says, "I don't know about you, but it scared the crap out of me!"

Even Niki laughs at this, arching her long neck back and letting loose a barrage of giggles.

The mood lightens, the talk settles into the familiar — the kids in our class, teachers, music and clothes.

I drift off, thinking about Buddhist monks. I'm trying to figure out what it takes to sacrifice your life for your beliefs. I imagine knights fighting duels on horseback for the love of a woman. Next, I'm wondering if I would ever fight a duel with Greg over, say, Samantha. I realize that probably wouldn't happen because in our world, Samantha would get to choose.

"We've got choices," I say, thinking out loud.

"What?" asks Greg who was speculating about whether or not a girl in our class named Laurie Methvan ever washes her hair.

"I was just thinking that's what separates us from other people."

All eyes turn to me. I know that they're thinking: He's strange. He's always asking serious questions.

"Which people are you talking about?" Niki asks knitting her brown eyebrows.

"People in the Middle Ages," I answer. "The people here."

They want an explanation, and I try to find the words. But my mind is more agile than my ability to express myself.

"Are you trying to say that there's a lesser probability of conflict when people have the right to choose?" Niki asks.

"Sort of. Yes." I want to go further. "What I'm trying to say is that when people make their own choices there still might be conflict, things still might get messy. But I think there's a greater probability that people will arrive at some natural kind of order, some sort of harmony with the way they're supposed to live."

Greg shakes his head, Samantha grins. Niki fixes me with piercing eyes. "You really believe that there's some kind of natural order? Some harmonious way of living?" she asks.

I never realized it before, but I do. Somewhere in my

subconscious I dream of such a place. I even feel like I've been there. "Yes."

* * * * * *

I'm still playing with this concept as I sit in church listening to Father McDaniel. He says, "Jesus said: 'I am the gate.' He said: 'If we don't know where we're going how can we find the way?'"

Afterwards, as I help him prepare sandwiches and rice balls to take to Saint Frances Xavier Church in Cholon, I ask about President Diem and the Buddhists.

He squares his shoulders. "Frankly," he answers, "I don't know what to think. I understand the need to express one's beliefs. I understand the need to protest when those beliefs are interfered with. I might even understand the need to sacrifice one's life in the most urgent circumstances. But I don't see what the fuss is all about. I mean, this all started because of a protest about the flying of a Buddhist flag. We don't fly Catholic banners outside of the church."

I'm confused. "Then what do you think is going on?"

Father McDaniel shakes his head. "I can only repeat what our friend Mr. Nhu told me. He says that Vietcong sympathizers have infiltrated the Buddhists. These sympathizers are agitating, creating cells, setting up headquarters in Buddhist temples, conducting crash courses in drafting tracts, slogans and distributing their propaganda in Vietnamese, French and English, which they print on mimeograph machines."

On the way to Cholon I ask, "Has Mr. Nhu communicated this to US officials?"

Father McDaniel says, "I believe so." Then, "Maybe you should talk to your father."

As we get out of the car at Saint Frances Xavier, I say, "I will."

Inside we pass out food to people with missing limbs and men and women whose faces and bodies are covered in fabric because they're suffering from leprosy. They take the food graciously and retreat into the shadows of the church where they eat in private.

* * * * * *

My father waits impatiently, standing before the open door of the Mercedes as I enter the gate. "Where the hell have you been?" he asks. "I have to pick up your mother from the airport."

"I was with Father McDaniel."

"Bullshit!" he bellows, pushing me so I stumble and fall on the gravel. "Look at your watch!"

Things happen fast. Dong opens the gate. Ti Ba ushers my brother and sister into the back seat. My father starts the car. My watch reads 12:45, which means that mass ended approximately an hour and a half ago. *Should I tell my father that I went to St. Francis Xavier afterwards to hand out sandwiches?*

He's already turned the car so it's pointed at the gate.

I run to his open window. He brings the car to a crunching stop and leans out. "Mr. Trong (our cook) is preparing a cake for your mother," he shouts. "When it's ready, bring it with you in a taxi to the Relafords. You have money?" His tone is surprisingly businesslike.

I check the wad of piaster notes in my pocket. "Yes."

"See you there," he says, pressing his foot down on the accelerator and speeding towards the street.

It takes a moment for the confusion in my head to clear. Palm fronds sway in the breeze; birds call joyfully to one another; the scent of hibiscus sweetens the air. I climb upstairs and lie on my bed. The house is deliciously pleasant and calm.

Music drifts up from the maid quarters where a radio is

playing. A Vietnamese man sings accompanied by a zither. There's an ache in his voice that transcends language. I translate the Vietnamese into English.

> With you it's love at first sight
> Is it the will of heaven?
> I love you for your pink cheeks
> Your lips that bloom like a flower
> Love strikes a deep chord in my heart
> Bred by your pride, talent and beauty
> Even stones would be moved by them
> How could a man's heart offer resistance?

I think about Ti Hai and Samantha, who fade into one another and into a dream about my grandmother. She smiles down at me with dark, weary circles around her eyes.

Downstairs in the kitchen I find Mr. Trong (our cook) in white shorts putting the finishing touches to his masterpiece. Wielding a pastry bag filled with yellow icing, he spells out "Welcum home," in perfect script as Ti Ba and Dong watch.

Ti Ba (Ti Hai's mother) shoots me an accusing look and leaves. I don't have time to consider what she's thinking, because Mr. Trong is giving me instructions in French, telling me how to carry the box, how to remove the cake, and where to place it so that it's not directly in the sun.

With Dong's help, I leave through the side gate and into a cab. Through the back window I catch a glance of Ti Hai in her *bao dai* and *non gai tho* holding a bicycle, and I wave.

* * * * * *

I'm seated in a chair next to Brad Jr.'s bed. He's showing me these really cool plastic knights on horseback that his mother bought for him in Hong Kong. He talks excitedly about the figures, handing them to me one by one, pointing out how the lances, visors, and all the other parts move and are inter-changeable.

"Neat. Very neat," I say.

He doesn't mention his injury or the white bandages that still cover the left side of his back from his armpit to his ribs. His injury seems to cast an unmistakable shadow over his bold blue eyes. He seems further away, confined to some kind of silent punishment by his family for bringing them shame.

Samantha arrives to announce, "Your parents are here." She's still friendly and pretty but different from the girl I took to the movies.

I hurry downstairs to greet my mother.

"Mom!" I gush, throwing my arms around her and kissing her cheek. She responds for a second but remains aloof. Her face is perfectly composed like that of a Japanese geisha. She doesn't even wear a bandage over her eye.

"They were wonderful," she says, turning her attention to Mr. and Mrs. Relaford. "The doctors there were so skillful, truly. I owe them so much."

She explains that just as they were preparing her eye for surgery, a new medicine she had been taking appeared to be working better than anyone expected.

"It was miraculous," she explains. "One day my eye was all inflamed and dangerous scar tissue was building up, and twenty-four hours later the retina was perfectly clear."

The grownups happily extol the virtues of modern medicine. It's probably not the best time to tell them about Ti Muoi and the pot of herbs she placed under her bed. But I do anyway, briefly, as their butler arrives with a tray of pink daiquiris.

My father, Bruno and Mr. Relaford don't even look up. The only one who gives even the slightest indication of having heard what I said is my mother who sighs and says, "Really, Michael, that's quite a story. Especially when we're talking about a completely incompetent woman who doesn't even know how to iron a shirt."

"Isn't she the one with the crossed eyes?" Mrs. Relaford asks, laughing and waving her hand.

"Exactly!" answers my mother.

"It's something to consider," I say, trying to sound as reasonable as possible.

My mother bats her long brown lashes. "If you want to consider it, Michael, you be my guest. I'm not going to waste my energy."

"It's something to think about," I say as I leave. "What's wrong with that?"

* * * * * *

I'm content to spend the rest of the day in Brad Jr.'s dark tile room playing with the knights on horseback and building a castle for them at the foot of his bed. Samantha and my sister interrupt us after we've finished lunch, which was brought to us on trays.

"Mom is cutting the cake," Maggie says with a wicked gleam in her eye.

"Okay."

"Don't you want to watch Mom cut her welcome home cake?" my sister asks.

"I'll be right there," I answer, then promise Brad Jr. I'll be back shortly with a big piece for him.

Downstairs, they're gathered around the table with my mother at the head holding a long brass knife shaped like a sword. We cheer as she cuts into Mr. Trong's magnificent chocolate cake. I tell her I'm glad she's all better and back home with us.

She smiles at me with strange indifference. Despite the goodwill that swirls around her, she remains indelibly removed. Her invisible shield is back in place.

At night when we return home, the day feels like it's been

long. And it's not over, because my father has sent Dong to summon me to the living room.

I find my parents seated together on a rattan sofa, my mother rubbing the back of her neck. Her eyes study the cushions on the chairs nearby, appraising their condition, all the time avoiding mine.

"I want to let you know that we had to let Ti Hai go," my father announces, his cheeks flushed from the drinks at the Relaford's house.

My body turns rigid as though it's been struck by lightning. "Why?"

"I think you know why," he says, turning to my mother who wrings her hands.

"No, I... I don't know why," I stammer. "I... I don't understand."

My father says, "We think it's best for all concerned. Ti Hai is a lovely young girl. Your mother is going to write her a positive letter of reference. I'm sure she'll find another job."

Confused, I ask, "Did she do something wrong?"

My mother nods.

My father says, "I'm not sure."

"I don't understand," I say again.

My father removes his glasses and looks at me coldly through small gray eyes. "Your sister saw you enter Ti Hai's room the other night," he says quickly. "I don't think I have to tell you what's wrong with that."

His words and everything about his manner and tone of voice seems designed to offend me. But it's the weight of my own guilt that is crushing. Shaking with shame and anger I try to defend her.

"That's no reason to fire someone," I say. "Punish me if you want, but it's not her fault. If you want to know the truth, I went to see Ti Hai to apologize for something. She didn't invite me in. Why was Maggie spying on me? Please don't do this. It's not fair!"

My parents don't respond. The gulf between us darkens and grows more treacherous and immense.

My father dismisses me with three words, "Go to bed!"

CHAPTER
FIFTEEN

A week has passed and I still feel terrible because I never meant to hurt Ti Hai.

The problem is the two separate sets of voices in my head: one expresses my own sense of right and wrong, and the other my mother's and father's points of view. They clash continually and overlap sometimes, which makes it hard for me to come to terms with what happened and move on.

Also, I fear that my credibility, especially as it pertains to my father, has been severely diminished. That's why I haven't approached him with what I learned from Father McDaniel. I'm waiting for his disappointment to wane and my confidence to grow.

I've made a terrible mess. Not only have I hurt Ti Hai, I've also offended her mother, angered my parents, and compromised my ability to get a decent hearing from my Dad.

Before my parents put me in the middle, each wanting me to take their side against the other. Now, they're united against me.

When I ask my mother about her miraculous cure, she says, "Please, Michael. I don't want to talk about that anymore."

They want me to swallow my shame like a man. But I can't because it feels like poison.

Standing on the edge of the light green soccer field, Mohammed senses something is wrong. Maybe it's the reckless way I'm playing defense, throwing my body into oncoming players, challenging the men with the ball. At halftime, he limps over on his bad knee to hand me a bottle of soda.

"You're playing with anger," Mohammed says, a hedge of tall bamboo swaying past his shoulder. "What's up?"

"I'm mad," I say catching my breath.

"Don't let anger disrupt you," he says without even a hint of reproach. "Don't let it take you out of your game."

After the soccer game, I go to the Cathedral and sit in the confession booth where Father McDaniel is waiting.

He listens through the wicker screen and says, "Tell me exactly what happened."

I explain the incident with Ti Hai, haltingly.

At the end he asks, "Didn't I warn you about this, Michael?" Then he doles out my penance of Our Fathers and Hail Marys, which I offer quietly in the empty church.

When my conscience still isn't relieved, I seek him out again and ask, "Father, is there something wrong with me?"

"Michael, hasn't your father ever spoken to you about this? Don't you know that all men have these feelings?"

"No, father," I answer realizing that he's saying that he's not only felt temptation like I have, but he's probably given into it, too.

"It's difficult to live as flesh and blood and find the path to God," he pronounces.

I think of my father, Sy, Mohammed, Dong and President Diem sitting in his room like a monk. I'm ready to thank Father McDaniel for helping me, when he takes my hand and asks, "What's really bothering you, Michael?"

"Ti Hai," I answer. "She lost her job because of me."

"Then you must help her."

"Thank you, Father. Thank you."

I think I know what I have to do.

* * * * * *

Monday morning, in the shop, I find Sy standing at the lathe watching a carpenter carve the leg of a chair. Wisps of wood shavings cling to his thinning hair. I tell him that I need help finding Ti Hai a job. He smiles slyly and says, "You can do that better than me."

"I can?"

He pats me on the head. "Yes. But if you need help, I'm here."

Later that afternoon when Mohammed and I inspect a house that's down the block from the Ambassador's residence, I ask the woman living there, Mrs. Morris, if she needs help around the house.

"No," she answers, her eyes pinched tightly in her head. "Do you know someone who is good?"

"Yes, I do," I answer. "She's excellent, honest, hard-working and discreet." I know that these are the qualities that my mother and Mrs. Relaford value.

"Can she do laundry?" Mrs. Morris asks.

"Oh, yes. Very well."

She says, "There's an older man, a bachelor named Mr. Mettier who lives two houses down. Talk to him."

Not only is Mr. Mettier a kind man with a bald head and a gray handlebar mustache, he's also eager to meet Ti Hai. When I get home, I find her mother Ti Ba in the kitchen. She takes the information with a wary look and promises to pass it on.

A week later, when Mohammed arrives to pick me up, I see him talking to our gardener, Van. Van's a wiry man with thin spindly legs, who does impeccable work and rarely says anything. Now he's waving his hands excitedly and pointing to the grass.

"What's he talking about?" I ask.

Mohammed turns his handsome head to me and answers, "Grubs."

"What are grubs?"

Van squats in his shorts and pulls at a fistful of grass that comes up easily. Pushing his hand into the dark soil he pulls out two white bugs the size of his thumb. He offers them to Mohammed, who studies them and then crushes them with his boot.

"We've got a problem," Mohammed concludes. "If we don't stop them now they'll destroy the whole yard."

Working together in the sun, we pull up the loose grass and dig out the grubs. By the end of the morning, the front lawn has yielded a bucketful of grubs. Van pours kerosene over them and sets them on fire. Then the three of us go down the street for a bowl of *pho*.

Van chatters the whole time. He's telling us that he once was a cook in the French army, and that the requirement of a good cook is excellent taste.

Good *pho*, he says, requires a clear and tasty broth, rice paste that is velvet soft and beef that is crisp, not rubbery. The soup should be flavored with lemon juice, hot pepper and shallot bulbs.

"A good bowl," he says with a grin, "will give you a taste of paradise."

Van judges the *pho* we've been eating as "not bad."

When we reenter the gate, I see my mother standing in the middle of the drive with her hands on her hips, surrounded by Ti Ba, Dong, Maggie and Corey. She looks at the bare front yard with disgust and asks me, "What have you done now?"

Mohammed steps forward and explains about the grubs.

"Don't you know your father's throwing a cocktail party tonight?" my mother asks me. "You're supposed to mix drinks. He's going to be furious!"

Mohammed's voice slides up an octave as he explains. "Put your mind at rest, Mrs. Sforza. We will put it all in order. We'll have it all in order before the sun goes down."

"You'd better," my mother says glaring at me like it's my fault.

It's amazing what we three accomplish in an afternoon, even when half of it is spent driving through monsoon rain back and forth to the nursery for sod. Working in our bare feet with our pants rolled up, Mohammed and I smooth the black mud and lay down the squares of sod. Van tamps and adjusts the seams of sod so they match.

By six-thirty, when Dong hurries to open the front gate for my father's Mercedes, the whole lawn has been replaced except for a little patch along the side of the house. Mohammed explains everything to my father.

My father looks at me skeptically and says, "As soon as you're finished, go inside and wash up."

I'm too tired to wonder if my father's annoyed.

"Hurry up," he says. "Get ready. The guests will be here in twenty minutes."

Kerosene lamps illuminate the driveway. Dong, Van and I set up a table on the patio and stock it with supplies — sweet and sour vermouth, gin, scotch, bourbon, rum, tonic water, soda, beer, cola, lemon-lime, ice, glasses, maraschino cherries and wedges of fresh lemons and limes.

Cicadas fill the air as men in white shirts and khaki pants and wives in cotton dresses with red lips and lacquered hair arrive. The night air reeks of kerosene and perfume.

My father drifts over to me holding a martini in one hand and puffing on a cigarette with the other like a movie star. "How are we doing?" he asks.

"Fine," I answer, trying to keep up with the drink orders.

I'm so busy, I forget my exhaustion and hunger. The space around me buzzes with activity and shreds of conversation. I hear Bruno's big laugh cutting through the chatter like a saw. In the midst of everything, one figure remains in the distance like an island apart. When the figure steps towards me I notice that it's Sy wearing a striped shirt that sticks out of his gray pants. His hair is disheveled.

"Don't you ever get a break?" he asks under his breath.

I'm on automatic. "Can I get you anything to drink?" I ask.

He hands me a glass that smells of rum, then points over his shoulder and says loud enough for my father to hear, "Nice job on the lawn. It looks a hell of lot better than it did before."

"Thanks."

Sy leaves with a wink. The crowd starts to thin. Chico trots by, trolling for fallen hors d'oeuvres. I lean against a palm tree and rest. Tiny sprigs of golden orchids tickle my ear. I close my eyes for a few seconds and dream I'm floating down a river.

Pieces of conversations reach my ears, many of which deal with the "political situation." I notice that the sentiment expressed is decidedly anti-Diem.

"Look at the way he treats his own people? Barbaric!" a woman says as though she knows.

"It's time to get rid of him," pronounces a man puffing on a pipe.

Mrs. Relaford's voice dominates the others. She tells a group of men and women how the Embassy Ladies' Club held a raffle to raise money. "After a great deal of discussion, we decided to use the funds to help a beautiful, young girl on Tu Duc Street. You know, that poor dear with the atrocious clubbed foot. We found out that there's an operation that fixes that. So we pooled our money and approached the family. The girl was very excited, but her father was decidedly not. Believe it or not, he refused our offer."

"Why?" a woman asks.

"He said that under no circumstances would he permit the operation. He said his daughter supports the entire family –

mother, father, grandfather, grandmother, great grandmother, four aunts and uncles and five other children."

"Unbelievable!"

"I was absolutely flabbergasted," Mrs. Relaford exclaims.

"Struck dumb!"

I'm two tired eyes and a pair of ears. If I were brave I'd raise my voice and call them hypocrites, because they haven't taken the time to learn anything about the people they say they want to help.

I could tell them about Dong, who wanders over with his thin black tie askew. I could explain how he and his wife and four children arrived eight years ago from Hanoi as refugees. How his oldest son is now a pilot in the South Vietnamese Air Force based in Pleiku. How he speaks with great dignity and accepts the life that fate has dealt him. How the wall of his room is covered with photographs of Washington, DC, San Francisco and chateaus in France even though he has never left Vietnam.

An hour later, as the party fades into twilight, Dong, Van and I lug the bottles back to the pantry. We pass Chico stalking the yard from a thick chain tied to a tree.

"That dog attacked a guest," Dong says out of the side of his mouth, in French.

"Chico?"

"*Oui!*"

"*Dinky dow,*" I say to Dong.

"*Oui.*"

* * * * * *

Two days later, Mohammed announces that Mr. Mettier's water heater isn't working.

An inspection accomplished with a flashlight and ladder reveals a burnt-out fuse, which we replace.

"Can I get you gents a refreshment?" Mr. Mettier asks

smiling beneath his bushy gray mustache.

"Yes, thank you," I answer quickly.

My heart beats harder as we wait in rattan chairs. I'm expecting Ti Hai. Instead, Mr. Mettier enters with two cans of Shasta and a mug of beer, explaining that it's the maid's day off.

Mohammed sees my disappointment. He knows me well, and poses the question I'm too embarrassed to ask, "How do you like your new maid?"

"Ti-Hai is a-okay!" Mr. Mettier beams, his eyes a-twinkle. He turns to me and lifts his mug of beer. "Thanks."

"You're welcome," I say feeling slightly jealous.

"See," Mohammed says when we return to truck. "It all worked out."

If Mohammed looks after me like an older brother, Sy's the wise older man who's seen it all and speaks honestly. He's fond of saying that he "doesn't play the game."

Friday afternoon, after Mohammed and I had worked for hours in the sun, helping workers pour a new walkway at the Ambassador's residence, Sy invites me to join him for a cold drink in the air-conditioned Cosmos Bar behind the Embassy.

We pass a group of Americans at the bar talking excitedly about a third Buddhist monk who's set himself on fire.

"Diem's a homo," I overhear one of them say.

We sit in back where it's quiet except for the gurgle from the pump of a giant fish tank. I tell Sy what Father McDaniel told me: that Mr. Nhu thinks the Vietcong are helping to foment the Buddhist protests.

Smirking, Sy answers, "Anything's possible."

Sometimes, I sense things. Like I get the feeling now that the men crowded around the bar — embassy officials like my father, eager-eyed, serious, white shirts, black shiny shoes — are lusting for the President's head.

I ask Sy, "Why do people at the embassy dislike President Diem so much?"

"Because they think they're supposed to pass judgment, but really don't know shit from shinola," he answers draining a bottle of 33 beer.

"What's your opinion of President Diem?"

Sy doesn't answer. Instead, he watches the waitress sashay past the red glow of the bar, shifting her hips from side to side. As she leans over the table with another bottle of beer, she teases him with a coy smile. Some sort of sexual understanding passes between them.

He told me a few days ago that he broke off his relationship with Chan, because her parents didn't like her spending so much time with an American without a proposal of marriage.

Now he gulps down another 33 beer, searching my eyes. Thrusting his chin towards the men at the bar, he whispers, "What do you think they're up to?"

"Maybe they're planning a coup," I answer. Until recently I didn't even know what a coup d'état was.

He grins. "You're a smart kid."

Thoughts, names and pictures collide in my head. Bruno, my father, Mr. Relaford, the meeting with the Vietnamese General Don on the boat. I think back to my first day in Saigon when I met Mr. Nhu and Father McDaniel in the Cathedral.

Outside, in the streetlight, I watch a woman with a long broom sweep a mixture of fruit and vegetable peels, fish heads, fish and chicken bones, coconuts husks and eggshells into a gutter. The wind makes strange music as it passes through the trees.

We drive past a big, red banner in Vietnamese that reads, "Human kindness is the milk of Vietnamese art."

"The people here love art, don't they?" I ask into the dark cab of the truck.

Sy nods. He stops at the side gate of our house where a vendor with scissors is selling long coils of funnel cake. "Careful with your father," he warns.

"Thanks."

I find him sitting on the edge of the bed pulling up his socks. I tell him the news I heard two weeks ago from Father McDaniel about the Vietcong fomenting the Buddhist protests.

Looking disinterested, he walks to the closet to get his pants. When I tell him the rumor some Vietnamese generals are planning a coup, his ears perk up.

"Who told you that?" he asks, closing the door.

"Is it true?"

He stares at me with penetrating eyes and asks again, stronger, "Where'd you hear that, Michael?"

"Nobody told me. It's a feeling I have."

"A what?" he asks.

"An intuition."

"An intuition?" he repeats in a mocking tone. "Do you think for one minute that any serious person would put the slightest bit of credence into the imagination of a thirteen-year-old boy?"

* * * * * *

Uneasiness roils inside me, even though the house is quiet and my parents are gone. It's after dinner and Corey and I sit on my bed playing checkers. Maggie lies on Corey's bed reading *Winnie the Pooh*. Lizards outside make an "uh-oh, uh-oh" grunting sound over and over.

Corey's thirsty so I tell him to go downstairs to the refrigerator in the pantry and pour himself a glass of milk.

"You have to come with me," he says. "I'm afraid to go downstairs in the dark."

He's a sweet boy with thick brown hair and very thick eyebrows. I take his little hand in mine and we descend.

There's a lamp on in the living room. The massive doors to the porch are locked tight. I hold open the swinging door to the pantry for him and turn on the lights. "Help yourself," I say.

"Thanks."

Wanting to talk to Greg, I cross to the phone that rests on top of the bar. I'm about to dial his number when I hear Corey scream, "Michael!... HELP!!!!"

I drop the phone and run, sliding across the tile floor and through the pantry door. Stark light from the open refrigerator bounces off the narrow walls. I see Chico on top of Corey with his jaws open about to attack his throat.

"NO!!!" I shout, pouncing on Chico's thickly muscled back. He uncoils like a spring, snaps his head back and bites my wrist.

"Corey, run!!!" I scream, pain shooting up my arm into my neck.

I watch him scramble to his feet and stumble backwards, holding his bloody hands to his collarbone and sobbing hysterically.

"Run, Corey! Run! Get Dong!" I scream trying to free my wrist.

With my other hand I squeeze Chico's throat with all my strength. He yelps and lets go of my wrist. But he's fast and furious and there's no room to maneuver in the tight space. Before I can get to the door, he lunges mouth-first at my chest. His sharp teeth sink into the flesh right below my heart.

I scream, unleashing a blot of anger that I use to rip his teeth free and throw him against the wall. He hits it with a hollow thud. I bring my knee up and kick him in the chest. Stunned, he twists and falls back-first to the floor.

Before Chico can recover, before he gets his feet under him, I dash out the door to the living room and bolt it shut.

Breathless, I run through the living room and out the back door to the breezeway between the maid's quarters calling, "Corey! Corey. Where are you?"

In my right periphery I see him being helped by Ti Ba and Dong. Before I inquire about my brother's injuries, I dash to the outside door to the pantry and make sure it's locked.

Chico glares at me through the distorted glass. He's vicious-looking, panting hard, with blood on his teeth. I watch him turn back and stick his nose in the open refrigerator door. The reconstituted milk Corey meant to drink stands on the shelf.

Corey sobs, shaking from head to toe. I hurry inside and call Dr. Silverman, who's half asleep. Then I try to calm Corey so that Ti Ba can clean the blood and we can see the extent of his wounds. There's a long one like an exclamation mark across his collarbone, which just missed his throat, and several deep bites in his arm.

Fifteen minutes later, Dr. Silverman arrives with a medical kit wearing a t-shirt and rumpled khaki-shorts, his sparse hair in a swirl. He works quickly and expertly with thin pale hands, repeating over and over to Corey, "I'm sure this hurts. It's not as bad as it looks. You're a very brave boy."

Time passes quickly. Corey's collarbone and wrists are covered with bandages and tape. His eyes are still red with tears. My sister Maggie is on the telephone upstairs trying to locate my parents who are attending a reception for a State Department official visiting from Washington.

Dr. Silverman turns to me and says almost matter-of-factly, "Look at your chest." That's when I realize that blood has seeped through my shirt. I'm holding my right wrist which seers with pain.

Dr. Silverman disinfects the wounds and dresses them.

"Do we have to go to the hospital?" I ask.

"No," Dr. Silverman says, calmly. "I checked our records, and Chico is up to date on his rabies shots, so I can take care of everything here."

After Dr. Silverman finishes applying the bandages and Corey is escorted upstairs to bed, my parents arrive.

"Where's Corey?" they ask together. My father's mouth looks distorted; my mother clutches her hands to her chest.

They run up the stairs with Dr. Silverman behind them. I

sink into a stuffed chair in the living room. Maybe I close my eyes. Some minutes later, my father stands over me and asks, "What the hell happened?"

I tell him calmly.

"Where's Chico now?" he asks.

"Locked in the pantry."

My father turns and takes a dozen long strides to the pantry door. I follow behind and cower when he opens it. Chico gazes up at him lovingly and wags his tail. My father smooths the dog's head.

"What happened, boy?" he asks gently. Then up at me, "Who left the refrigerator open?"

I recount with some urgency the savagery of the attack and end by saying, "He was going for Corey's throat."

"You told me that already," he says.

My father takes Chico by the collar and leads him outside, where he chains him to a tree. I wait in the living room until my mother returns and announces that Corey is asleep. Together we thank Dr. Silverman who leaves in his car.

Then my mother turns to me and asks, "Are you okay, Michael?"

"I think so. It was frightening."

My father passes on the way to the bar, where he pours himself a glass of scotch. "What possessed Chico to attack you boys?" my mother asks.

"I don't know. He went berserk," I answer, my hands still shaking, Chico's strength and fury still vivid in my mind.

From the bar, my father flashes an ironic smile. "No," he explains. "He didn't go berserk. Chico thought that Corey was taking his food."

I feel my anger rising. "He attacked him, Dad. He was going for Corey's throat!"

"What were you and Corey doing in that refrigerator in the first place?" my father asks.

"Corey was thirsty and wanted a glass of milk."

"Dogs are territorial," my father explains like the teacher he once was. "They're protective of their food. You should never go into that refrigerator when Chico is nearby, because that's where we keep his food."

I want to scream at him, but I'm too tired. My mother tries to check us with soothing words, "It's over now. Let's forget it. Thank God nobody was badly hurt. Let's all go to bed."

I don't want to argue about what happened, or why it happened, but I know one thing irrefutably, Chico has to go. He can't stay in this house.

"Go to sleep," my father orders.

I don't move. "What are you going to do about Chico?"

"I'm not going to do anything about Chico," he groans. "Now, go to bed."

He stands over me threateningly. I stand my ground and say again: "Dad, Chico can't live here anymore."

"I said, Go to sleep."

"Not before you promise."

"Do I have to smack your face?" he threatens. "Or are you going to bed?"

"Go to bed, Michael," my mother pleads.

I'm not going to move until I'm ready. I say, "If that dog isn't gone when I get up in the morning, I'm going to get my baseball bat and bash his head in."

"Michael! You wouldn't!" my mother gasps.

"Yes, I will. It's a promise."

With that, I go upstairs and fall asleep. In the morning when I sit down for breakfast, Chico is gone.

CHAPTER SIXTEEN

Sometimes the world seems perfect and happiness and beauty hang in the air like songs waiting to be sung. It's a glorious Sunday morning. The air's fresh when Huang meets me after church.

He's dressed in white with carefully combed hair. His face beams with goodwill as he talks about his love for his bride-to-be, Kim, as we walk to the zoo.

It's a peaceful place where friends, lovers and children come to observe the animals, laugh and act silly. We pass cages filled with Siberian tigers, monkeys, ostriches, crocodiles and elephants, then pause in a thick patch of shade. Flowers whisper to each other. Birds sing. Huang sketches out his dreams, which stretch far into the future —a house filled with children, laughter, hard work, intelligence and art.

"Everything positive. Everything must be strictly positive," he says.

He talks as though the war and political tension can be magically held at bay. He giggles as monkeys scratch their butts and lick their fingers.

He's a good man who deserves to get what he wants and tries to think the best of everyone. He says he's my friend because I love people and try to make things better.

His bride-to-be waits for us in a white tiled restaurant in Cholon, which is the crowded Chinese part of town. She's petite with a round face, little lips and nose and tiny hands. Everything about her is pleasing down to the perfect white bows in her hair.

She sits upright near a white cooler stocked with ice-cold sodas and beer.

Huang proposes a toast, "To love and friendship, which are the two most powerful forces in the world!"

As I drink the cold, sweet orange soda, I hope that love and friendship can resist the darkness that gathers around us like the storm clouds outside. We eat crisp slivers of vegetable with tender fish and chicken spiced with lemon grass as thunder shakes the glass window. The lights go out and the cooler sighs.

We sit in grey, woolly darkness illuminated by flashes of lightening, which bounce off the walls and turn the narrow streets blue, silver and white. Rain beats relentlessly, pounding the tin roof above.

I imagine the whole city being washed away — trees, houses, taxis and oxen. The rain and darkness don't seem to intimidate Kim, who smiles throughout.

"She says she's very glad that you're my friend," Huang translates, "and wishes you would honor us as a special guest at our wedding."

I'm flattered. Given the experience with my father and Mr. Relaford and the party at the shop, I hesitate for a second, because I don't want to disappoint them. Reasoning that their wedding has nothing to do with Mr. Relaford and the Embassy, I answer, "Yes! I'm honored to be asked."

After a dessert of pineapple and lichee nuts, we share a cab to the center of town. They say goodbye on Tu Duc Street and enter an arcade in search of gold wedding rings. The world doesn't seem as good now that they're gone.

The truth is: I'm just a boy with no responsibilities, which according to my father means that I don't know much of anything.

What I do know is that everything about me is changing. My body has stretched to six feet. My pants aren't long enough, my shoes don't fit. I barely recognize my face in the mirror. My mother says that my features are out of proportion.

My father's always telling me: Think. Think. Use your head.

When I think a lot, I'm flooded with fears and concerns.

Who is managing this magnificent world of ours? I ask myself. It seems like too big of a responsibility to be left to men.

Hands in my pockets, I push through the shade to the harsh light of the intersection. Even the bunches of flowers seem garish and wrong now. Bees buzz around them, hungrily, lustfully.

I wonder if my father really did return Chico to the man who gave him to us, like he said.

Today the plaza around the Cathedral is dense with heat and the sour smell of exhaust. The pavement is dotted with old women selling balloons and girls selling cigarettes.

I turn right onto Dai Lo Thong Nhut. Lately, my father has been threatening to send us away to live in Bangkok or Hawaii. My mother, sister, brother and I would stay there until his tour of duty is over.

The prospect fills me with unease, because my mother would depend on me and want me to help her feel safe, which would be impossible.

Men with big wide brushes swab white paint on the trunks of the trees that line the boulevard. *Why am I made to feel responsible for the insecurity that dominates our lives? Why am I always worried about my parents' feelings?*

My mother says my father will never be happy living on

his own.

In the still, thick afternoon change threatens to overcome everything. The red banner hanging across a side street reads in Vietnamese, "They must often change, who would be constant in happiness or wisdom." It's a quotation from Confucius.

Danger lurks everywhere. Even the seemingly peaceful people who glide past on bicycles could really be vicious Vietcong killers. Their smiles could easily change into savage grins. Their hands could be used to manufacture bombs instead of making rice cakes and painting pictures.

While I think these thoughts, the present whispers soft and languid, and passes. *Where does it go?*

I look down at my white sneakers, dropping one after another on the sidewalk.

Mohammed says he believes in reincarnation and has lived as many as 10,000 lives. He says each life represents a small step forward in consciousness, through the thicket of karma. When we are clear, unencumbered and fully conscious, we join creation, or God.

Counting the cracks in the sidewalk, I try to trace the steps back to when I was an infant. I remember candles on a cake at my third birthday party and my grandfather's smiling face. I remember stepping outside with my mother into the sunshine. But when I try to peer farther back, I get lost.

Greg says that I should become a philosopher or a priest. "Your head is in the clouds, Sforza," he says. "You ask so many questions. Why don't you do like other people and occupy yourself with details?"

I'm back home listening to my father and his friends analyze their golf games, shot by shot. The dogleg to the left on fifteen, the water hazard on nine. They're drinking beer, eating fried shrimp chips and throwing dice.

My father has heard through the grapevine that I've been invited to Huang's wedding. He asks me if I plan to attend.

"Yes," I answer.

"Do you think that's a good idea?" he asks.

"Well, he invited me and I'm his friend. I think it would be rude if I didn't go."

"You'll be the only American boy there," he warns.

"So?"

* * * * * *

The night of the wedding reception, I enter the floating restaurant in a suit that I borrowed from my classmate Alain Perry. It's gray with thin white stripes and makes me feel grown-up. I'm shown to one of a dozen round tables covered with white tablecloths, crowded into a rectangular room with drawings of birds and dragons on the walls. Mohammed sits beside me looking dapper and happy. My parents are with the Relafords on the other side of the room with their backs to a window, whispering to one another.

Huang and his bride enter to the sound of a gong. We stand and applaud. Everyone smiles together; our hearts open. Kim, the bride, wears a lovely white dress covered with tiny pearls. Huang parts the veil and kisses her lips as cameras click and flashbulbs pop.

Out of the corner of my eye, I notice Bruno in khaki pants and a matching shirt trying to appear inconspicuous as he slithers across a wall like a lizard. He kneels beside Mr. Relaford and whispers. Our eyes meet for an instant. Bruno nods and slinks out the way he came.

I'm not the only one who has noticed him. But the good will is so strong it washes over everything, including the interruption and the fact that the guest of honor, Mr. Relaford, is frowning and talking excitedly to my father who appears tense.

The Chinese banquet begins with velvet corn and chicken soup and green papaya salad. Then we're offered courses of abalone, shrimp, monkey's brains, pigeon, fish and chicken. Mohammed tells me that the curls of red pepper at the center of the table clear the palate and relieve the sensation of being full.

Every ten minutes or so, our eating is interrupted by toasts in Vietnamese and French, which are accompanied by glasses of rice wine and whiskey. I'm drinking Coca-Cola, but the man on the other side of me, a driver named Mr. Phat, sneaks rum into my glass. Every time he spikes my drink, I hear him giggle. My face turns hot and I feel like being silly. But I would never embarrass my dear friend Huang.

Scanning the sea of faces, I notice that Mr. Relaford has left and Sy still hasn't arrived.

"Didn't Sy say he was coming?" I ask Mohammed.

"Yes," he says nodding. "Do you think something's wrong?"

"I don't know."

The room tingles with goodwill and laughter. Huang and his bride float from table to table to drink more toasts. A five-tiered pink and white wedding cake is wheeled out to huge applause.

"You make a beautiful couple!" I exclaim when they arrive at our table. "We're all so happy for you."

Serious adult faces have transformed into those of children. When Phat discovers that the liquid in Huang's glass is water, not rice wine, the men at our table tease him and make him replace the water with wine.

By the time Huang reaches the last table, he's wobbling and has to hold onto his bride. When I try to stand, I stagger, too. My head feels like it's filled with mercury that is sliding from side to side. Mohammed helps me to the door where I'm confronted by my mother's tight smile. I have an urge to tickle her and make her laugh. I see my father standing with Mr. Bowers, both looking grim.

My father says, "I've got to take care of something. Mr.

Bowers is going to take you and your mother home."

Something is wrong.

Seated on the back seat of the Impala, I marvel at passing colored lights. Later, I sink into the mattress like it's a cloud. I hear an intricate trumpet solo in my head and imagine that I'm playing it. The crowd grows excited. Then the whole scene explodes into the softest white snow.

* * * * * *

When I wake the next morning, the world outside is quiet, except for the sweet patter of birds. Time feels like it's ground to a halt. The clock on the night table reads 11:05.

I stretch, shower, dress and glide downstairs. I sit down at the table set for one and bite into a piece of sweet papaya. There's no sign of my family or the servants.

Almost on cue, Mohammed walks in from the pantry. His eyes are tight with worry. "Sy's in trouble," he says standing over me.

"What kind of trouble?" I ask, remembering that Sy never arrived at the wedding.

"I don't know."

He wants me to go with him. I finish my toast and juice and join him in the truck. It doesn't register immediately that we're headed for Sy's house. When we arrive, two American men with crew cuts stop us on the front lawn.

"You can't go in," they say.

"We've come to get the refrigerator," Mohammed responds cleverly.

The men give us the once over then wave us in. Sy's house is low and dark and furnished with standard rattan furniture provided by the Embassy. We pass his bedroom, where we see another American man leaning over a suitcase.

In the kitchen, Sy's maid weeps. "They took him away," she says in broken French. "He'll never return."

"Who took him?" I ask.

"Americans," she answers.

Working together, Mohammed and I unplug the GE refrigerator, hoist it on a hand truck and carry it to the pickup. Armed Forces Radio plays *My Bonnie Lies Over the Ocean* as we drive away.

"I've got to tell my Dad about Sy," I say to Mohammed. He leaves me at the Embassy. I enter, pass the Marine Guard and take the elevator to the 5th floor.

I find my father looking taller than usual and wearing a white short-sleeved shirt, gray pants and black shiny shoes even though it's Sunday. He seems happier than when he's at home and more at ease.

"What brings you here?" he asks with a friendly grin.

"Dad, something happened to Sy. He's gone."

He quickly waves me into his little office and shuts the door. Venetian blinds dissect the light in narrow slivers that fall across the desk and floor. A poster on the wall shows a stalk of bamboo being pulled by the wind and the message: Bend with the wind, but never break.

My father leans back in the leather chair and says, "You're old enough to understand, so I'm going to tell you. But this is strictly between us men."

"Okay."

"Sy was caught in a compromising situation with a Vietnamese woman. He'd been drinking. This wasn't the first time. He's been ordered back to the States."

My mind retrieves an image of Chan standing with her back to the sun.

"What's going to happen to him?" I ask my father.

He lights a cigarette with his Zippo lighter. "He'll go back to Washington DC, probably take some R & R. The State Department will give him another assignment."

He sends a stream of white smoke tumbling past my ear. "The whole thing will blow over," he adds. "Sy will do just fine.

Don't worry about him."

On the street in front of the Embassy, Mohammed listens and shakes his head. "A Vietnamese woman?" he asks with his hand on the stick shift. "No, Michael," he answers. "They wouldn't send him away for that."

That night, after my parents have left to attend another reception and I'm reading *The Sun Also Rises* on the front porch, I stop and wonder: *Did Sy get in trouble because of what I said to my father? Did my father tell somebody that Sy told me that some Embassy men were planning a coup?*

Angry with myself for opening my mouth, I get up and pace. The trees stand like dark totems, witnesses to my naivete and stupidity.

What have I done? I ask myself.

The idea that I can't trust my father – the man our lives depend on – seems too terrible to consider. I try to accept his explanation, but it doesn't make sense. I'm left on middle, uncertain ground. I don't have enough information to arrive at the truth. I wish I knew a way to talk to Sy.

Feeling bad, I call Samantha. She listens sympathetically.

"It's so hard being thirteen and living like this," she says. "Our parents don't get it."

Her voice reassures me and fills me with hope.

"You're lucky," she says. "You get to go out. You have lots of friends. You get to do something useful. I feel like I'm sitting inside this house waiting. What am I waiting for? I don't know."

I tell her that I think our world is different from that of our parents. Ours seems softer, kinder and more about feelings and the future. Theirs is hard, rational and filled with compromises and patterns from the past.

"Am I wrong?" I ask Samantha. "Am I hopelessly naïve?"

She says, "Michael, if I have to live like them, I'll die."

Her words hit me hard. "We have to find another way to live," I tell her. "We'll find one, Samantha. We will. We must,"

I say like I'm trying to convince myself.

In an instant, it seems as though my life's path has been set: To find a way to live honestly and free of the hypocrisy and moral compromises made by our parents. To find a place for intuition and feelings in their world that's tightly defined by reason.

I express all this to Samantha, then immediately start to question if I have the will and strength of character to follow my life's path.

Her words surprise me. She says, "I believe in you, Michael. You have empathy. I think I'm falling in love."

Tears come to my eyes; my tongue grows thick and heavy. I can barely get out the words to ask her to the movies.

"I want to, Michael," she answers. "I'll see what I can do."

I fall asleep dreaming of her and Huang and his new bride Kim. Together the four of us visit the zoo where we find that animals have been replaced by people living in cages.

* * * * * *

On Sunday I escort my sister Maggie to mass at the Cathedral. She wears a round straw hat with sprigs of yellow flowers and smiles as we walk together. She's happy to be out of the house on a beautiful morning.

I light a short red candle for my friend Leroy who died at Pershing Field, and another for my grandmother, who taught me to help the people around me.

The priest at the altar repeats words from Jesus in French. "Love your friends like your own soul, protect them like the pupil of your eye."

Maggie and I kneel next to one another at the altar to receive communion. I feel my heart open to God's grace.

Jesus said, "Those who seek should not stop seeking until they find. When they find, they will be disturbed. When they are disturbed, they will marvel and reign over all."

Questions swirl in my head. *What drives men to hate and kill one another? What happens to your soul when you do? Can killing someone be as simple as punching a hole in that person's skin and letting their blood run out?*

Father McDaniel greets us at the end of mass and hands Maggie a white lily. He pats me on the head and says, "You seem less burdened today, Michael."

Maggie takes my arm and we walk down the steps together, into whirring traffic and noise that stirs the thick noon air.

"Thanks for bringing me," she says with a smile.

"You're welcome, Maggie."

I gaze up at the sky where rain clouds are starting to gather. She tightens her grip on my arm. "Look," she says.

To our left, at the edge of the plaza two rows of Buddhist monks with shaved heads and saffron robes have gathered. They sit in lotus position along the curb, their heads bowed in prayer. A crowd of onlookers gathers. Then a taxi stops and three monks get out. One of them carries a yellow bucket. A second one spreads a mat on the street in front of the row of monks.

"What are they doing?" Maggie asks.

A murmur runs through the crowd as a third monk assumes the lotus position on the mat. The monk holding the bucket pours gasoline over the monk on the mat and steps back. As he lights a match, the crowd gasps.

A huge orange flame shoots up from the monk. It rises as high as the roof of the Cathedral. Birds take to the air urgently and soar over the spires. Simultaneously, sunlight breaks through the clouds.

"Michael!" Maggie screams, clutching my side.

I cover her eyes and watch in horror as the flames crackle and the monk burns. It's incredible. The monks watching from the curb bow their heads and chant. The monk on fire sits perfectly still. Our noses fill with the stench of gasoline and burning flesh.

Within what seems like seconds, the flames start to diminish. The monk's body remains black and rigid. It hasn't moved from its original position. A breeze sweeps up Tu Duc from the river, knocking the burnt body forward onto its head. Then the neck cracks and the body starts to break apart. People scream out and cry.

I hurry Maggie to Thong Nhut Boulevard and into a taxi. She weeps in my mother's arms when we get home.

"It's okay, darling. It's okay, darling girl," my mother says, smoothing Maggie's hair. "He didn't feel anything. He wanted to die."

"Why, Mommy? Why?" Maggie asks.

"It's what he wanted," she answers. "It's part of his religion."

When my father returns, he grabs my shoulder and squeezes it until it hurts. "I don't want you taking Maggie out with you again," he says. "Understand?"

"She asked to come to church with me," I answer.

"Don't act like an idiot," he growls. "Don't do it again!"

CHAPTER
SEVENTEEN

I hold too many questions. I'm trying to make sense of everything at once. I'm struggling to make connections like maybe Plato did. But he was a great thinker. Or like Athanasius Kircher who I read about, whose mind traveled from Egyptian hieroglyphics, to perspective in painting, to labyrinths, magnetics, to God and the Bible. I'm just a teenage boy who is acutely aware of how little he understands.

For a week now a bird has started chirping outside my window at 4 AM in a plaintive way that sounds like a warning.

A dark cloud of change is gathering. I can feel it in the streets. I see it in my father's eyes. I sense it at the Cercle Sportif.

I'm sitting in the shade with Greg and Alain. The sun is so hot that no one dares venture out of the shade. Bathers under straw hats and umbrellas quietly discuss the political situation.

Rumors of a coup are everywhere. Last night my father and I watched from the roof of the Embassy as a fire burned on the other side of the Ben Nghe Canal. I worried that it would reach our warehouse and Mohammed and the rest of the workers would lose their jobs as a result.

When I asked my father if the Vietcong had started the fire, he shrugged and answered, "Difficult to know."

We watched as the amorphous yellow and orange mass seethed and stretched out like a dragon, consuming houses, wooden shacks, sampans and warehouses like ours. Sometimes the flames shot up like a geyser, and my father said that the fire had probably reached a barrel full of kerosene.

By midnight it seemed like our warehouse would be next. At the last minute the wind shifted south and the rest of the waterfront was spared.

I look at the empty pool as Greg and Alain tally up the names of our friends who have left because of the deteriorating security: Charlie, Matt with his dirty drawings, Ann, C.J., Debbie and our teacher Mrs. Fisher.

"My father says that they might have to close the school for lack of teachers," Alain reports.

Greg's father expects to be assigned to a new post in December.

Alain and Greg's main concern is who is going be at Niki Clifford's birthday party. As long as Samantha's there, I don't care.

Greg and I walk over to the bar to ask after Bobby Ho. The bartender's a Frenchman with longish hair that curls over his ears. He starts a blender full of ice and waves us away as though we're annoying gnats.

"Asshole," Greg groans as we return to our place in the warm grass. From there I watch the bartender shovel the yellow slush into two glasses and top them with triangles of pineapple. He places them in front of a tall American with a red face and a Eurasian girl in a white bikini. They suck on the straws, kiss and then rise together leaving their drinks at the bar.

I wander over and ask again, "Sorry to bother you, but have you seen Bobby Ho?"

The bartender stops wiping the dark wood with a white and blue-striped towel. He looks up and says, "Bobby Ho is dead. The VC got him. Tortured him for three days, cut his head off and sent it back in a box."

I feel a clutching in my stomach. "No!"

"Yes."

I remain silent for the rest of the afternoon, thinking: *Bobby Ho is dead. Who's next?*

After the sun disappears and the city cools, we kids gather in Niki Clifford's living room like moths. There are six of us: Greg, Alain, me, Samantha, Niki and Sally.

Sally announces, "We're the survivors."

"Or the morons!" Alain replies. He's the tallest at 6'2" and thinks it's cool to be fatalistic.

Niki's parents are out for the night. They said that they felt they could trust us. Maybe they just wanted to get away. Whatever the reason, their confidence in us is misplaced. Because before the party even gets started, Alain opens a bottle of Polish vodka that he took from his parent's stash and empties it into the fruit punch.

A song by The Searchers plays on the stereo. Sally puts her arm around Alain and tries to get him to dance. Greg sits on the sofa grinning like a goofy Buddha. The spiked punch makes us feel silly, sloppy and dangerous.

Samantha clings to Niki's side watching everything carefully and whispering into Niki's ear.

Sally spins by herself in the center of the room like she's in a trance. Greg tosses a pillow at Alain that hits him in the face, and soon the two of them are wrestling on the floor.

Sally grabs Greg by the leg and shouts, "Let's take off his pants!"

Greg kicks wildly and screams for help. I try to pull Sally off him. She accidentally grabs me between the legs and I double over. Everyone is breathing hard by the time we stop.

"Let's get drunk," Alain declares, downing another glass of punch. Niki quietly takes up the challenge. Samantha turns up the volume on the stereo which plays *The Little Old Lady from*

Pasadena.

Sally peels off her sweater revealing a sundress and cleavage. Greg wags his tongue like a dog.

Niki says, "Let's play spin the bottle."

Her abandon surprises me.

Alain finds an empty vodka bottle in the trash. Soon we're all sitting on the cool tile floor facing one another with a strange sense of fear and expectation.

"Does everyone know the rules?" Alain asks.

"Does a bear shit in the woods?" Greg asks back.

Niki goes first since it's her birthday. The bottle points at Samantha. Niki blushes as she kisses Samantha on the cheek.

Then it's Samantha's turn. Her spin lands on Alain. She leans over and kisses him on the forehead.

He groans, "Come on! Do I look like I have leprosy or something?"

The bottle spins 'round and 'round. The kisses move from cheeks to lips and start to linger. We all cheer when Sally French-kisses Alain.

Niki, whose face has turned bright pink, says demurely: "Maybe we should stop now."

Despite loud protests from Greg and Alain, we pause to watch Niki open her presents — new 45s, a silver bracelet, a book of poems by Emily Dickinson.

We drink a toast to her turning fourteen. Then another. Someone asks Niki when her parents are returning home.

"Not before one," she answers. The clock on the modern credenza reads ten forty-five.

Greg and Alain whisper and call me over. Then, Alain asks Niki for a deck of cards.

"Who wants to play strip poker?" he announces.

Sally is the first to raise her hand. Alain and Greg lift theirs. Then, I raise mine and Samantha follows. Niki is last.

"But we can only go down to our underwear," she warns.

Now the room is charged with an even thicker sexual

tension. We're about to venture into uncharted territory. I imagine all of us sitting naked, then avert my eyes.

Greg loses three times in a row. Then Sally loses once. Then me. Round and 'round we go shedding our shoes, socks and shirts. After Alain loses his pants and we finish the punch. Greg goes to the kitchen to look for beer and Niki and Samantha retire to the bathroom.

"They're going to chicken out," Greg warns, opening a large bottle of 33 beer.

"You can't do that!" Alain shouts at the bathroom door.

Niki emerges and beckons me further inside the house with a finger. "Samantha wants to talk to you," she says. "She can't play anymore."

There's a groan from the others as I stand to leave and Niki returns to the circle.

I find Samantha outside on the dark porch wearing a sweater that she didn't have on before. She explains that she wants to play but had to stop because she "can't right now."

I tell her that I don't mind and hear Sally squeal inside.

Peering through the door, I see Alain removing his underpants – which I can't believe is happening.

Samantha and I sit on a couch that overlooks a garden. She removes the sweater as a cacophony of cicadas and lizards call from the trees.

"I was thinking about what we talked about the other night," Samantha says, her smooth features half-hidden in the darkness.

"It's not that I'm really afraid of growing old. There's nothing we can do about that. It just that I don't want to become bitter and hate myself for accepting things that I know are wrong."

I reach over and take her hand. "Don't worry, Sam," I say. "We'll find our own way, somehow."

"Yes..." Our lips meet and the hardness that surrounds us dissolves. We stop so I can wipe away her tears and use my finger to trace the outlines of her lips. I run it over her little chin, down the slope of her neck and stop. She leans her head back and sighs.

Her mouth remains open, posed like an invitation. I run my finger lower through the space between her collarbones, across her chest, down the front of her dress to the gap between her breasts. Our lips meet again.

I run my hand over her breast and leave it there. She stirs and holds me tighter, sucking on my tongue.

I squeeze gently and feel soft skin yielding under the smooth, hard outline of her bra. She takes my hand and guides it under the front of her dress, then shudders as I push my hand further between her bra and the very tender skin. I find the hard little nipple and rub it gently between my fingers. She slides down lower on the sofa, thrusting her tongue into my mouth.

I hear a series of sharp sounds on the glass behind us.

"Oh, Michael..." Samantha moans. I fumble with the straps of her dress and try to pull them down off her shoulders. Again we're interrupted by the sound of someone knocking.

Niki stands at the window, waving and beckoning me inside.

I let go of Samantha and stand. "No, Michael," she purrs.

But Niki looks like she's in extreme distress. Hiding the protrusion in my pants with my hand, I hurry to the door.

"You've got to stop them!" Niki shouts, pulling me inside. She stands in white panties and holding a man's shirt up to her chest.

Before I can ask anything, she leads me to the living room and says: "Do something! You've got to stop them!" Her terrified blue eyes point towards Sally, Alain and Greg writhing on the floor in a pile of clothes. I take a step closer, so I can see past a chair. Sally lies on her back, kissing Alain while Greg sucks on her breast.

"Are you alright, Sally?" I whisper.

She looks up at me with one eye like I'm crazy. Pushing Alain's head aside, she waves at me to join in.

"Are you sure you're okay?" I ask again.

She nods and reaches down under Alain's underwear and grabs his cock. He lets out a cry of ecstasy as she proceeds to pump him up and down.

Niki screams, "Sally, please stop!"

Instead, Sally kisses down Alain's chest, to his stomach, into his crotch.

"I can't watch this!" Niki shouts, pulling me with her to the porch. She stands crying, shaking and holding onto me all at once.

"What's wrong?" Samantha asks.

"It's okay, Niki," I say, trying to calm her down. "If that's what they want to do, it's their business."

"I'm stupid. I'm so stupid," Niki says. Then, looking up at me, she adds: "Please, tell them to leave."

I take a step towards the door and stop.

"Michael, please. I can't let this happen in my house!"

Inside, the lights are off and the air is thick with the musk of sex. Sally's naked backside faces me. She's on her side with her face buried in Alain's crotch. Alain kisses her white stomach and thrusts his fingers between her legs. I hear Greg groan loudly. Then, Sally screams with ecstasy. Then Alain, too.

Feeling like an intruder, I look back at the curtains and wait for the moans to subside. When I turn back a minute later, their bodies lie still, arms and legs intertwined in the mess of clothes.

I say, "I think we'd better go."

The four of us leave together without saying goodbye, leaving Samantha alone with Niki. Greg and Alain peel off and share a cab and it falls on me to escort Sally home. She leans her head back against the rear seat of the taxi and stares at the ceiling as though she's lost in reverie.

"Don't you dare tell anyone," she warns when we reach her house. "I'll kill you, Michael. I swear to God, I'll kill you." Then she kisses me quickly and runs to her front gate.

* * * * * *

I wake the next morning to find my father looking down at me disapprovingly. I imagine he's heard about the party last night. Instead, he tells me to eat breakfast, shower and get ready to go to the Relafords.

A sweet breeze plays with the shuttlecock and net in their back yard. Brad Jr. and I are beating Bruno and my father at a game of badminton. The score is nine to six. The women sit under umbrellas sipping daiquiris and watching. The younger kids play tag on the other side of the yard.

Mrs. Relaford wears a big straw hat and shouts orders to the maid in broken French. Hamburgers and chicken sputter on a grill. In the distance, we hear the low thud of mortars. With the match tied one game to one, we break for lunch.

While we're eating dessert, Mr. Relaford brings out his monkeys, Yin and Yang, and lets them free in the yard.

I step inside the screen porch looking for Samantha, but I run into Bruno instead. He's chewing on an unlit cigar. "I heard about your friend," he says. "That's a shame."

"Which friend?"

"I liked Sy," he says studying me over this cigar. "He's a guy you could talk to. He had a sense of humor. He wasn't always judging things the way that most people do."

"Someone judged him," I say like moving a piece forward on a chessboard.

His little eyes narrow. "What'd you hear?"

"My father told me he was caught drunk with a Vietnamese woman and fired."

Bruno scoffs. "I heard he was sent home because he was spreading rumors that the Embassy was planning a coup."

Still angry about what happened to Sy and looking for a comeback, I say, "They can't be rumors if they're true."

Bruno steps closer and grabs my chin. "You think you're a smart kid, but you don't know shit. All of us here are expendable. Me, your father, Relaford, the Ambassador. We're fighting to defend something that's bigger than all of us."

I could ask what that something is, but he's even closer so that his hot breath is in my face.

I say, "Maybe your methods don't work."

Bruno throws back his big head and laughs. "Maybe you're a boy who has a lot of growing up to do. Maybe you should learn to keep your big mouth shut."

He grabs my face with his right hand and shoves me backwards so that I lose my footing and stumble against the wall. With the cigar still clenched in his teeth he steps through the French doors to the living room.

I sit on the floor trembling with anger and watching the ceiling fan spin lazily overhead. Outside, Mr. Relaford calls after his monkeys and my mother and Mrs. Relaford laugh.

I don't feel like facing their forced frivolity and their smiles, so I pick a paperback off the shelf and start to reread *Lord Jim* by Joseph Conrad. I lose myself in another man's challenges in a very different set of circumstances. Jim's a romantic like I am. People like him, but things don't go well.

Twenty minutes later my mother breezes in with Mrs. Relaford and announces gaily, "Oh, here you are!" They chatter something about the monkeys getting away and Mr. Relaford and my father chasing them down the alley.

None of it really interests me, so I return to the *Patna* and Lord Jim and the vastness of the ocean.

Sensing someone standing in the doorway, I look up and find Samantha looking as though she doesn't know what to do with herself. I wave her over, which she does only after peering past her shoulder like a deer.

"We can't talk here," she says in a hush, which seems to

get caught in the sadness that swirls around her.

"Are you okay?" I ask as she stands over me.

She casts her eyes to the floor, her long braid shimmering in sunlight. She reminds me of a horse pawing the ground. I take her hand.

"Not here!" she whispers.

"Where?"

"I don't know. My mother is suspicious."

"Of me?"

"No, of me." She starts to back away delicately like a ballerina leaving the stage.

"Would you like to go to the movies on Saturday?" I ask, taking in the sweet scent of her hair.

"Yes."

"The matinee?" I ask.

"I'll meet you," she whispers, pausing on her toes in the doorway. "What's going to happen to us, Michael?"

I start to answer, but she's already gone.

* * * * * *

On Sunday, after mass, I wait for Father McDaniel in the rectory. I tell him that Mr. Nhu and his brother might be in danger because some generals are planning a coup. Father McDaniel removes his black robe to the white cassock underneath and pours himself a glass of wine.

He says, "Mr. Nhu knows that already. What can he do?"

All through the week and into Friday, I sense something dark and dangerous gathering around us. In the burned-out neighborhood near the warehouse, people sort through the rubble, recovering anything they can find: Pieces of metal, porcelain bowls, scraps of books that miraculously survived. As soon as space is cleared, new houses go up made of scraps of wood, cardboard and corrugated tin.

I'm reminded of ants, who immediately go about repairing

their hill seconds after someone has stepped on it.

Vendors with portable carts sell fresh vegetables and *pho*; barbers set up their chairs and cut hair; children laugh and play the way they did before.

Traveling with Mohammed in the black Chevy pickup, I realize how much I've grown to love this city with its wide avenues, big trees and flowers. How much I admire the women for their grace and beauty. How much I admire the men for their intelligence, determination and wit. And how much I admire all of them for their appreciation of poetry and art.

When I watch the painters standing on cans painting the ceiling, I'm reminded of Sy.

Weekdays flow easily, working with Mohammed, moving from job to job. Arriving home at night tired and hungry I fall asleep easily knowing that tomorrow there are more tasks to complete.

Although I live with my family, we're apart. My sister has girlfriends who come over once or twice a week and play in her room. My brother prefers to be by himself, building houses out of blocks. My mother avoids everyone, sticking to her bedroom, emerging only to accompany my father to parties and receptions.

My father doesn't talk about work. Evenings, he arrives home angry, slams down his papers and waits for Dong to bring him a drink.

Sometimes I feel like I have more in common with Huang and Mohammed. I'm beginning to realize that my parents don't love me the same way I love them.

Maybe it's the pressure of this place. Maybe if we lived somewhere else we'd be happier and spend more time together.

Two big gray clouds meet in the sky as I approach the modern Kinh Do theatre in a taxi. A crowd of civilians in short sleeves and GIs in khaki uniforms mill outside on the sidewalk.

There's no sign of Samantha.

"All hell's about to break loose," I hear one of the MPs guarding the door say as he points to the sky.

I poke my head inside the modern, high-ceilinged lobby, but she's not there, either. The clock above the ticket counter reads 1:47.

Big drops start to pelt the sidewalk. I have to step away from the door to avoid the crush as the crowd hurries inside. I stand under the concrete overhang with the two MPs with holstered 45s on their hips and wait. Little beads of water gather on the smooth toes of their black boots.

The thickly built one with the broad chest and wide face that the sun has turned the color of toffee looks at me and smiles.

"I'm waiting for someone," I explain. "A girlfriend."

"Nice," he says.

Sheets of silver rain pound the sidewalk and trees. Day has been changed into night with visibility reduced to a few feet.

"How long you been in 'Nam?" he asks.

"Nearly a year," I answer.

"A year," he repeats to his taller friend who nods and keeps staring straight ahead. "Him, a year and a half." Then poking a finger in his chest, says, "Me. Six months."

"You like it?" his friend asks.

"Yes," I answer. "A lot."

I try to imagine his life — guarding buildings, sleeping in barracks, looking at every passing Vietnamese as a potential VC, measuring how quickly he can draw his gun before he's blown up by a grenade.

I think of introducing them to my friends Huang and Mohammed and the men at the shop. Maybe then they would see the country from a different perspective. It would probably make their jobs more complicated, too.

I'm gazing down at my feet, watching rivulets of water dissect the sidewalk, when he taps me on the shoulder and points to Samantha running towards us through the silver rain and holding a white sweater over her head.

She stops beside me, out of breath, her hair and face wet, the straps of her yellow dress clinging to her shoulders.

"Sorry, I'm late," she says, her blue eyes turning silver as lightning flashes in the distance.

A peal of thunder rushes through the cool air and shakes the trees.

Winking, the MP pushes the door open to let us in.

I purchase tickets, while Samantha runs to the bathroom to dry off. Emerging with a handful of brown paper towels, she dabs her hair. I escort her into the dark theater. The end of the newsreel illuminates a sea of heads. A man is speaking in a deep voice about the Alliance of Progress and President Kennedy. On screen, children cheer as we make our way down to the front row center.

"Is this okay?" I whisper to her in the dark.

"I guess so," she answers, nodding.

Her chest heaves as organ music swells. A lion roars. The movie is *Phantom of the Opera* starring Herbert Lom. Samantha turns and smiling at me, sweetly, lays her wet head on my shoulder.

Forgotten are my parents, their struggles and the war outside. The rain that has been pounding the roof eases and stops. We're transported to London and the Opera House, where a disfigured violinist falls in love with a soprano named Christine. She's pretty, delicate and unsure of herself. The conductor is harsh, and the disfigured violinist (the Phantom) wants to protect her.

When their eyes meet, Samantha squeezes my hand. We kiss and hold each other tight. Her mouth tastes vaguely of salt and the sea.

"I love being with you, Michael," she purrs into my ear.

"I love to be with you, too."

We watch the Phantom being chased through the sewers

of Paris by an evil dwarf. The music swells and crashes in wild crescendos that push our hearts into our throats. I run my free hand over her hair and forehead, across the bridge of her nose to her soft lips. She gently bites my finger. There's a heavy, dull explosion to the right of the screen that pushes us back abruptly into our seats.

"What was that?" Samantha asks.

The noise itself isn't especially alarming, but the smoke and pressure I feel in my ears are. Women scream. A man yells out: "Cover your heads!"

The movie sputters and stops and the film melts as plaster falls from the ceiling, brushing past our heads. I'm not sure what is happening and hold Samantha against my chest to protect her.

"What's happening, Michael?"

Behind us, people hurry to their feet, shout, talk excitedly and cough. Our throats are clogged with smoke that tastes like burnt sulfur and plaster.

"Look out!" a man screams. Above us, a chandelier pitches from side to side in the cracked ceiling and a big chunk of plaster falls into the seats directly behind us.

"We're under attack!" I hear another man shout.

Samantha trembles deeper and holds me tighter.

"We're going to be okay," I tell her. "We'll be okay!"

Past my shoulder, I see people rush for the two exits, climbing over chairs, pushing one another and clawing in panic. The fear on their faces incites mine.

"We're all going to die!" a woman cries out.

Samantha looks up at me, pleading silently with her eyes.

"We'll be alright," I say again.

Her blue eyes are big and frozen. She coughs from the smoke and dust.

"We'll wait here," I say handing her my handkerchief. "I think it's... better... if we wait."

She stares at me numbly, the handkerchief over her

mouth. Something in her eyes starts to fade.

The white screen turns black and the theater is completely dark. I hold Samantha's head close. Her forehead is wet, I assume from the rain.

The noise behind us has become an indistinct roar that my brain can't decipher. It's obliterated by a deeper, sharper blast that numbs my ears. The whole theater lifts off the ground, shakes and crashes. My whole body trembles. We cling to each other desperately, air and dust rushing past us, so that it's hard to breathe.

For a moment I think we're going to suffocate and imagine my grandmother waiting for me in heaven. I'll only leave if Samantha does.

I gasp the bitter air and pray. Beyond us, the roar is gone, replaced by a moan like a cat pleading for milk. It's someone crying. Other moans come from the direction of the lobby. I hear a man calling: "Someone, please help me." I cover my ears.

My head is spinning. Samantha stares ahead in horror, her hair and face white.

Tears have started to leave furrows on her cheeks. There's a wet spot on the right side of her forehead. When I take my hand away and hold it up to my eyes, I notice it's red.

"Samantha, are you hurt?" I ask.

She doesn't answer. She just stares ahead at nothing. I hug her to my chest and we tremble together.

I'm vaguely aware that I'm sitting in the front row of the theater, but my mind travels to a brook where I'm watching friends set up a picnic. A woman with red hair is taking things out of a basket carefully and setting them on a blanket. Sandwiches, potato salad, watermelon. The woman looks up at me. Her are lips moving. She's asking me something, but I can't hear.

Someone is shaking me and is separating me from Samantha. The woman wears a white medical mask.

"Are you hurt?" she asks in a muffled voice. "Are you injured?"

"I think she is," I say, pointing at Samantha, who is being examined by a man with glasses. He applies wads of white gauze to her head and forehead and moves her hair aside carefully. She holds onto me again like she doesn't want to let go.

My eyes have been seeing everything in shades of gray. When another man appears with a flashlight, the first color I notice is red. Dark red lines like smears of lipstick extend down the right side of Samantha's head to her dress. The field of yellow is splattered with red splotches and dots.

Men are examining me now, patting my chest and head. They're talking, nodding, helping me up from the seat.

"Take her outside," the first man tells me. "Hold her," he says. "Be careful. Be very careful. She'll receive medical attention outside."

They leave us to examine other bodies lying on the floor behind us. I stand unsteadily in the darkness and make my way to the aisle. An electric lantern that's been placed on the floor casts strange shadows against the shattered wall. I stumble forward to catch up with Samantha who is being held up by a woman with red hair.

The aisle near the exit is clogged with lady's purses, shoes, a man's briefcase, berets and discarded bags of popcorn. A man wearing a medical mask helps us step over them into the lobby.

"Don't look down," he warns. "Eyes straight ahead."

But it's too late. It's as though we've stepped into the scene of a horror movie. It seems unreal at first. White walls splattered with blood. Bodies thrown into the corners, some missing heads and limbs. Smoke rising from the center of the floor. A gaping hole where the doors used to be. Metal rails twisted into exotic shapes; chunks of concrete; part of a hand on the first step with only three fingers; hair, fluid and blood.

A horrible, ripe, thick smell cleaves at my nostrils and enters my lungs.

Samantha's mouth forms a horrible shape. Her whole face is distorted. She looks like she's screaming, but nothing comes out. The medical man holds a hand over her eyes.

I remember the two MPs standing guard somewhere near there, then everything inside me turns numb. Hands at our sides, helping, hurried voices. I purposely don't see anything. Just the jagged hole in front of us and a sliver of blue sky.

As we step outside, I hear a strange, joyless cheer. A willful cheer, not one of celebration. It comes from a crowd of people standing among ambulances and rescue vehicles that have parked on the sidewalk. Red and blue lights flash.

"What happened?" I ask the man holding my left arm.

He looks at me like I'm crazy. At my feet, I see the body of the tall MP, his face covered by a light blue shirt.

"There were two MPs. What happened to the other one?" I ask.

No one speaks. We enter the crowd; eyes press around us. Hushed voices and whispers like they're afraid to wake up the dead.

I spot my parents at the edge of the crowd. *Can they really be my parents? What are they doing here?*

They take Samantha and escort her to an area where doctors are treating the wounded.

"What are you doing here?" I ask my father when I catch up with him.

"What are you doing here?" he asks back.

"We went to the movie."

"Your mother and I were across the street at the bowling alley when we heard the first explosion," he explains.

I hug him but he doesn't respond. Everyone seems to be acting strangely.

"Wait over there," he says pointing to the curb, then walking away.

I have to sit for a moment to get my bearings. Then I remember Samantha.

I look for her face among the crowd of strangers. Their expressions are confused; some are weeping. I push my way to the area with the doctors and nurses.

"Where's Samantha?" I ask.

No one answers.

To my right I see my father and mother helping her into the back seat of a blue car. My mother climbs in after her. My father stops, looks around, then he gets in the front passenger seat and closes the door behind him. The side of the car says "Security." It starts to pull away.

"Samantha!" I yell at the blue car. "Samantha, wait!" I start to run after it, but I only get as far as the curb. My legs are too thick and heavy to carry me further. I'm too exhausted.

I don't know how I crossed the street to the bowling alley. I assume I walked; maybe I was carried. I stand in the bathroom, confronting my face in the mirror. It's seems like my face, but I'm not sure it's mine. The process of recognition takes a minute, and I realize I look older, duller, less alive.

A man in a uniform hands me a towel. "Here," he says.

I take it and dry my face and wipe my head, face and neck over and over until the dust is gone. "The smell won't go away," I tell him.

"What smell?" the man asks, screwing up his freckled face. "I'll get you a drink. Wait there. Sit. I'll bring you a soda."

I sit at a table in front of alley number six. Someone left a score sheet that stops at the fourth frame.

The Shasta soda tastes like metal. As soon as I finish it, I want to leave. The building has filled with panicked voices reverberating off the walls and ceiling. Men shout into walkie-talkies, and wave pistols and submachine guns.

I exit unnoticed looking for Samantha, asking, *Where did they take her? Why didn't I protect her? Why didn't they take me, too?*

The more I think about her, the angrier I get. I overhear a man outside the bowling alley explain. He says the Vietcong placed plastique explosive on the outside wall of the emergency exit to the right of the screen. This went off first, sending everyone in the theater running for the lobby. Meanwhile, other Vietcong shot the two MPs guarding the front entrance and rolled more explosives into the crowded lobby, which inflicted the greatest damage.

The image in my head is of Vietnamese men in black pajamas with bandanas tied around their heads. They could have looked like any of hundreds of men I see passing in the streets every day. I turn cold inside. An invisible wall goes up around me. The city groans.

I lose track of time and distance. My feet take me home. When I get there, I shower and climb into bed.

CHAPTER EIGHTEEN

I'm chasing the blue car through the jungle. I follow it over mountains, across a dry plain and into a city. It pauses at an intersection. I run to catch up. Just as I'm about to touch it, the traffic light changes and the car races off again.

Samantha looks at me through the back window. She looks to be in distress.

"Samantha!" I call out. I run until my legs grow tired. I drag myself along the ground.

"Samantha, where are they taking you?" I shout.

I wake in a pool of sweat. My father looks down at me and places his hand on my forehead.

"He's on fire," he says to my mother who stands behind him shaking a thermometer. He takes it from her and places it under my tongue.

"Samantha," I murmur.

"Don't talk," my father orders. In my mind's eye I see the blue car. It pulls up to a tall building. A group of children come out and escort Samantha inside.

"Wait!" I shout.

Long furrows appear on my father's forehead.

I hear my mother say, "It's one hundred and four."

"A hundred and four?" my father repeats slowly so the

impact will register. "You'd better call Dr. Silverman."

I try to sit up, but I'm too weak. The actor Herbert Lom stands at the door of the tall building. He's wearing a white coat and eating a green apple. He slowly removes his mask; he's not the Phantom anymore.

I hear children laughing inside the building where bright lights burn. "They took Samantha," I say to him, tugging at his coat. "They took Samantha. She's my friend."

"Don't worry..." Herbert Lom says before his face dissolves into that of my mother. She runs a cold washcloth over my face.

"Don't worry, Samantha is being taken care of," she says. "She'll be fine..."

Her eyes look away. Her voice sounds artificial.

"Really, Mom? She's fine? Where is she?"

"She's been evacuated to Okinawa," she says. "The doctors there are excellent... I should know."

I have to leave. Samantha is calling me. Her voice echoes through the yellow hallways. The floor is wet. I find her in a golden room surrounded by children dressed in white. Samantha lies on a blue bed. Her skin glows like porcelain.

It reminds me of a scene out of the movie *Snow White and the Seven Dwarfs*. But these aren't dwarfs, they're little kids. Lots of them, smiling, laughing and jumping up and down on beds.

As soon as I sit next to Samantha, the children start singing. I start to weep.

"Please don't cry," Samantha says.

"I don't want you to leave," I say. "I love you."

"I'll never leave you, Michael," responds Samantha. "It's only temporary."

What does that mean? The children stop singing. A pretty girl steps forward and hands me a shiny brass trumpet. I put it to my lips and blow. Magically, notes come out that slowly weave into a ragged lament. Low and sad like the moan of a river.

I master the trumpet, and make it sing. "Happy trails to you, until we meet again…"

The floor opens and I start to fall. I fall for days and days and days.

When I wake up I see Ti Hai. She's sitting across from me reading a book, mouthing the words: "A happy boy listens to his mother. A good boy… washes his hands," like she's learning English. The sun shines through the window and plays with her long hair.

I think it's a dream at first, a strange dream that's meant to mock me.

"Ti Hai," I say. She looks at me and smiles with sparkling white teeth. "Ti Hai, are you real?"

She covers her mouth and giggles. A shiver runs up my spine. "Yes, Michael. I visit you. I hear you sick."

I sit up against the pillows. My back aches and my elbows are stiff. "Your English is good," I say. "It's much better."

She pronounces the words carefully: "Thank you, Michael. Thank you very much."

"I'm so glad to see you. Are you… well?"

"Very well, Michael," she says smiling. Everything about her is grace and sweetness. "Mr. Mettier… very kind. He hire for me… one English teacher. He send me to school at night."

She stands in a maroon tunic and white silk pants that float over her lithe body. For an instant, I remember her lying on her side. She steps closer with her hand behind her back. Bowing, she hands me a cone made of light blue paper.

"Thank you, Michael," she says.

Pealing open the paper I'm overcome by the sweetest perfume. Inside are a half-dozen tiny tiger orchids. Their beauty and perfection produce emotions that clog my throat.

The next time I awake, Ti Hai's mother Ti Ba, stands over me rearranging the pillows behind my head.

"Was Ti Hai here?" I ask her. She points to the vase of tiger orchids by the side of the bed.

Dr. Silverman stands beside my mother who looks pale and lost.

"Are you feeling better, young man?" he asks.

"I think so. Yes."

He turns to my mother and asks, "Does he know what happened?"

My mother acts as though she didn't hear his question. She's chewing the inside of her mouth.

"I wasn't allowed to stay with Samantha," I explain. "I was with her and these children. I was playing a song on the trumpet, when the floor opened up and I fell."

Dr. Silverman frowns. "Delusions from the fever," he says to my mother. "You've contracted dengue fever, Michael. You need to spend the next week or so in bed."

My health improves in fits and starts. I pass a week playing checkers with Corèy, reading *A Farewell to Arms* by Ernest Hemingway and writing thank you notes to the people who have sent me get-well gifts — including Mr. Nhu. When Mohammed visits, he brings a dozen mangosteens which are my favorite fruit.

No one mentions the bombing. No one talks about what happened or how many people were injured or killed. When I ask my father about Samantha, he tells me that the Relafords have returned to the States.

"Why?" I ask.

"Why didn't you tell us that you were taking her to the movies?" he asks back.

"Because..." I stop. I feel anger rising from my stomach, filling me with energy. "What difference would that have made?"

My father looks at me like I made a big mistake. He has no solace to offer, just disapproval and suspicion. I ask him to leave.

"Why?" he asks.

"Because I have to rest."

Two and half weeks after the bombing, I'm strong enough to walk around the yard. A month later, I sit in my room looking out the window thinking that the bomb robbed me of something that I want back.

* * * * * *

Mohammed drives the black Chevy truck and wears a clean, white shirt. His dark arm rests in the open window. The sun shines through the trees casting a lattice pattern on the street ahead.

The city seems duller than before, as though it's been cleansed of vitality and hope.

Danger seems to lurk in every shadow, in the face of every motorcycle and taxi driver who pulls up beside us. I keep waiting for the dull roar, the huge release of energy that sends bodies flying everywhere. I feel vulnerable and exposed.

"This came for you," Mohammed says as he reaches into his pocket and hands me a letter.

The writing is crooked and difficult to read. It's from Sy. "Dear Michael and Mohammed," it starts.

> "Your old friend is back in Fairfax, Virginia, waiting for the start of the football season. Saigon seems like a dream. I miss you guys. I miss Saigon. A part of me is still there with you. I want to let you know that I'm okay. I've been instructed not to talk about my sudden departure. Let's just say it was unexpected. I'm trying to figure out what I'm going to do next. I don't think I'm cut out for government service. As you might have noticed, I'm not a company man. I have a hard time following people's orders. Big surprise, huh?
>
> After I square away my pension and all that I'm thinking of moving down to Florida and opening a

business. Say hi to the guys at the shop. I never got a chance to bid them a proper farewell. Write when you get a chance. Maybe I'll get to see you Michael, when you return to the States. I miss you guys. Your friend, Sy."

* * * * * *

The new Ambassador's residence reminds me of the Kinh Do theatre. It's modern and made of the same beige stone, with the same rectangular windows and covered with the same patterned wrought iron. I'm reluctant to enter at first. But the smell of new paint and the patter of familiar activity beckon.

Inside my legs wobble, and I feel like I might faint.

Painters wave from the scaffolding. Electricians look up from their work and nod. I take a deep breath and follow Mohammed into the living room, where Mr. Bowers stands next to a thin, pained, shriveled woman with short gray hair. She's the new Ambassador's wife, Mrs. Lodge.

She shows no interest in me. Instead, she's handing Mr. Bowers a bolt of red and white checked fabric and saying, "I want this hung on that wall," in a high, pinched voice that cracks and wobbles.

"Hung like a curtain?" Mohammed asks.

She frowns at him like he's stupid. "No, hung like wallpaper, of course."

Mr. Bowers rubs his big stomach and clears his throat. I'm sure he'd rather be sitting in his air-conditioned office eating doughnuts. "I don't think you have enough," he says uncertainly.

"There's plenty more where that came from," growls Mrs. Lodge. Her voice reminds me of coils of barbwire.

We follow her inspection of the rest of the rooms. She has precise ideas about everything — where to place the refrigerator, where to install the air conditioning units, how many coats of white paint to use on the ceilings. She makes Mohammed record all of them on a sheet of paper attached to a clipboard, then checks the list and corrects his spelling.

In the front hallway she stops and groans. "Everything must be completed by next Friday so that we can move in on Saturday, September 11th."

Mohammed opens his mouth to stay something. Mr. Bowers interrupts him. "We'll have to add more men and work around the clock," he says.

"Yes."

"Everything will be to your liking, Madame Ambassador," Mohammed says, bowing.

"Of course it will," she brays as she shoos us out the door.

* * * * * *

We work feverishly for a week and a half. Each night I fall asleep as soon as my head hits the pillow. Seven AM Saturday morning when the trucks arrive with the new Ambassador's furniture, Mohammed and a crew and I are still scrubbing paint off the floors.

"Good work," Mohammed says when he drops me off at home. I sleep until the afternoon and meet Greg at his house at six. He greets me at the door with a fake Chinese proverb: "Man who run in front of car get tired."

We can't go to the movies because the Kinh Do theatre is closed. And we can't stay out past midnight, because President Diem has imposed an 8 PM curfew. So we sit in Greg's room and read comic books: the *Magnificent Four, Sergeant Rock, Spiderman*. Greg's parents are in Bangkok for the weekend shopping for Thai silk.

"Man who run behind car get exhausted," Greg says with a grin.

I say, "Man who eat many prunes get good run for money."

When Greg laughs his eyes become narrow slits. We're

eating hamburgers, when his voice turns serious. "What have you heard about Samantha?"

"Not much," I say in a low, heavy voice, remembering the last time I saw her,

"It's really messed up," Greg says. "It's kind of depresssing."

"What's depressing?"

"What happened to her."

I hold my breath. "You heard something?"

He nods.

"Is... she... dead?" I ask struggling to get the words out.

He shakes his head. "No. But she might as well be."

"Why? What happened?"

I brace myself for bad news. I've heard my parents whisper her name and seen them stop talking when I enter a room.

"When they took Samantha to Okinawa, she slipped into a coma," Greg says slowly. "She was out for ten days. Now she's with her family... in the States."

He stops to look at me and sees that I'm in a state of shock.

"Michael," he declares. "She was in a coma."

He doesn't mean to be cruel. He's my friend and he thinks I should know.

"Do you know what that means?" he asks.

"Not really. No."

"She might never recover," he says. "She can't do anything for herself now. They have to dress her, feed her, wash her, take her to the bathroom..."

I've stopped breathing. I feel myself slipping out of consciousness. I wake up seated on the sofa. Greg's maid offers me a glass of water.

"Are you okay?" Greg asks as he watches me drink. His face is pink. He says, "I'm sorry."

"No, Greg..."

"I feel... real bad about... everything."

"It's not your fault."

It's too awful to think about. Night after night I call out her name in my sleep. "Samantha! Samantha!" like she's waiting somewhere and it's my job to find her.

I seek out Father McDaniel at the Cathedral after mass. He has a plate of fresh pineapple and a cold Coca-Cola waiting for me in the rectory.

"It's good to have you back," he says putting a hairy arm around me. "I don't know what worried me more, the bombing or the dengue fever."

I drift back to the Kinh Do theatre and the walk through the lobby. I'm trying to see through the haze and fit the shards together into a coherent picture.

I explain to Father McDaniel that I think the dengue fever was a reaction to the bombing.

"I believe it's transmitted by a mosquito," Father McDaniel says like a doctor.

It's impossible to separate one incident from the other in my mind. *Didn't my whole system shut down? Didn't I need the time after the bombing to rest, to reconcile and recover?*

I clear my throat and tell Father McDaniel how the bombing has caused me to question my belief in God.

Father McDaniel folds his hands in his lap and says, "I understand, Michael. I question Him sometimes myself."

"How could he let something as horrible as that happen?" I ask. "And why Samantha?"

He tells me that we don't know enough to judge God. He says that it's like asking a monkey to explain advanced physics.

He says, "A monkey doesn't have the vocabulary, his conscious mind doesn't extend that far. It's the same with man and the Almighty."

CHAPTER NINETEEN

Because of the martial law and curfew, I'm not allowed to leave the house after dark. When I venture out during the day I find myself planning every aspect of my journey, retracing it over and over in my head. I see myself getting into a taxi, I imagine where I'll get out, which entrance I'll use to enter a particular building and how I'll escape if it comes under attack. I even work out different exit scenarios should that happen – climbing through windows, crawling over debris, fighting my way past the attackers.

I anticipate everything, scanning the crowds, paying special attention to groups of men, their expressions and body language. Sudden, loud noises send adrenaline rushing through my veins.

Seeking a form of diversion from the concerns in my head, I go downstairs and look for Dong. Last night we talked about his hobby, photography. He showed me scrapbooks filled with photographs of pretty girls in *bao dais* posing on bridges and in front of trees in blossom that he took with the old Kodak camera he keeps on his dresser.

Tonight he's slowly pressing my father's shirts with an iron that's been stripped of its American plug so that bare wires can fit into the French socket. With an unfiltered cigarette clutched in his teeth, he looks at me with glazed eyes that bulge from his high forehead. Everything about him is relaxed and limp, including his spine.

When the ash has consumed half the cigarette and it falls narrowly missing the sleeve of my father's white shirt, Dong brushes it away without even looking.

Lizards hiccup in the garden. The leaves hiss. A dog barks from across the street. Somewhere a woman is complaining in a high-pitched wail of invective.

"One moment follows another," a night bird sings. "One after another... into infinity. Never back, always... ahead..."

Upstairs, I try to follow the story of Gulliver and ignore the dull voice in my head – the one that wants to convince me that there is no such thing as love and God has abandoned us to die randomly and crumble into dust.

Armed Forces Radio introduces "the number one hit from England" called *She Loves You*. Though know about the Beatles, I've never heard their music before. It's happy and invigorating and leads me to the entrance of a shimmering new place.

When it ends, I pick up a pen and paper and compose a letter to Samantha. It's my third in two months. The first two have gone unanswered.

"Dear Samantha," it starts. "How are you? I hope and pray that you're feeling better. Things aren't the same with me. I try to be hopeful and enthusiastic, but my efforts fall short. Why? I'm not completely sure. I have the feeling that something is going to end here. I also know that I miss you a lot. I think about what happened to us every day. Over and over, back and forth. Sometimes we're laughing, sometimes we're covered with dust and tears are running down our faces. We're always together. No matter what else happens in my life, I'll never forget you. You'll always be in my heart and mind. I only wish I could have protected you better. I was sick myself for a while with dengue fever, but I'm better now. I still see Greg, who says hello. Every time I see him, he's got a new funny Chinese saying, like, "Man who chase car get exhausted." All the rest of our friends are gone. Niki, Alain, Sally all left with their families at the start of martial law. Please write and say hello to your family, especially Brad Jr. I miss you a lot. Love, Michael."

* * * * * *

Sunday morning, when I wake up *She Loves You* by the Beatles plays in my head. Dong is outside sweeping the walk and humming to himself.

Passing to the maid's quarters, I spot a long white pipe on top of his dresser next to a picture of a holy-looking man with long white hair.

Inside the kitchen, Ti Ba stands on a box counting brown eggs and placing them carefully in a bowl beside a long, ripe papaya filled with shiny black seeds. Since it's the cook's day off, it's her job to make breakfast.

"I'm going to bake muffins," I tell her in French.

Although I've never made muffins before, it's simply a question of following the directions on the box. Before long, Ti Ba lines up a dozen steaming corn muffins on the counter and I reach for the Bisquick and read the instruction for making hot cross buns.

"What possessed you to do this?" my mother asks sitting at the table in a green silk bathrobe, her hair wrapped in a red scarf.

"I felt like it," I answer.

Everyone in my family is pleased, even my father who regards me with suspicion because baking hot cross buns and muffins is not something he would consider doing in a million years.

After breakfast after Maggie and Corey have gone upstairs to play dominoes, I hand my father the letter I wrote to

Samantha and ask him to mail it through the Embassy A.P.O.

My parents steal a glance at one another. Then my father asks, "Why do you keep bothering those people?"

I practically choke. "Bothering them? I'm not trying to bother anyone. I'm just... writing to my friend."

My father sighs with exasperation and turns to my mother for help. She looks at the white wall where a thin gray lizard clings like an exclamation mark.

"Michael," she starts slowly. "I'm sure the Relafords appreciate your concern, but—"

My father interrupts. "The Relafords have been through living hell!" he exclaims.

"It's been terrible for them," my mother adds. "Brad Jr. badly burned, their daughter traumatized and injured —"

"I think you understand what we're saying," my father brays jutting his jaw out and shaking his head.

I say, "I don't see what the problem is... in sending a—"

My father is about to lose his temper. My mother grabs his wrist.

"Forget about the goddamn letters!" he shouts.

My mother tries to soften the charge he's left in the air. "Be patient, Michael. Give them time to deal with this alone."

They make it sound like I'm violating the Relafords. Like I've done something wrong.

"Despite what you think of them," my father continues, "the Relafords are good, decent people. I can't tell you what a help and support they've been to me and your mother."

My mother folds her hands in her lap. "True," she adds. "Very true."

I'm overwhelmed with conflicting emotions — anger, confusion, frustration and sadness. I don't know where to start. "Are you saying... I don't respect... the —"

My father slams the table. "For christsakes, Michael!"

We met each other eye to eye. His anger confronts my profound frustration.

"Give them some goddamn room to breathe. If after a couple of months, you still want to correspond with their daughter, maybe. We'll see."

My father stands abruptly, scraping the chair against the floor. My mother follows.

I'm reeling, trying to calculate the implications of what has just been said. "Just one question," I say as they reach the doorway. "Did you send the other two letters I gave you?"

My father glares back at me with eyes loaded with bullets. "What do you think, Michael? What the hell do you fucking think?"

* * * * * *

Last week was my birthday. We didn't have a party to mark the occasion, only chocolate cupcakes baked by our cook, Mr. Trong, and a hurried singing and blowing-out-of-candles before my parents left for a reception at the new ambassador's residence — the one with the checked fabric on the wall.

Today, the sun rises gently, spreading its golden fingers as bells in the distance toll for All Soul's Day — a day of remembrance for our ancestors. My parents say nothing when I mention it at breakfast. They seem preoccupied with things they don't share. My father, who is in a hurry, complains about the coffee. My mother folds her hands and looks up at him with eyes dark, pregnant with worry.

Last night I heard him shouting over and over into one of the radio transmitters, "The chickens are out of their roost. The chickens are out of their roost." I wonder who the chickens are but dare not ask.

It's a Friday, but my father says that there's no school today and no work with Mohammed.

"Why?" I ask.

"Just stay here and keep an eye on your sister and brother."

Once my father leaves, my mother repairs to her room and the house is still.

My sister sits in her air-conditioned room, reading, and my brother is playing with cars. So, I retreat to my workshop — a little room hidden in the front corner yard that once housed the men who guarded Emperor Bao Dai's mistress.

I start building a stool for my brother Corey to stand on while he's brushing his teeth. I cut four eight-inch legs with an old bow saw. It takes roughly thirty minutes to assemble the legs and struts, by which time my arm is tired.

I consider returning to the house to get something to drink, when I hear the clatter of tanks. Exiting the workshop, I climb up on the flat cement roof to get a better look. From this vantage I have a clear view of Rue Phan Than Gian.

People have dismounted bicycles. Others point north towards the bridge. The rumble grows louder. Then the first tank rolls into view.

I've seen tanks and processions of soldiers pass before on their way in and out of the city, but these are different. The soldiers' faces are grimmer. They grip their weapons with a determination that says they're ready for combat. For a second, I wonder if they're VC. But the familiar yellow and red flag of the Republic of Vietnam flies from every tank and truck.

I count five M-41 Walker Bulldog tanks and six two-and-a-half-ton trucks filled with soldiers. They stop right in front of our house and soldiers get out. Some shout orders, others hurry into the city carrying M1 carbines and Thompson submachine guns. I hear firing farther down the street.

I duck lower. Incoming bullets slam into walls and buildings, sending up little puffs of concrete. They ricochet wildly off the street and ping against our iron gate.

I lay down prone on the flat roof, thinking that this seems unreal, like I'm watching a movie. A vendor runs by with a cluster of red balloons. A bullet hits a woman on a bicycle. She screams and jerks the rest of her body away from her leg. A red spot spreads from her thigh of her white silk pants.

Without warning, the tanks and soldiers start firing all at once. There's a terrible racket and lots of smoke that smells unpleasant and burns my eyes.

I feel like it's important for me to find out what the soldiers are shooting at. I raise my head carefully, because they're firing almost directly below me. I hear someone shout my name.

Suddenly, it dawns on me that they're shooting at the police station two blocks away. This is very important. It must be the coup d'état!

The voice behind me belongs to Dong. He looks almost comical standing on the front lawn in his white t-shirt and shorts with his hands cupped over his mouth trying to shout over the machine guns.

I take a last look at tanks rolling into town. Jeeps arrive towing howitzers, which soldiers disengage and aim towards downtown.

"Get your camera," I shout to Dong in French. "The coup d'état has started right outside our gate!"

When I climb down, he takes me by the shoulders and pushes me towards the front of the house.

"You must go inside!" he shouts in French.

My mother lies curled on the living room sofa. She barely lifts her head.

"Your father just called," she says. "He told us to stay away from the windows. Some parts of the army have revolted. They're going to overthrow the president. Your father says it will be over soon."

The first howitzers fire from in front of the house, rattling the windows and lifting everything up from the ground. "Where are Maggie and Corey?" I ask.

She points under the stairway to the bar. I find them cowering behind it, shivering.

"Are they going to kill us?" Corey asks.

"No, Corey. They're not going to hurt us. They want to overthrow the president. That's all."

With Dong's help, I lock the big mahogany doors and move the sofas to form a six by eight-foot rectangle in the living room. Then I direct everybody to sit inside.

Dong runs upstairs to bring us books and a deck of cards.

"Maybe we should play war," Corey says with a twinkle in his eye as he shuffles the deck.

The howitzers fire in clusters — a series of concussions that turn our inner ears numb. A bullet splinters the mahogany door and my sister screams, "We're going to be murdered!"

It's not that the thought hasn't crossed my mind. But hearing her say it makes me mad. "Shut up, Maggie!" I shout. "Keep your stupid mouth shut!"

Maggie throws herself into my mother's arms and sobs.

"I'm sorry, Maggie," I say.

"It sounds like they're in our yard," my mother warns.

I explain that the howitzers are in the street, just beyond our gate.

"Do you think they'll remain there?" she asks.

"I don't know."

The fan above us stops turning and slowly comes to a stop. "They've shut off the electricity," I announce.

Soon the air is thick and hot and laden with the heavy smell of sulfur.

"I wish Daddy was here," Corey moans.

"Well, he's not," replies my sister.

"Call the Embassy," my mother instructs me in a dull, far-away voice. "Tell them to send someone to rescue us."

It's a good idea, except the telephone behind the bar is dead. And I don't know how to operate the radios upstairs.

Back in our sanctuary, Ti Ba serves us tuna salad sandwiches and lemonade. Afterwards Dong and I slip upstairs on a reconnoitering mission as Corey, Maggie and my mother try to nap.

It's 2:30 in the afternoon. The guns are quiet. Through a crack in the shutters, I see tanks and cannons lined up haphazardly on the street. All have their barrels aimed into the city.

Soldiers mill about. Some lean against the walls and rest. Businesses and windows are shuttered.

"What are they doing?" Dong asks.

"Nothing, right now."

We collect flashlights, a transistor radio, chocolate bars, crackers and bottles of boiled water. When I check the telephone in my parent's room, I only hear one long hiss of air.

Downstairs, we deposit everything in the sanctuary created by the sofas. Then I go to the maid's quarters at the back of the house where I find Ti Ba and the girl who does the laundry, huddled inside the kitchen listening to a radio, where a man speaks excitedly in one long, fast, slurred line of Vietnamese.

"What is he saying?" I ask in Vietnamese.

"He's asking President Diem and his brother to surrender. He says he's with the Army and they have the city surrounded," Ti Ba answers.

I invite them to join us in the living room. But the new girl wants permission to return to her family.

"Now?" I ask, trying to imagine the danger she'll face if she bicycles through the streets.

She nods with her jet-black hair pulled back into a tight knot and her thin lips clenched.

"It's too dangerous," I say. "You should wait."

Soon, the firing starts again. The maids elect to stay in the kitchen where they can huddle around the radio and drink tea.

Back in the living room, I tune our transistor radio to the US Armed Forces station. Military marches play. Then, without any news or announcements, they run down the Top

40 – *Surfin' USA, Walk Like a Man, Be My Baby, It's My Party,* etc.

Corey is reading a book about dragons. I tell him that the Vietnamese believe that a dragon is a symbol of good luck.

"Do dragons really exist?" he asks me as howitzers thunder in the distance. Every so often an airplane passes over at low altitude and we duck our heads.

"I don't think so anymore." I answer. "Maybe in the past."

I tell him a Vietnamese legend about a lonely dragon that entered a land of unsurpassed beauty and was so happy that it took human form. He became a man and almost immediately met and fell in love with the daughter of a local dragon lord. They married and had a beautiful son.

Corey has closed his eyes and snores gently beside my mother and sister. There's no one to talk to until my father returns, which happens as the sky starts to darken. He's even more tense than usual and his eyes are red.

He reports hurriedly, "The phones are working again. This whole thing should be over soon."

He asks my mother what she wants Ti Ba to fix for dinner since Mr. Trong (our cook) never made it to work.

She answers, "Nothing. My stomach is upset."

Outside, the shooting grows more intense and all three of my father's radios bark at once from upstairs. "Red Rooster. Red Rooster, this is Uncle Remus. Come in. Over."

"Alfa One, this is Station Central."

"China-Eagle-Two, this is Lone Star. China-Eagle-Two, this in Lone Star. Come in."

"Don't worry," my father says, pointing his chin in the direction of the front gate, "the fire's not directed at us."

I know that already, because if it was, we'd all be dead.

He tucks a .45 automatic in his belt and hurries upstairs. "Just in case," he says.

In case of what?

After a dinner of fried chicken and mashed potatoes, he

takes me to the roof to watch the fighting. The lights of the city sparkle with excitement and expectation. Green, yellow and blue tracer bullets fly in straight lines and long, beautiful arcs. Most of them are directed to one general target approximately two miles away.

"The Gia Long Palace," my father pronounces.

I feel sad as I remember our dinner in the white dining room with the soft linen napkins and heavy silverware. We watch P-51s dive over the palace and drop bombs. The whole area lights up gold and fades.

Somewhere around midnight, Dong brings news from the Vietnamese radio that the generals have been victorious. The firing outside starts to diminish. I go to Dong's room to listen to the radio and fall asleep on his bed.

* * * * * *

He rouses me at 4:30 in the morning. All I hear are cicadas and lizards calling outside. "Your father wants to see you," Dong says in French.

I find my father at the bar drinking a cup of coffee. He points to the telephone receiver. "Someone has called you twice. I think its Father McDaniel."

I pick up the receiver. "Hello?"

There's noise in the background like breaking glass. Then, I hear Father McDaniel's voice, "Michael, is that you?"

I'm still half-asleep. "Yes, Father."

"Michael, it's Father McDaniel. Are you and your family safe?"

"Yes, we are."

"Thank God." He sounds tense. "Do you understand what's going on?"

It seems like a strange conversation to have so early in the morning. "Yes," I answer. "Some generals are trying to overthrow the president."

"They <u>have</u> overthrown him, Michael!"

I think back to the radio message in Vietnamese with the whining martial music in the background that I listened to with Dong.

"They've succeeded, I'm afraid," Father McDaniel continues, "with the help of the United States."

He's American, too, raised in Dayton, Ohio, but his last words sound bitter.

"Have you heard anything about President Diem and Mr. Nhu? Are they okay?" I ask.

"The generals are searching for them," Father McDaniel reports urgently. "President Diem and Mr. Nhu are hiding. That's why I called you, Michael. The situation is extremely dangerous for them. They need your father's help!"

My heart starts to race. I'm fully awake. I turn to my father seated at the bar sipping coffee.

"My father?"

"I need to talk to him," Father McDaniel repeats. "You think he can be trusted?"

I don't know what to say.

"Tell him that I'm with President Diem and Mr. Nhu," Father McDaniel continues. "They're willing to surrender if your father and the US Embassy can arrange a plane to fly them out of the country."

The hair on the back of my neck stands up.

I turn to my father. He looks back at me with a combination of curiosity and annoyance.

"What's he want?" he asks pointing at the receiver.

I quickly explain the reason for Father McDaniel's call. My father lowers his brow in concentration.

"He wants me to make arrangements for an airplane to take them out of the country?" he asks, summing up.

"Yes." My heart thumps hard and fast, and my mind wants to race ahead.

My father studies me as he considers — not like I'm his

son, but some strange interloper that he's been forced to deal with.

"Is he with the president now?" he asks, sliding off the stool.

"I don't know."

My father says, "Take down his number and tell him that I'll call him back."

He retreats upstairs to his bedroom and his radios and shuts the door. Twenty minutes later he emerges, his face red and his forehead beaded with sweat.

"Give me the number," he orders.

His manner bothers me. "Have you made the arrangements?" I ask back.

He glares down at me and almost snarls, "Give me the goddamn number!"

I read him the number and he dials the phone. Then he waves me away.

I retreat behind the door and listen. I hear him tell Father McDaniel that he has spoken to people at the Embassy and they can have an airplane ready in several hours. He asks Father McDaniel for the location of where President Diem and Mr. Nhu are now.

My father says, "President Diem and Mr. Nhu will be safe. First thing we'll do is send an armored column to rescue them and bring them to a secure place in the Embassy...while arrangements are finalized to take them out of the country."

Minutes of silence pass. My heart is in my throat.

After half a minute my father calls out, "Michael, come. Father McDaniel wants to talk to you."

I hold the warm receiver up to my ear.

"Michael, do you remember the church we went to where we handed out food?" Father McDaniel asks.

"You mean the one in Cholon?" I ask back.

"It's called Saint Frances Xavier. Tell your father to send some American soldiers here before it's too late."

The line goes dead.

"What did he say?" my father asks.

"He said that they're waiting at Saint Frances Xavier Church in Cholon."

He rises quickly and pats me on the head. "Good," he says.

Then everything moves like a blur. I follow him up the stairs and ask him what he's doing.

He stops and shouts, "Go downstairs! I have to call Bruno."

"Why Bruno?"

He pushes me hard, so I lose my footing and crash into the wall.

* * * * * *

I sit in the kitchen with Dong listening to the radio. Cars horns blare from the front gate. I follow Dong outside and stop.

The gate is open. My father stands with Bruno beside a military jeep. Another jeep enters and several armed Vietnamese soldiers get out and stand guard. I see General Minh's big head standing with Bruno.

My father orders me and Dong back into the house. I hide behind the palm trees near the front porch and watch. More jeeps arrive with Americans in civilian clothes and additional Vietnamese soldiers, followed by an armored personnel carrier. I see Father McDaniel being helped out the back. His hands are tied behind his back and there's a black bandana tied over his eyes. I run over to where he sits on the gravel. A Vietnamese soldier holding a pistol stands over him.

I say, "Người đàn ông này trong bạn của tôi." (This man in my friend.)

The soldier laughs at me like I'm crazy, then shows me that the pistol isn't loaded. No one else is paying attention. They're all focused on the back of the armored personnel carrier. The door is open, and the Americans crane their necks to look inside.

I kneel beside Father McDaniel and ask in a whisper, "What happened?"

He looks up. His cheeks are pale and slack. "It's over, Michael. It's all over."

"What's all over?" I ask.

"The president and his brother are dead."

I feel like I'm going to be sick. My head is spinning. It's too much for my mind to process.

Time skids forward. I'm on my feet, watching an American with blond hair help Father McDaniel to his feet, remove the blindfold and untie his hands.

I watch as Father McDaniel is helped into a car at the front gate. He stops, turns to me and makes the sign of the cross. Then he gets in and the car drives off.

My father stares at me like I'm a stranger. His expression says, *You see now? This is what life is really like. It's not the way you want it to be, is it? Too bad.*

I turn and walk out the gate. I hear Bruno call after me, but don't look back. I continue past the tanks and artillery, past spent shells and victorious soldiers having their pictures taken with well-wishers and friends.

Only a few civilians have ventured out—men on bicycles, a handful of women running to fetch water from the public pump. I continue down the street dotted with brass bullet casings, spent clips, jammed rifles, discarded belts, cigarette boxes and soda bottles. A burnt-out jeep lies on its side with a charred body still gripping the wheel. Boys poke at piece of a shredded leg sticking out of a boot.

Up ahead, barefoot kids swarm around the ravaged entrance to the police headquarters. Some carry out souvenirs — boots, helmets, metal chairs, umbrellas, even rifles that they drag behind them. Men in cars stop to snap pictures. The first thing I see inside the courtyard is the bloody chest and head of a policeman who was blown in half and placed on a pedestal that once held a marble bust of the president. The half corpse still wears a policeman's white helmet and has a cigarette clenched in its teeth.

A little boy in dirty shorts offers to sell me a Thompson submachine gun with a live clip. "One dolla. One dolla!"

I move numbly towards the center of the city. In the back of my mind I know that I'm seeing it for the last time.

It's only when I pass the Cathedral that I realize where my feet are taking to me – Gia Long palace. There's no celebration on the streets, only curious people like myself, vendors going about their business and soldiers resting, smoking cigarettes and eating soup.

The closer I get the more pockmarked buildings, splintered trees, smoldering trucks and jeeps I see.

Most people are moving in the same direction as I am. We're like a tide of silent witnesses. We walk and ride bicycles, motorbikes and pousse-pousses. We pass felled utility poles and crumpled steel fences. Whole pieces of houses and buildings are missing like some monstrous hand grabbed them and snatched them away.

A big crowd has assembled around the palace. Smoke rises from it in thin gray plumes. We stand before the empty ruin and imagine what it means and how it will affect our futures. Windows are broken and blown out, stately trees are shattered, and the façade is covered with thousands of pockmarks. There's a huge hole ripped in the front that's big enough for a tank to drive through.

Angry and empty, feeling as though I'm standing on the verge of something new, I wander the city all day and into the evening, pausing only to rest at the river and watch the green-brown water drift by.

CHAPTER
TWENTY

We're on a jet plane headed home. Outside the window the lush, rich green landscape changes into aqua, then deeper and deeper shades of blue. Boats reduce to tiny specks in the water. As the jet climbs higher, Vietnam recedes behind us.

Anger burns inside me. My heart is heavy with feelings for the people and places I've left behind —memories both sweet and terrifying, and my friends Mohammed, Father McDaniel, Huang, President Diem, Mr. Nhu, Leroy and Samantha.

I sit seething with questions: *What's going to happen to them? When will I ever return to Vietnam? How can I live with my father? Where can I escape to? Where will I go?*

I vow to honor the memory of my friends, whom I imagine somewhere, listening and watching. I've learned that I'm not like my father and will never be like him. And I realize that I'm going to have to blaze my own path.

My father's shadow falls over me like a cold fog. "Look at what I'm doing," he announces as he stands in the aisle. We've been careful to avoid one another during the past three weeks. He holds a red-and-white pack of Marlboro cigarettes and looks pleased with himself.

"What?" I ask, resisting the impulse to pick up the fork on the tray in front of me and shove it into his thigh.

He calls the stewardess, who sashays over in a tight blue uniform with a matching blue bonnet. "Yes, sir."

He hands her the pack of cigarettes and turns to my mother on the other side of the aisle.

"Please, throw these out," he says to the stewardess loud enough for all of us to hear. "I won't be needing them anymore."

His gesture seems strange and inappropriate given what happened back in Vietnam. But I know that my father doesn't see it that way. He's proud of himself. He's glad President Diem and his brother are gone, and a new government headed by General Minh has been installed. He considers it a victory. I think what we've done is wrong.

My sister turns to me and asks, "What's Dad so happy about? He's acting weird."

"He threw away his cigarettes. He's not going to smoke anymore."

"So? Who cares?"

Bruno Gelbart and his wife came to the airport to say goodbye. He hugged my father and kissed my mother but avoided my eyes.

I overheard my father say to Bruno, "I feel like we've taken positive steps towards saving this godforsaken place. We've accomplished something."

I wanted to scream. To shake the tiles loose from the ceiling so they fell on their heads and buried them.

Mohammed would say that they have left behind a lot of bad karma. People have been killed, lives have been violently uprooted and changed, as a result of our interference. *Why? To show the world that the United States is powerful, and we will stop communism no matter what the cost?*

How does that make the world a better place?

I want to better understand how men like Bruno and my father think. I need to grow stronger and become smarter so I can reason with them and prove them wrong.

I've learned some things. My parents have taught me that there are different kinds of love. I've learned that there's a lot of confusion and darkness in the world. I've learned that real love and compassion make life clearer, richer and more beautiful.

Jesus said, "There is light within a person of light, and it shines on the whole world. If it does not shine it is dark."

A red light flashes above me. Then the pilot's voice comes over the PA to make an announcement. In a grave voice, he says: "Ladies and gentlemen, I have very sad and tragic news. We've just heard over the radio that the President of the United States, John F. Kennedy died today in Dallas, Texas. He was struck down by an assassin's bullet."

A collective shudder passes through us. We sit stunned.

CHAPTER
TWENTY-ONE

President John F. Kennedy is being buried today and the entire city of Washington, DC is in mourning. On the street and in the lobby of the Fairfax Hotel, people pass silently with blank looks on their faces and muffled screams in their eyes. It's as though a part of them has been desecrated and destroyed.

"There go our dreams of Camelot," I hear a man groan as he watches the funeral procession on television. "Our innocence is gone," a woman says as she dabs tears from her eyes.

My family sits with the others watching the TV that's been set up in the dining room. Waiters, chambermaids, guests and bellhops are gathered behind us, clutching handkerchiefs and each other's hands.

I tear myself away and climb to the fourth floor, not out of disrespect or fear of being overwhelmed by emotion, but because I'm expecting a call from Brad Jr. at one PM. It's 12:58 already.

I stare at the beige phone beside the bed and will it to ring.

Tomorrow we're leaving for New York and six weeks of R&R (rest and recuperation) while we wait for my father's next assignment. He says there's a good chance we're going to Spain.

Maps of Madrid and books about Spain lay on the light

blue bedspread. I leaf through one of them, but my eyes keep being pulled back to the clock. It's 1:05, then it's 1:07.

I tell myself that I'll give him ten more minutes, explaining that his watch might be set wrong.

At 1:12, I can't wait anymore, so I pick up the receiver and dial the number I've committed to memory, knowing that if the wrong person answers my plan could be sunk.

"Hello," says the voice on the other end. It's soft, tentative and indistinct.

My heart pounding in my throat, I take a deep breath and ask: "Brad, is that you?"

"Yes."

I don't hear exactly what he says next — something about waiting for his mother to leave the room — because I'm so relieved. Then he says, "My grandmother and I are leaving in a minute. Can you meet us in front of Sibley Hospital in half an hour?"

Without thinking of how I'm going to get there or where it is, I answer, "Yes."

"I've got to go," he whispers in a rush.

"Sibley Hospital?" I ask. "It might take me a while to get there."

All I hear is a click on the other end, followed by uninterrupted buzz.

I move quickly down to the lobby with its dark wood paneling and high-backed velvet chairs. At the concierge's desk, I ask how to get to Sibley Hospital. He's a pale, thin man in a green coat with epaulets. He looks up from the magazines he's sorting with a long jaw and sunken eyes.

"Bus or taxi?" he asks dully.

"What?"

"How are you getting there?"

I count two dollars and change in my pocket. "Bus."

His eyes are as blank and impenetrable as mud. "Walk down to the corner and wait for the MacArthur Avenue bus.

Ask the driver to let you off at Loughboro Road. Take a right on Loughboro and walk up the hill. Sibley Hospital will be on your left."

"Loughboro Road?" I ask. "How long does it usually take?"

"Twenty-five to thirty minutes."

"Thanks."

I've decided not to tell my father. But he's waiting by the front desk like a bad dream, standing between the front door and me. He's with a tall man with a red flattop and clashing rust-colored plaid shirt. When my father sees me, he stops me with his right hand.

"Michael, I want you to meet Mel Sanders."

I smile and take the man's hand as the seconds tick by in my head.

"Mel served with Sy in Mexico City."

"That Sy's one strange cat," Mr. Sanders says turning to my father, looking for agreement. "Marches to the rat-tat-tat of his own drummer. Did I tell you about the time Sy got into it with the Ambassador's wife?" Mr. Sanders asks squinting at us through tiny blue eyes.

I imagine the MacArthur Avenue bus pulling away from the corner without me.

"Dad. Mr. Sanders. Please excuse me," I say. "Someone is waiting. I've got something I have to do."

I step around Mr. Sanders, who nods as though he understands. "Sure, son. Nice to meet you."

"Nice to meet you, too."

Frowning deeply, my father blocks my path.

"Where do you think you're going?" he asks.

I'm trying to think of a good answer and plot my way around him at the same time.

"I'm in a hurry," I blurt out.

He grabs me by the shoulder.

"You aren't going anywhere," he says sternly. "I need you to stick around and keep an eye on your sister and brother.

Your mother is taking this whole thing very hard and..."

He pauses to look at his watch. I take this an opportunity to slip past. "I'll be back in a little while. I promise."

"Where do you think you're going?" he growls, reaching back and clutching my arm hard. "What the hell is going on?"

I try pleading. "I need just half an hour. I'm going to see a friend."

"Which friend?" he asks. "Which friend?" he demands, squeezing my arm harder and shaking me.

I meet his eyes and feel rage stir inside me. "Let go. You're hurting me."

"Which friend?" he asks again, his voice wobbling and losing control. "Brad Jr.? Samantha?"

I say, "Dad, if you don't let go of me right now, I'm going to walk out of this hotel and never come back."

Instinctively, he starts to raise his fist. I don't flinch. I've already decided that if he hits me, I'll go live with my aunt and uncle in New York.

Our eyes meet and a curious change comes over him. He relaxes his grip. Then, shaking his head from side to side, he says, "You've done it now. Boy, have you done it."

* * * * * *

Throughout the bus ride I bounce back and forth between fear and exhilaration. The minute the driver lets me off on Loughboro Road, my attention shifts to Samantha. As I climb the hill, I remember all the precious moments we spent together — our talks, the day we went bowling, the bomb. Her bright smile and the smoking shell of the movie theater lobby flash in my head. Images tumble on top of one another. At the top of the hill I stop to gather myself and catch my breath.

Brad Jr. waves from the shaded front of the Sibley Hospital. We shake hands like old friends. His grandmother waits for us in the lobby — round, kind and gray with twinkling blue eyes like Samantha's. I like her immediately.

"I've heard so many wonderful things about you," she says, warmly.

"It's a pleasure to meet you," I say back.

A nurse in a crisp light green uniform escorts us down a long corridor to the Rehabilitation Unit. Brad Jr. and his grandmother walk ahead. My legs grow cold and stiff, because the enormity of what I'm about to face starts to hit me.

What if upon seeing her, I break down and weep like a baby, or even worse, shut down completely?

We push through double doors. At the other side, I stand and shiver.

Brad Jr. waits beside me, hands in his pockets, looking at his shoes. It's a big room with green paint halfway up the walls, which are cut by a swath of wide windows. Sunlight streams in.

I notice his grandmother has entered from another door to our left. She bends over and whispers to someone in a wheelchair. I crane my neck to see who it is, expecting to see a very old person or a child.

All I can make out is a little face shrouded in white. The hollowed, haunted eyes seem familiar.

Oh, God!

I have to catch myself from falling. For some reason, I never imagined Samantha in a wheelchair. But I know those eyes. They're bigger and darker now. They're no longer light blue. The rest of her seems to have shrunken.

I step forward tentatively holding my breath. She's dressed in a white gown with a white cap on her head. Her hair has been cut very short and her chin is held up by a smooth piece of metal that's attached to the arm of the wheelchair. Her mouth is twisted into a question mark as though she's trying to comprehend where she is and what's going on

"Samantha..." I say, bending at the waist and trembling.

"It's me, Michael."

The whole world stops as she turns her gaze towards me and her eyes light up

with recognition. Eternity passes as we touch each other deeply, all the way to our souls.

"Samantha..." I gush and take her hand.

Her very thin arm trembles. Her lips move but nothing comes out.

Her grandmother whispers, "She can hear everything you say, but can't speak."

I nod. "Samantha," I say. "I'm so glad to see you. I've missed you very much."

She grips my hand tightly. Her's is small and tender like that of a child.

Although I expected to feel sad, maybe even devastated, I'm filled with enormous energy. Her eyes tell me that she wants me to speak. I talk about everyone and everything, picking up my life from the moment we parted in front of the theater to the present. It's one long, continuous stream, with words flowing easily one after the other.

She nods, encouraging me, then her mouth moves awkwardly as though she's trying to form words. Thin trails of tears dissect her cheeks. I'm weeping, too, but my heart is happy.

I'm holding both of her hands now. It feels like we're the only ones in the room. Time and circumstances are unimportant.

I'm telling her about the coup d'état and the call from Father McDaniel, when her eyelids flutter and her eyes float back into her head.

"She's getting tired," her grandmother whispers.

A nurse with blond hair steps forward and tries to push between us. "I'm sorry," she says, taking my wrists. "You can visit another time."

I cut off my story, but Samantha won't let go. She looks at

me as though she's waiting for me to tell her something.

I say, "I love you, Samantha. I'll always love you. I have to leave tomorrow with my family. But I'll write to you and I'll visit the next time I'm in town."

Her lips tremble as they try to form a smile.

I have to stop myself from looking away. I have to hold myself from falling apart. I repeat, "I love you so much."

Her hands squeeze hard, then go limp, and the nurse quickly maneuvers between us, releasing the brake and turning the chair. I'm staring at the spot where the gray rubber wheels meet the floor, biting my lower lip, wondering what to do next.

It's like I'm dreaming and have lost track of time. All I see are wheels moving and the back hem of Samantha's garment, her thin, pale arms hanging awkwardly at her sides.

The chair stops and I raise my eyes. The nurse and the grandmother bend over Samantha. They're watching her write on a pad of white paper. She writes slowly, concentrating hard as they whisper words of encouragement. The nurse takes her hand and helps her form the letters.

Samantha tries to raise her arm again but can't summon the strength to continue. As the nurse releases the brake and starts to move the chair a terrible strangled sound issues from Samantha's throat. Everything pauses. The nurse pulls the paper from the pad and hands it to me.

There is one word written awkwardly: "em..path..y." It says everything.

"Yes, Samantha," I cry out nakedly. "I won't forget." My mind is racing back over all the things we talked about and everything we pledged to one another. "I won't forget what happened, what we saw and the promises we made to one another... how we said we're going to live differently. We will, Samantha... with empathy... yes."

ABOUT
ATMOSPHERE PRESS

Atmosphere Press is an independent, full-service publisher for excellent books in all genres and for all audiences. Learn more about what we do at atmospherepress.com.

We encourage you to check out some of Atmosphere's latest releases, which are available at Amazon.com and via order from your local bookstore:

Twisted Silver Spoons, a novel by Karen M. Wicks

Queen of Crows, a novel by S.L. Wilton

The Summer Festival is Murder, a novel by Jill M. Lyon

The Past We Step Into, stories by Richard Scharine

The Museum of an Extinct Race, a novel by Jonathan Hale Rosen

Swimming with the Angels, a novel by Colin Kersey

Island of Dead Gods, a novel by Verena Mahlow

Cloakers, a novel by Alexandra Lapointe

Twins Daze, a novel by Jerry Petersen

Embargo on Hope, a novel by Justin Doyle

Abaddon Illusion, a novel by Lindsey Bakken

Blackland: A Utopian Novel, by Richard A. Jones

The Jesus Nut, a novel by John Prather

The Embers of Tradition, a novel by Chukwudum Okeke

ABOUT
THE AUTHOR

Ralph Pezzullo is a *New York Times* bestselling author, and award-winning playwright and screenwriter. His books have been published in over twenty languages and include *Jawbreaker, Inside SEAL Team Six, The Walk-In, Plunging Into Haiti* (winner of the Douglas Dillon Prize for American Diplomacy), *Zero Footprint, Left of Boom, Ghost, Hunt the Leopard* and others. The son of a US diplomat, he lived in Saigon, Vietnam from 1963 to 1965.